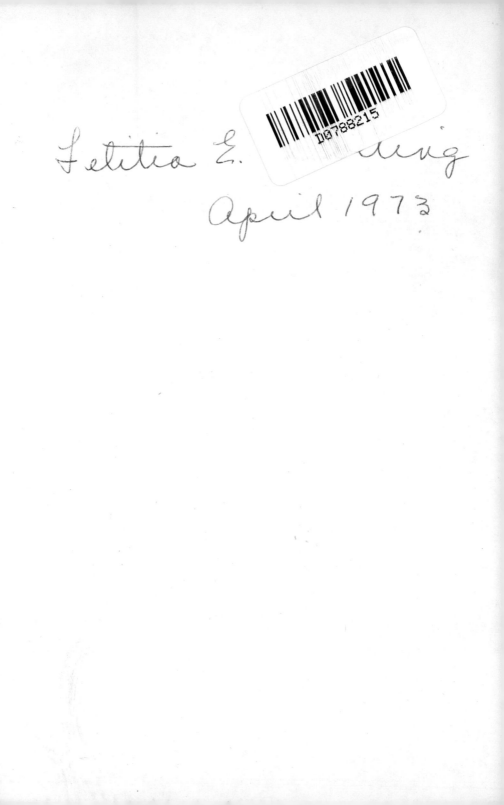

Letitia E. _____ _____

April 1973

Also by CECELIA HOLLAND

THE DEATH OF ATTILA

THE
DEATH
OF
ATTILA

CECELIA HOLLAND

ALFRED A. KNOPF
NEW YORK
1973

Library of Congress Cataloging in Publication Data

Holland, Cecelia.
    The death of Attila.

    I. Title.
PZ4.H733De3   [PS3558.0348]   813'.5'4   72–8386
ISBN 0–394–47309–4

For Bobby

THE DEATH OF ATTILA

ONE

B EFORE THEY REACHED THE
river, the horses had grown used to the corpse. Tacs had not.
Of course it was cold enough except at the height of the day so
that the dead flesh hardly smelled, and Tacs had bound it into
a tight wrapping of his and the dead man's cloaks, to keep the
spirits from getting at it. Still, at night, when Tacs was camped,
Marag troubled his sleep.

On the morning of the sixth day after Marag's death, four
days after they left the mountains behind, they came within
sight of the river. Tacs had the grey horse on a long tether so
that it could graze while it traveled. Seeing the glitter of water
in the distance, he jerked on the tether and reined in his black
pony, and for the space of two long breaths he sat motionless
staring at the undulating line of trees that marked the river
bank. The sight of the river overwhelmed Tacs, even more than
if he had met another of his own people. In four months the
only other Hiung he had seen was Marag, and now Marag he
saw too much of, in the night.

He nudged the pony with his heels and gave the grey horse's
rope a shake, and with the rope swinging between them the
two horses started down the slope again. The river sank out of
sight beyond the next rise. Although this steppe seemed level
it actually rolled in long waves from horizon to horizon. Now
in the middle of autumn the plain was crisp and brown. The
dry grass rustled under the black pony's hoofs. Brown birds
marked with white, brown mice and rabbits appeared and dis-

appeared among the patches of weed and the stands of high grass. Everything smelled of dust and drying.

The grey horse stopped to scratch its shoulder with its teeth. Tacs kept on, his eyes moving constantly. With the river so close he knew he rode under the Kagan's protection. But the habit of watching was strong in him and Germans lived on this plain as well as Hiung. Tacs had seen that the soldiers of the Romans were mostly German and he could see no difference between the Roman Germans and the ones who served the Kagan. They were all dogs. The pony reached the end of the grey horse's leadline and Tacs was almost jerked from his saddle. He yanked on the rope; the grey horse broke into a trot to catch up. The black pony climbed in short lunges up the next slope into the roar of the wind.

There the river lay, apparently no closer, but now Tacs could see where the Roman bridge crossed it, well to the east. While the two horses walked on, taking him slowly down again into the trough of the plain, he thought uneasily of other ways to cross the river. Here it ran swiftly, deep between treacherous banks, and so late in the autumn the water would be freezing. He could not swim it, and the nearest ford was days away. He knew that the bridge was guarded by Germans, probably by Gepids. It had been Ardaric, the King of the Gepids, who sent Tacs and Marag away from the army in Italy and so caused them to be left behind when the Kagan suddenly retreated. Now Marag was dead in consequence. It was unclear to Tacs whether such a death required vengeance; he would have to talk to a shaman about it.

The high wind stirred up a whirl of dust as tall as a man and drove it skittering along the crest of the next rise, picking up dead leaves and bits of branch. Its careening path headed roughly toward the bridge. Tacs followed it. He had no choice —if he went north looking for a ford or an unguarded bridge, he would have to spend at least two more nights with Marag.

Throughout the rest of the day, he rode steadily toward the

river. In the blue arch of the sky an eagle appeared and
circled him awhile, perhaps waiting for him to leave the dead
man. Tacs wondered if he might not now make a burial platform and leave Marag on it, here within the boundaries the
Kagan had declared his, and thus have served Marag properly.
Through the early afternoon he tried to argue himself into it,
although the taboos and ritual of their people required three
witnesses to bury a warrior. Gradually he became aware that
he could not bury Marag here anyway because it was not truly
land of the Hiung, and he switched to thinking of how he
would catch frogs to eat, once he reached the river. The frog
was one of his totems, and eating its meat made him agile.

In the late afternoon he came to a worn path in the plain,
the road that led to the bridge. Turning to follow it, he rapped
his heels against the black pony's ribs. At first the pony only
pinned back its ears and snorted. Tacs kicked it harder, and the
pony bucked, and Tacs smacked it across the ear with his open
hand. Sulking, the pony stepped out into a brisk trot, towing
Marag's horse along after him.

They came within sight of the bridge, and through the
trees along the far bank Tacs saw a camp with a fire and a line
of picketed horses. They had to be Germans; no Hiung would
tie a horse with the whole wide plain to graze it on. Almost at
once the men in the camp saw him coming and rushed forward
to bar the bridge. They came on foot, running, half a dozen
men. Tacs reined in. The Germans swung the wooden bar to
close the bridge and stood watching him, talking among themselves. Most of them carried bows, and one or two even had
swords, like the Romans.

"Come forward," one of them shouted, in German.

Tacs looked from side to side. There was no other way to
cross the river. He reeled in the lead rope until Marag's horse
stood with its head almost against his thigh and started forward.

The black pony caught the scent of the Germans and flung

up its head and neighed. At its high squeaky neigh the German horses beyond the river surged and lunged against the
picket rope and whinnied in answer. Tacs kicked the pony forward again. It pinned back its ears and Tacs patted its neck.
He had taught it to hate Germans. Those at the bridge were
waiting for him; one man came forward toward him.

"Who are you?"

"A Hiung," Tacs said stiffly, in German. "I go to Hungvar.
The Kagan is my chief."

"So you say," the German said. "How do we know that you
are not a spy, sent by the Emperor?"

They always said this. It was a German trick to try to keep
him here, perhaps even to turn him back and force him up-
river. Tacs choked down his anger. The Germans were all
laughing at him, their teeth showing in the midst of their
blond beards.

"I am the Kagan's man. My name is Tacs, my father was
Resak, my brother is Ras, we are of the frog clan of the
Mishni Hiung and our—"

"What's that?" another German said, going toward Marag's
horse.

"Leave that alone," Tacs called.

The German leader lifted his pale bushy eyebrows. His red
lips curved into a smile smooth as a woman's. "What could
be in that bundle? Something you don't want us to see?" With
his men crowding after him, he went up and reached for the
rope that held Marag on his horse.

Leaning across the grey horse's back, Tacs grabbed the
German by the wrist. "No. Don't—"

The German struck him with his fist. Hands seized him from
behind and dragged him down out of his saddle. The black
pony reared. A German had hold of its bridle; the pony
lashed out with its forefeet, shrilling, and the German stumbled back. Wheeling, the pony galloped off into the plain,

away from the bridge. Tacs cried out. On foot he was helpless. He flung his weight against the arms that held him, but the Germans held him fast; they were much bigger than he was.

"Don't kill him yet," the leader called. "Let us see what he was bringing to Hungvar."

With a knife he cut the rope and pulled the wrappings from Marag, and Marag slid rolling down into the dirt of the road.

Outraged, Tacs whined in his teeth. The Germans recoiled. Marag, covered with dust, lay almost at Tacs' feet. A sour stench leaked from the body. One of the Germans yammered out an incantation. The men holding Tacs let him go, hacking away; their leader's face was twisted and he licked his lips.

Tacs knelt down beside Marag and pulled the cloaks around him again. To touch Marag filled him with fear, and the odor made his stomach heave, but he could not bear to see him lying covered with dust in the midst of Germans. He wrapped the cloaks carefully around Marag's feet and tucked his rigid arms inside and drew the thick folds of bearskin across his face. Seeing Marag's face, even stiff and distorted, reminded him again that he was alone and his friend was dead, and he straightened up and beat his body with his fists and wailed in grief and loneliness.

Their faces whey-colored, the Germans had backed off around him. Tacs lifted Marag up in his arms. The body was frozen in the shape it had taken while lying across the grey horse's back. It was hard to lift but easy to return to its place on Marag's saddle. The rope lay in two pieces on the road. The Germans deserved all the ill luck that cutting a rope would bring them. Tacs knotted the rope together and tied the body fast. Taking the reins of Marag's horse, he walked back along the path, away from the bridge, and whistled for the black pony.

When he had gone almost a hundred steps along the road, the pony came trotting up to him. The dust had irritated

its eyes so that the rims showed red and gritty. It jogged up to
the grey horse and sniffed its muzzle. Tacs picked up the trailing reins and mounted.

Seeing him turn toward them, the Germans moved away
from the bridge, going either way along the river. Tacs lifted
the pony into a lope. Marag's horse, short-led, trotted along beside for a dozen strides and broke into a canter. The bar of the
bridge appeared before them, and Tacs felt the pony start to shy
and tightened his legs on its barrel. Half a stride ahead of
the grey horse, the pony leapt easily over the bar. They galloped across the bridge and onto the plain beyond, and Tacs
swerved to follow the course of the river, but he slowed the
horses only when the bridge was out of sight and the Germans
well behind him.

Hε COULD FIND NO FROGS;
they had all died for the winter. In the dark, crouched around
his little fire, he fought off sleep all night long, while the skin
of his back crawled over his spine, and his whole body twitched
at the merest sound behind him. Marag in his wrappings lay
tamely on the far side of the fire; the horses alternately slept
and grazed along the river bank. Tacs' eyes grew hot from
lack of sleep. Once he dozed and woke just before he would
have fallen into the fire.

With the rising of the sun he rode north, following the
slow windings of the river. After the long months of being
alone and far from the shelter of his own people, the river
seemed like a friend to him. He listened to its voice and even
sang to it once or twice. Now that the sun shone in the sky
he no longer felt tired. Overhead the sky glistened as blue as
the paints the Romans used on the walls of their houses. He
and Marag had spent the night once in a deserted house in the
hills, in Italy south of the City, and stared at the pictures on
the walls half the night. With torches they had gone arguing

through the whole house and found all the pictures. The people drawn on the walls were strangely lifelike but not real-looking at all. Marag had stubbornly refused to admit that they were pictures of demons.

He began to organize his memories of the journey in his mind, as a finished thing, so that he could tell his friends when he was safe among them. Marag's family would have to know everything of importance. The black pony trotted steadily along, the rein looped over its neck. Tacs took the feathers and pebbles from his long black hair and combed it out with his fingers. In his shadow he saw how long his hair had grown.

In the late summer his hair had been much shorter, back when he and Marag returned to the Kagan's campground, expecting to find thousands of men, and found only dead fires and blowing dust. At first they had hoped to catch up; racing after the army, he and Marag had killed one horse and nearly finished another, but the Kagan always moved fast and had a month's lead, and no one had waited.

He tucked the pebbles into his belt pouch and braided the feathers back into his hair. The river dipped down into a hollow on the plain, and the bank turned to half-frozen marsh: two storks, late migrating, drew themselves slowly into the air on their long wings and rose away from him. Underhoof the ground crunched and the pony stepped short to keep from slipping. The sound of the river changed to a quieter note.

He had felt about the trail of the vanished army much the same way that he felt now about the river murmuring and lapping at the bank beside him—as long as he followed it, he was safe. They had stayed close to the army's track all the way out of Italy, although the game there was gone and the grass eaten away. But in the high passes of the mountains, lashed with snow and the shrieking wind, they lost the army's trail. Two days later one of their horses slipped and fell over a cliff; the next morning Marag was sick. By midafternoon he was too sick to ride. They camped in the lee of a cliff. Both of them knew Marag would be dead by morning—Marag talked of dying and asked Tacs to take word of his death to his father. In the afterdawn Tacs lashed his body to his saddle and rode on. That afternoon he killed a white goat, scrambled across a snow-field to reach it, and ate the heart and tongue raw.

It would snow on this plain within the month, but before then he would have come home. He kept his eyes moving, in case more Germans patrolled his side of the river. In the late afternoon he saw, far off, three wagons drawn by oxen and followed by a herd of four or five horses: a family moving south out of Hungvar for the winter. The men herding the horses reined in to watch him ride by. Tacs lifted his hand in salute and the two horsemen threw their right arms up in answer. The sight of them and the brief communication filled him with triumph. He had come home. Winding in and out of the fringe of trees along its banks, the river led them along, and he sang it a song about following the Kagan's trail out of Italy.

THE BLACK PONY TROTTED steadily along. Tacs could hardly see the road, it was so dark. The deep night chill pierced him like needles. Ahead, on the crown of the hill, light showed on the high walls of the Kagan's stockade. There were more lights on the lower hilltop west of the river, but Tacs thought that to be the camp of the Gepids' king. The pony strode along without hesitation, its nose aimed precisely toward the stockade.

All afternoon the north wind had risen steadily; now Tacs could see how it churned the naked branches of the oak tree at the gate to the stockade, and when the pony carried him up the last steep stretch of the road, he could hear the branches rattling together. All along the back of his head, the hair stirred and stood on end. He looked hastily behind him, but in the dark he could see nothing except the lights across the river. He turned his face toward the patch of lights before him, on the Kagan's hill. He had been mad to keep going when the night came, he should have stopped and waited until morning.

The grey horse loped along beside him. The cold wind rose in a gust and howled around him, shoving him forward; on the grey horse's back, the wrapped corpse shifted and moved, and Tacs whispered under his breath. Once he had known magic against the dead, but he had forgotten everything except some fragments of the incantation. Although the words alone were of no use he had taken to repeating them anyway.

The pony carried him directly under the oak tree, turned a corner, and stopped before the great gate into the stockade. Tacs drew a deep breath. The wind screamed and gibbered at him; the gaunt branches of the oak rasped together over his head. The gate was shut, of course, and they would never let him in so late. But he could not stay out here, in the open, in the dark. He leaned sideways and pounded with his fist on the gate.

"Let me in. Oh, let me in."

He could go out to one of the camps on the plain around the stockade, but in the dark he might as easily ride up to a German, and he knew he could not face a German now. No one answered his call, and he beat on the gate; it was made of logs split lengthwise, with the bark left on that muffled his knocking.

"Go away," a voice called from the top of the wall. "It's after dark, the gate is closed at sundown. Go away."

"Yaya!" Tacs cried, relieved. "It's Tacs. Let me in." He strained forward against the gate, pressing on it with both hands, as if he could wish his way through the wood.

Up on the wall, Yaya swore in a panicky voice. Tacs glanced over at the grey horse. It shone with a strange pale radiance. The wind and the dark buffeted him, chuckling around him, full of demons. His skin crept at their touch. They wanted Marag's body to eat. The pony danced from hoof to hoof, its ears pinned back, and Tacs patted its neck.

"Tacs is dead in Italy," Yaya said, just the other side of the gate. "Are you truly his spirit, or do you take his voice to lure me out there?"

"I'm not dead. It's me, Tacs, alive, no demon. Yaya! Please let me in."

"It's his voice," another man said, beyond the gate. "If you open the gate, Yaya, it will suck your blood. It spoke your name."

Tacs cried, "And yours, Monidiak. Let me in—there are true demons out here, will you leave me to them?" He knew if he mentioned Marag's body they would never let him in. "Yaya, please—"

"No," Monidiak howled. "It's a demon—no—no—"

Something heavy fell against the gate, and there were sounds of struggling. Other feet came running. Tacs banged his fists on the gate, so that they would not forget him. Around him the wind and the dark wound full of voices like a river. The gate creaked open, and the black pony bounded forward through it, dragging the grey horse after. Tacs grabbed a handful of the pony's coarse mane, and it lunged to one side to let the gate slam closed. Men with lances and bows surrounded him. Tacs held up his hands.

"It's Tacs. See? If I were a demon you could not kill me anyway. The dead one is there behind you. Yaya!"

He leapt off the pony into Yaya's arms; Yaya shouted something and gathered him up. Tacs could not breathe for pleasure. Others crowded around them, laughing, and hugging Tacs and Yaya both and making jokes about demons and the wind that screeched and tugged at the gate, shaking it on its leather hinges.

"Is this Marag?" Monidiak called, in a steady voice.

The voices and the laughter quieted. Tacs turned toward

him. Monidiak stood at the grey horse's shoulder, one hand on the wrapped corpse.

"He died in the snow coming back," Tacs said. Grief filled him, and he cried out.

"Pigs," a woman shrieked, from a second-story window in the Court of Women. "Sons of snakes and demons. Can't you let people sleep?"

"Ssssh," they all said to each other, laughing.

"Come along," Monidiak said softly. "Let's get inside to talk over all this. Let the gate guard itself. Is that your pony? Yes." He slapped the black rump. "He can watch over himself. We will bring Marag inside, safe from demons. Wait until the Kagan knows of this."

TWO

⊂⊐

ARDARIC SAID PATIENTLY,
"Yet the same problems will pertain, my Kagan. Before we can hope to take Italy, we must solve those problems that led to last summer's failure."

"Puh," the Kagan said; he made a gesture with one hand, like throwing something away. He put his head against the tall back of his chair. "Unimportant."

"My Kagan, I cannot see how—"

"Last summer we failed because we were given a lot of gold money to fail. The next time, maybe we won't take the money."

Ardaric laid his hands down flat on the table in front of him. "My Kagan, the army was starving. Dying of plague. We could not find a way south through the mountains and the swamps. There was no game and no grass and no way to find more supplies. Italy is treacherous country. If Constantius tells the truth it took the Romans themselves many years to conquer it. And the next time, Aetius might not be caught unprepared."

The Kagan's expression never changed. For a moment, he stared at Ardaric, and Ardaric, knowing how Attila hated men who could not meet his eyes, stared back, although he disliked to and thought it rude. He rested his weight on his elbows on the polished oak of the table between them. In any case, they could not march again until the spring, when the passes cleared through the Alps, and so they would spend a long winter arguing, snug in this little room with its fire and its tall pitchers of mead and Roman tribute wine and its furs to cushion the wooden benches. Ardaric prided himself on his patience.

"Excuse me," the Kagan said abruptly. "Scottas!"

The door to the right of the Kagan's chair opened, and Scottas came in and bowed. Scottas was second in command of the Kagan's guard and always stood sentry there. Attila shifted his weight onto one ham and spoke to him in a low voice, his body cocked toward the other man. Ardaric gave Scottas only a glance and politely looked away. Like all Huns, even Attila, Scottas was squat and round, barrel-shaped, and ugly, and like all Huns except Attila he was fatally stupid. Ardaric, who was a Gepid, was tall and strongly built, with luxuriant golden hair and a beard he kept neatly combed and even, on occasion, perfumed.

A slave came in from the door to the left of the throne and put more wood on the fire. Ardaric turned to face the great brick hearth behind him. Usually Edeco would have been here for such a conference as this one, and what other Huns and Germans the Kagan believed knowledgeable of the subject, but Edeco was in Constantinople on a mission and no one else of sufficient rank was near Hungvar.

"King," the Kagan said, and Ardaric swung back toward him. "Until this morning I agreed with you. It looked mindless to attack Italy again so quickly. Now I am not so sure." He made a gesture toward the door; Scottas went to it and out. "Do you remember Tacs?"

Ardaric frowned. The name sounded familiar, but he could not place it—a Hun name, connected in his mind with Italy. "My Kagan, you know my memory for names—"

The door opened, and Tacs came hobbling through the door. Immediately Ardaric remembered him. Tacs was even shorter than the average Hun and his legs were crooked from some disease, so that he could barely walk. In Italy he had served as a scout—Ardaric, who had commanded certain reconnaissance, had found him useful several times. He averted his gaze, but through the corner of his eye he studied the little Hun curiously. He had taken for granted that Tacs was dead, left behind in Italy with another man whose name he had forgotten. More than a dozen Huns had been left behind when the army pulled out. None had returned before.

Tacs' lank black hair hung down below his shoulder blades and was tangled with feathers and berries and stones, and his tunic was of some indistinguishable, grimy fur, and he smelled. The Kagan leaned down over the arm of his chair to speak to him. It was the same Tacs. Ardaric wondered how he could still be alive; perhaps the Romans had captured him and sent him back as a favor to Attila. The Roman commander Aetius and Attila were old friends, so it was possible.

"King," Attila said. "Ardaric. You remember Tacs." The Kagan took Tacs by the shoulder and shook him. "Last night they almost would not let him in for fear he was a demon."

The Kagan put his head back and laughed, and Tacs smiled, his narrow eyes on Ardaric. Ardaric could not imagine what had been said that was funny, but he smiled to be polite.

"When we retreated from Italy," the Kagan said, "Tacs and his friend Marag were riding south, not north with us. It was more than a month before they discovered that we had gone, and by that time the legions of the Emperor were prowling around again, Vandals and Goths. They all hate Hiung. Marag died but Tacs has come home at last."

Ardaric looked at Tacs. "Admirable." But surely it was a lie.

"He knows Italy," Attila said. He leaned forward to reach his ivywood cup, standing on the table, and the little Hun beside him turned his head and watched, bold as a dog. "He has lived in Italy, by his own hunting, through the bad autumn weather, and he knows the countryside south of Aquileia. He knows which marshes are impenetrable to large bands of men and which passes are safest and where the best graze might be found."

"Ah," Ardaric said, at last understanding. "How far south did he go?"

"Ask him. He speaks German." The Kagan drank from his cup and leaned back, putting one foot up on the edge of his chair, the wide leather boot planted on a black and white African fur.

"I went to the sea," Tacs said, and smiled, exactly as if Ardaric were a child to be encouraged. His German was slurred with his accent.

"There is sea all around Italy," Ardaric said impatiently. "What town did you come to? Spoletium? Narnia?"

"I don't know towns. I went to where I could see Africa."

The Kagan cuffed Tacs across the back of the head. "He exceeds his instructions. I told them to go to Rome, you remember."

"We did," Tacs said.

"He exceeds much," Ardaric said, keeping his voice level. "Including possibility. There is nowhere in Italy from which one can see Africa."

Tacs shrugged. "I went south to salt water and looked across and saw land. I thought it must be Africa." Instead of the German for salt, he used the Hun word with a German ending. Twisting to look up over his shoulder, he said to Attila, "May I sit? My legs hurt."

"Sit, little frog."

The Hun scrambled up onto the table opposite Ardaric and sat down, dragging his warped legs around so that he sat on them. "The salt river was called Messin."

Ardaric sucked in a breath and held it. This one was lying, they all lied, thieves and liars and lazy vermin, all Huns except the Kagan. "That is the narrow sea between Italy and Sicily."

"I thought it was Africa." The Hun shrugged and looked back at Attila, who smiled at him, a peaceful, secret smile like a father's to a favored child. Ardaric cleared his throat. His mind was clogged with contradictions; he got up and went to the table under the window, where the pitchers of mead and beer and wine stood waiting. To reach it, he walked into the sunlight pouring through the window, and he stood a moment looking into the yard behind the palace, where the Kagan's children were playing. In his mind, the long placid winter months shrank to nothing, and he foresaw another campaign in Italy, another attack on Rome, summer full of dying and burning. But the little Hun was lying. No one could live for so long in hostile country, go so deep into unknown country—a Goth, perhaps, because there were Gothic villages in Italy, but not a Hun, alien to them all. He poured himself a cup of red Roman wine and carried it back to the table.

"You wonder why I have done this," Attila said. "Tacs has the knowledge you will need to form a plan of attack. You have the craft at forming such plans. If I put you together—" He laced his fingers into a knot, clasped his hands, and smiled. "So. Tacs will attend you whenever you wish to talk to him. When Edeco comes back from New Rome you should meet, as well. But Edeco will not come back for some while."

"I am yours to command, my Kagan," Ardaric said.

The Kagan looked down at Tacs. "Little frog. You may go. I will see you back among my guard when you are rested."

Tacs climbed down from the table. "Yes, Attila." He went out the door, and the sentry Scottas who had stood inside the door all the while followed him out.

The Kagan lifted himself out of his chair. In the past few years he had put on flesh; sometimes Ardaric thought he saw a tinge of grey under the tanned sallow skin, and a small indefinite sense of alarm stirred in him. The Kagan walked slowly around the little room and paused before the fire to hold out his hands to its warmth.

"Tacs has some very heavy magic to escape from enemies," Attila said. "Do you believe what he says, that he and Marag went so far south?"

"I have to think about it, my Kagan."

"What a strange journey—how full of stories. It seems impossible. But I believe him. He doesn't lie. How else would he be here now unless it happened as he says?"

"Indeed, my Kagan." Ardaric had always wondered where Huns got their reputation for reticence; he knew by the tone of the Kagan's voice that Attila had already decided that Tacs was telling the truth, and that he was talking to fill up the stillness while he thought.

"I have noticed this magic of his before. Once, while we were raiding in Gaul . . ." The Kagan turned slowly, warming his body. Light glinted in the sparse hairs of his beard. With his forefinger he scratched his stub of a nose. "I do not believe he had it of his father. Resak was an unlucky man with no success in anything. But Resak's brother was a fine shaman, speaking almost every day in incomprehensible languages. Perhaps Tacs learned the magic from him. His brother is also fortunate."

"Eh," Ardaric said cautiously. The door behind the throne opened, and two of the Kagan's sons came in—Ellac, the eldest, and Dengazich, the son of a Gothic princess, nonetheless as ugly as a full-blooded Hun. Ardaric hated the Kagan's sons, but he was pleased to see them, because it meant that he would soon be dismissed. It exhausted him to listen to the Kagan speak of things such as magic. From experience he knew that it could go on all morning, talk of bewildering things; choosing answers was like straining to understand a foreign tongue. The two young Huns stopped behind the throne and leaned against it, waiting for their father to notice them. Ardaric said nothing. Through the window on the yard, a shriek came, and sounds of a wild children's game, and all three Huns turned their heads to look in that direction.

"Tacs is not particularly clever," Attila said, his eyes on the window. "Yet one need not be clever to dissemble about magic. I have often thought that magic is strongest in those not so clever. I suppose we could trick him into revealing what he knows, but I don't want to. It pleases me that one of the few men left of that clan and totem should still have powerful magic in these days."

Squat, ox-faced Ellac stared at his father, but Dengazich turned his head and looked at Ardaric, boldly, with his rounded Gothic eyes.

"Each man's magic is his own possession," Ardaric said, because he had to say something, and Dengazich smirked at him. Furious, Ardaric said, "My Kagan, allow me to leave you alone with your sons."

"Yes," Attila said. His voice sharpened with sarcasm. "With the heirs of my body."

He had turned to face the fire again, his head bowed. Through the window came sounds of children playing. Ardaric made his obeisance, his hands laid together palm against palm, and went out. Even the Kagan disliked his elder sons. In the corridor, away from their eyes, Ardaric let his face sag out of its set polite mask and sent the first slave he met to bring his horse to the porch steps.

THE HUNS BELIEVED THAT A white deer had led them into the west, but Ardaric did not believe it, because a white deer was a sign of the Lord Jesus Christ and the Huns weren't even Christian. A few years before, a Hun shepherd had found an old sword half-buried in the steppe north of Hungvar, and Attila had made an elaborate show of it, calling it the sword of the War God and concocting stories of how it had come to be there and what the finding of it meant. But once when Ardaric was alone with him the Kagan made fun of the sword and the story; only foolish people believed it.

The tales Ardaric's father had told of the coming of the

Huns were easier. At first there had been only the Germans, north of the river, and the Romans, south of it, all living in peace and trading with each other. But one morning the eastern horizon had turned black with oncoming peoples—the Ostrogoths and the Visigoths, the Alans, fleeing from the Huns; and next the Huns themselves, driving all the people of the plain before them as if before a fire storm. Some had escaped into the country of the Romans but most of the Germans had been beaten in war and forced to pay tribute to the Hun kings, who at that time were many, six or eight, and none so strong as the Kagan Attila was now, who ruled half the world.

Ardaric mounted his horse before the Kagan's wooden palace and rode across the front yard toward the gate. Among the crowd of Huns beside the open gate was Tacs, drinking from a jug. With others of the palace guard, he sat at the foot of the gate post, warming himself in the sun. Ardaric swung his horse wide to his left to enter the stream of people going out the gate; Tacs saw him but looked hurriedly in the other direction.

Every day in this season merchants set up a marketplace in the yard before the Court of Women. Carts and men carrying packs on their backs were leaving the stockade now to go on to the villages around it. Ardaric on his white horse had to rein down to keep from trampling a man in a striped gown and a red headdress, who led slaves carrying bundles of cloth. Some people said that the Parthians traded in other than cloth: opium and hashish and other filth, smuggled in between layers of silk.

Beyond the gate, the pounded earth of the road split into three branches—one ran off to either side, and one ran straight on down the hill toward the river ford. Dense brush lined either bank of the river. Hun children played in it and in the dirt under the enormous oak tree that stood just outside the gate. The Parthian in his red and yellow gown called to his slaves in a rattling, clicking tongue and led them off toward the Hun village north of the stockade. Ardaric rode down toward the river.

When Hungvar had been only a crossroads marketplace, before the Kagan built the stockade there, the roads had curved like bows to avoid the marsh. The Kagan had filled the wet, sunken places with rock, dirt, and slabs of wood, and now even in the spring mud the road was firm. Now, in the cold, the marsh had shrunk away from the road on either side; ice coated the grass. The voices of the children playing in the trees along the river rang with laughter. In the leafless branches they looked at first like the winter nests of squirrels, until they moved.

Four or five Huns were crossing the river single file at the ford. On the rippled surface of the water their reflections moved in ripples. Ardaric slowed his horse to let them pass, and they rode up the bank and broke into a fast trot, and their leader raised his hand to Ardaric. Ardaric jerked up his arm in answer. He could never tell one Hun from another; he saw so many of them. Crossing the river, he rode along the edge of the marsh toward his own village, which stood on the hill beyond the marshes, opposite the Kagan's hill.

The white horse carried him up the last stretch of road, between the two banks like a miniature gateway where the comings and goings of people had worn the path deep into the lip of the hill. His first glimpse of his village, as usual, moved him to pride. In neat rows the houses covered the high ground, each with its own garden; every bit of land was fenced and used. Bright paint covered the carved wooden windowframes and the doorposts of the houses, the eaves of the roofs, the little porchways, cut as elaborately as lace.

He rode into the village, going to his own house. The chatter of women reached him from the brewhouses. He imagined the vats bubbling, full of beer and caked all around their rims with yeast, and the gossip flying back and forth over the slow-stirring paddles. The village children played seek-and-find in the street—pale-skinned, fair-haired children. Probably it was only that their skin and hair were so dark that Hun children always seemed dirty to him. The color of beer, their skin was, dark amber. He turned his horse around a corner and rode up to the gate to his stockade. It was smaller than the Kagan's, of course, much smaller, with no Court of Women, but as well-made, and more intricately decorated inside and out. Ardaric had refurnished it entirely with things taken in the raid into Italy.

Before the palace stood a statue he had found in a villa outside Milan: a boy made of white marble without flaw, half life-size. Its outstretched arm had fallen off at the elbow on the trip home. Ardaric dismounted and hung his reins over the boy's shoulders. At once the palace door opened, and Dietric, his only son, came out and down the steps.

"Where have you been?" Dietric asked. "Gundhar and Eidimir have been here since before noon, you said you would be home for dinner."

"The Kagan needed me." Ardaric made a face. For nearly a year Gundhar and Eidimir had been quarreling over ten brood mares and sixty sheep. "Are they still here?"

"They won't leave," Dietric said. His hair was sun-bleached the color of tallow; on his lean cheeks the silk of his first beard grew more red than blond. Taller than Ardaric, he was willowy, without his father's substance. "Neither of them will be the first to go." He went down to get Ardaric's horse.

Ardaric went up the steps. In the palace doorway, he turned and watched Dietric lead the horse over to the barn. Some of Ardaric's house-men were walking through the palace yard; although they passed within a few yards of one another Dietric did not greet them, nor they him. Turning, Ardaric walked into the noisy heat of the palace.

The two men on sentry duty were sitting just inside the door on the floor, eating. When Ardaric came in they got to their feet and saluted him. Ardaric waved to them. The inside of his palace was one large room, three times as long as it was wide, with the hearth in the middle made of slabs of rock, and a loft for sleeping. Someday he meant to cut up all this space into smaller rooms, like the Kagan's palace, which he knew was modeled after the palaces of the Romans.

His high seat stood at the western end of the room, under a window, and he went down toward it. Surrounded by their witnesses and kinsmen, Gundhar and Eidimir waited for him; their faces turned toward him, and they stepped forward, eager. An excited babble of talk rose among them.

"Well," Ardaric said. He climbed up onto his high seat and sat down, under the wooden canopy, which he had brought from Italy. The open window behind him breathed cold onto the back of his neck. He saw Dietric come in the front door and beckoned to him.

Dietric walked up quietly between the two mobs of witnesses and sat down on the little stool beside Ardaric's left knee. Eidimir waited until he was settled; his eyes flicked up from Dietric to Ardaric and he lifted his chin.

"My lord Ardaric, you promised us that you would give judgment today on this issue between me and Gundhar. Now, as you know—"

Ardaric put his elbow on the leather-covered arm of the chair and braced his chin on his fist. He had been listening to one side or another of this argument since the death of the uncle whose stupid legacy had caused the whole problem, and he had long since decided that there was no justice in it. Both of them equally deserved the legacy. It hardly mattered what he said or did, because the loser would immediately go to the Kagan, and a Hun would make the real decision. Rather than allow this, Ardaric had been putting the issue off for months.

Eidimir, lean and old, white-bearded to his waist, finished his version of the story and raised his arms for the approval of his witnesses. They all nodded and called out that they agreed. Flushed, Gundhar pushed forward, his hands outspread. His eyes stabbed once maliciously at Eidimir and swept up to Ardaric.

"My lord King, great son of Risimir, most excellent of men—"

Dietric was braiding the fringe on his wide blue sleeve. Gundhar's smooth speech, heavy with phrases, flowed on like bad music. Outside the open window, two women began to speak, sharing gossip: some girl was meeting a young man in the storehouse at night while the husband served in Ardaric's hall. Dietric was staring fixedly at the near wall, obviously listening. Ardaric leaned back and swung the window shut.

Tomorrow he would have to meet with Tacs. He would take Dietric with him—Dietric would like that, the Huns fascinated him. There was a moral lesson to be made, too, a good teaching. They could take another herd of the cattle due the Hun village. The Gepids were responsible for supplying the local Huns with meat, they considering themselves too superior to find their own. Perhaps it was his own fault Dietric took so little interest in the affairs of kingship; if he involved his son more in his commonplace business, Dietric might warm to it.

Gundhar stopped talking, and his witnesses clapped and nodded and said loudly that he was right and his claim proper and just. Ardaric jerked his mind back to the problem before him. They were watching him expectantly. Dietric, too, was waiting, his body twisted from the hips toward Ardaric. Ardaric opened his mouth, and suddenly the solution came to him. The sudden inspiration startled him, so that he had to cough while he straightened his words out.

"Eidimir—Gundhar. I have listened to this case for one year now, and it seems to me that each of you has a true and honorable claim to the herds. Therefore I find that the only just decision is to divide up the stock equally between you. That is my decision. You will divide the herds on the day after the coming Day of God, and my son Dietric here will oversee it."

That was honest enough; Dietric at least was a competent herdsman.

Eidimir and Gundhar stood with their mouths open, stunned. Ardaric tapped his index finger impatiently on the chair. It seemed to him that the decision was clear and just, and he expected them to applaud it, not to stand there gasping. In unison they burst into loud objections, glared at each other, and pressed toward the high seat. Ardaric lifted his hand. Reluctantly they let their voices die.

"That is my decision. Take it. Go. I will hear no more."

The two men stepped backward, looked at each other, and turned back to Ardaric. In a shrill voice, Eidimir cried, "Very well, then, I for one will bear my grievances elsewhere. The Kagan shall hear of this."

"And from me as well," Gundhar said. "We shall take this to the Kagan for justice." He gave Ardaric a vinegary stare and bowed stiffly; with their witnesses around them they marched out, past the women bearing in the loaves of bread for supper.

Ardaric muttered an oath. "There is no way to make men happy anymore."

"I thought it was fair," Dietric said. "But to them, maybe it seemed . . ."

"They are greedy," Ardaric said. They had no respect for him, for their own king, no humility before his decisions. He felt hot and prickly, as if their dissatisfaction had rubbed him to a rash. "Go get me something to eat."

THREE

B EFORE DAWN DIETRIC
went out with some of the other men and brought up the cattle for the Huns from the lower pastures. A light snow had
fallen during the night; against the white ground the red
cattle seemed like a child's cloth animals. Dietric sent two of
the men up to ride the point and with the other herders rode
along on the flanks of the herd to watch for strays. It was much
colder after the snow; the wind cut through his sheepskin coat
and made him shiver.

He knew he should not be so excited about the prospect of
going into the Hun village, but he had never been there and
he had met only one other Gepid who had. The sun rose and
warmed him slightly, and he tugged off his gloves. Blowing
on his hands he thrust them into the front of his coat to warm
them and wiggled his toes inside his boots to keep his feet from
freezing. Up ahead, on the hillside between them and the ford
across the river, his father waited on his white horse. Hastily,
Dietric pulled on his gloves, so that his father would not shout
at him as if he were a child still, caught doing something
wrong.

Ardaric was waving to him. He lifted his reins and swung
his black gelding away from the herd. While he rode up
toward Ardaric he looked over the cattle again, pleased: they
were fat, strong two-year-olds, most of them, worth all the care
they took. He reined up before his father and saluted him.

"You should have waited for me," Ardaric said. "You aren't really needed here."

Dietric said, "I'm sorry," and felt himself start to blush; that embarrassed him and he blushed harder. His neck and forehead burnt as if in the sun.

"Now, listen to what I say," Ardaric said. "When we meet the Hun, say nothing. Especially do not ask any of your silly questions. They are easily insulted and I don't want to offend him. If you disobey me I shall send you to stay with the horses."

"Yes," Dietric said.

"Be careful what you do, if we go into his hut. They have many customs that make no sense but some of them still take them seriously. Don't look at any of their women or children. Don't take out your knife, even to cut your fingernails. Don't show the sole of your foot. If anyone offers you food, decline it once. He will offer it again, and you may accept it then."

"I thought I couldn't speak," Dietric said.

"Don't be so rude to me, or you won't go at all."

"Yes, Papa."

"Don't eat or drink anything if you don't know what it is. When he speaks to you, meet his eyes."

"Yes, Papa."

"They are a people of ritual," Ardaric said. He and Dietric had reached the river; the herders were moving the cattle in a tight knot across the shallow ford. With Dietric behind him Ardaric rode up beside the nearest herder, one of the older men, who smiled and nodded when Ardaric hailed him.

"We had some snow last night, my King."

Ardaric looked up into the pitch of the sky, squinting. "More to come. We'll have snow to the eaves of our houses by the day after tomorrow."

"Well, then, it's good we're getting these steers across the river. No telling what they'd do if they had no meat in when the deep snow came."

Talking of the Huns, he gestured toward the Hun village. As if by signal, the three of them started forward, riding down into the ford behind the cattle. The point of the herd was already turning east, back in the direction of the Kagan's hill.

Ardaric and the herder went on talking solemnly of the weather, the herds, the stored hay, and the next crop of calves. Dietric took a deep breath of the air, so cold it tasted like ice water. Ahead, beyond the dreary patch of willows at the edge of the marsh, the stockade rose against the slate-colored sky. To the south of it, the ground fell off sharply into a short cliff. The herders were guiding the cattle to pass beneath this embankment. The Hun village lay on the far side of the hill; they would not see it until they had passed the stockade. The embankment itself was a kind of boundary, beyond which Dietric had been forbidden to go since he was old enough to ride.

The point of the herd had swerved to clear a finger of the marsh and was even with the leading edge of the embankment. Ardaric put out his hand toward Dietric. "Watch, now," he said; his voice was sharp.

Surprised, Dietric looked for something to see. At first there was nothing save the cattle and the distant stockade, but while he watched, a file of Huns came riding down between the stockade wall and the rim of the embankment. Their short, curved legs pressed into the shaggy sides of their horses. Their hair was decorated with feathers, bright stones, and metal, and a few of them wore tunics trimmed with shredded gold. Watching them, Dietric realized how awkward he still felt on his horse, even after years of hard work; he grew miserable with envy of their horsemanship.

"There is my Hun," Ardaric said. "The third from the front."

That Hun looked like all the rest, except that his horse was smaller than the others.

"Tacs," Ardaric shouted. The Hun flung up his arm and his

horse carried him out of line. The other Huns stopped, while Tacs cantered down the short slope toward Ardaric. The herd of cattle trudged steadily up between Ardaric and the file of motionless riders, and Tacs had to swerve to avoid them. Ardaric's herders were turning the cattle into the embankment to stop them.

One of the Huns on the hillside let out a cry, and the hair on the back of Dietric's neck unaccountably stood on end. Like a bird leaving a high branch the Hun wheeled his horse out of line and galloped down toward the herd. A red feather flashed in his black hair. Ardaric's men backed hastily away. The Hun carried a lance trimmed half its length with squirrel tails, and he raised it over his head and shook it and again gave the wild cry. Plunging into the herd, he scattered the last half of the herd back toward the river.

Dietric turned his horse and rode down to collect the frightened cattle together again. He shouted to the other Gepids to help him; across the herd he could see the Hun with the red feather forcing a spotted steer away from the others. The cattle lowed in fear. Other riders galloped up around Dietric, and he turned to call to them.

They were Huns, not his own people. He reined in. The Huns swept past him, gathering the cattle together into a herd again. Dietric rode at a gallop back to his father. Looking over his shoulder, he saw the Hun with the red feather beating the spotted steer on the flanks with his lance. Finally the steer turned and ran away from the herd, its muzzle out.

The Hun chased it, leaning out to strike it now and again. Dietric drew rein beside his father; the Hun Tacs was already there, on Ardaric's other side. Dietric studied him an instant, shyly. Tacs was watching the other Hun chase the spotted steer across the plain. All Huns looked much alike. Their yellow faces, sunken-eyed, showed no expression. Dietric looked back toward the spotted steer.

A short way from the herd, near a dead tree, it was doubling back, and the Hun swerved his horse to meet it. His body flowed smoothly with his horse; only the tumbling red feather showed how abruptly he moved. The steer lunged away. Its horns swept threatening toward the Hun horse. The rider goaded it with his lance, and the steer lumbered around and ran again. Leaning out from his horse, the Hun drove his lance into the steer's belly.

The steer bellowed in pain. It staggered and for a moment Dietric thought it would fall. His own heart jumped in sympathy and horror. The Hun jabbed it in the flanks with the point of the lance and the steer heaved itself up again and rushed on. Blood dribbled from cuts on its flanks. The Hun forced it into a dead run. The long pink entrails streamed from its slit belly, entangling its hind feet so that it slipped and stumbled.

Ardaric grunted. Dietric chewed the inside of his cheek. Why did they not kill it? The Hun was holding his horse tight-reined to a choppy gallop, to keep from outrunning the steer; he made no effort to kill it. Trampling its own guts, the steer floundered weakening across the plain. Blood and offal marked its path. Now the soft pink tissues of its insides were black with dirt. It sank to its knees. Its muzzle dipped to the ground, and bloody froth poured from its nostrils. Dietric realized that he was clutching the pommel of his saddle, that he was holding his breath. The Hun wheeled his horse around the steer like a crow settling to carrion. The steer collapsed over on its side; its legs shook and went limp. Beside Dietric, Ardaric let out his breath in a long sigh.

Turning to the Hun, Ardaric said furiously, "Why do you people do that?"

Tacs' tilted eyes rounded slightly. "We aren't allowed to hunt anymore." His shoulders moved, as if putting off some burden; his small slots of eyes looked elsewhere. "Do you want to talk here?"

"No," Ardaric said curtly. "It's too cold."

Tacs shrugged. "My aul will be full of people. We can sit on the palace porch in the stockade." He made no move that Dietric saw, but his black pony backed up and turned toward the stockade wall.

"We aren't going to the village," Dietric said.

"No." Ardaric started after Tacs.

In his disappointment Dietric at first did not move. The Hun at a quick trot was riding up the slope, with Ardaric a few strides behind; the other Huns were taking the cattle off around the bottom edge of the embankment toward their village. The dead steer lay on the plain, a shapeless bleeding mass. From the direction of the Hun village, a group of women came carrying baskets and knives, to butcher the carcass. Dietric slammed his heels into his horse's ribs and galloped after his father. He began to think of excuses to go back home, without having to sit through a boring session of military talk. But when he drew even with his father, he saw by the look on Ardaric's face that he should not speak, and so he had to ride along fuming beside him into the stockade where he had been a dozen times before, tether his horse with the others, and walk up onto the wide roofed porch that sprawled along the front and one side of the Kagan's palace. Tacs led them to the far end of the porch, out of the wind, and they all sat down. Ardaric began immediately to ask questions about the roads through some marsh in northern Italy.

The Hun answered slowly, as if he were envisioning the place in his mind. For a while Dietric studied him curiously. There was a red and black symbol painted on the Hun's forehead: it looked like a shovel with a staff drawn across it. On each cheek he wore the deep scars that, Ardaric had said, Huns gave their children at birth, to teach them to bear pain before they tasted milk. Dietric had always thought that interesting, like a reverse baptism.

The porch floor under him quivered, and he looked around. Another Hun was coming toward them, carrying a clay pot of coals and a jug of wine. He set the brazier down between them, smiled, and strode away without waiting for thanks. Dietric craned his neck to watch him go, amazed. A red feather swung from a braid in his black hair: it was the same man who had killed the steer.

DID YOU GO NEAR ROME?" Ardaric said. "How close?"

"We spent two days there. There was a big crossroads, we had to find out how much traffic passed."

"Two days? Did you go inside the city?"

Tacs looked surprised. "Inside? No—how could I? They had soldiers on the walls everywhere, and on the roads, too, I told you. We could only travel at night because of it. South of there we had no trouble."

Ardaric grunted. Like all Huns Tacs had an excellent memory for details of terrain, and through the long morning he had answered all Ardaric's questions patiently and usefully. Ardaric could not tell if the Hun were tired, but he himself was, and he wanted to stop for the day. He looked off into the yard. Under the porch, two dogs were growling over a bone, almost directly beneath him. He banged on the porch with his heel to scare them away. The thought of Rome drew him back to the Hun.

"What did you see of Rome?"

"Walls." Tacs shrugged. "It was like Sirmium, only older."

Ardaric heated with rage. This stupid man could not see the difference between a provincial fortress and Rome. Before he could speak, Dietric laughed. Ardaric looked at him, who had been silent all morning. "Why do you laugh?"

"You speak of Rome as if it were a place," Dietric said. "Like Hungvar."

"Like Hungvar! Rome is twenty times as great as Hungvar."

"Of course," Dietric said. "Half the world is Rome. Everything is either Rome or not Rome, isn't it? Everything we want is Rome." His voice faltered. "Like Heaven. Isn't it?"

In the stillness that followed, Ardaric could hear the dogs whining and growling under the porch. Tacs was drawing a piece of plaited rawhide through his fingers; his eyes were fixed on Dietric. Two horsemen rode by in the yard, talking. Inside the palace a door slammed.

"I can see how you would think of Rome in that way," Ardaric said at last. "It is an arresting idea. But it isn't true. Rome is a city, a real place like Hungvar or Sirmium, except that it is the center of the world. All good comes from Rome."

Now it was Tacs who laughed. The back of Ardaric's neck grew hot and rough. "It is true! Why do you both laugh at me?"

"All that comes from Rome is tribute," Tacs said, "to pay Germans to feed Hiung. Rome is like all cities, with nowhere to hunt and nowhere to graze horses, and all the water is kept standing in jugs so that it turns bad."

Dietric pulled at his chin. "There are more important things than that."

"Yes," Tacs said, "but none of them come from Rome either."

"Laws come from Rome," Dietric said. "The books of Christ come from Rome, and—" He looked at Ardaric. "What else?"

"Don't bother," Ardaric said. "Huns have no sensitivity for such matters."

Tacs laughed again. Ardaric set his teeth on edge. Flushed red to the hairline, Dietric said, "Are you laughing at us?"

"How can you say the books of Christ come from Rome when it was the Romans who tried to turn Christ into a tree?"

Dietric for a moment did not move. At last he turned his wide blue eyes toward Ardaric and slowly back to Tacs. "What?"

"I am no Christian, of course I know little of the totem. The Romans tried to turn Christ into a tree, because his magic was so strong. So the Romans were his enemy and must be yours. Isn't that why you wear that totem?"

Ardaric rubbed the back of his hand across his face. He felt as he did when the Kagan spoke of magic. He had never before heard a Hun speak of Christ. Tacs settled himself more comfortably on his heels and wound the plaited rawhide around his wrist.

"Besides, all the monks who come here are from New Rome, and the monks of Rome are their enemies, they kill each other. Isn't that so?"

Furious, Ardaric said, "New Rome is part of Rome. You understand nothing."

"You have never seen Rome," Tacs said. "What do you know?" He smiled, showing his eyeteeth like a dog.

Ardaric bit down on his tongue. It occurred to him that Tacs was playing with him. His palms were sweating and his heart beat raggedly in his chest. He knew the red and black mark on the Hun's forehead; it was a sign of mourning. Perhaps Christians had murdered the Hun's friend in Italy. Perhaps Tacs blamed Ardaric for his friend's death.

"If we were all Romans, there would be peace and everyone would be rich," Dietric said. "Aren't we all supposed to strive to be Romans?"

"Why?" Tacs asked.

"Because then there will be peace."

Tacs shrugged. "I have never heard that before. The Fluteplayer says—"

"The Fluteplayer!" Ardaric cried. "A lazy, painted shaman —who listens to him?"

"He says that the Romans have no magic left since the Visigoths sacked the City. The Fluteplayer knows everything."

"Why do you call him The Fluteplayer?" Dietric asked.

Tacs gave him a wary look. "Because he plays on a flute."

"Just the walls fell," Ardaric said. "Dietric is right, in a way; Rome is a way of talking about what is excellent and to be wished for in the world." He gathered himself to go, to get away from this.

"Well," Tacs said, "whatever happened, Rome has no power left, all the demons and spirits have gone, and the Romans took their totems to Ravenna. I thought we were talking about how to conquer Rome, anyway."

"We deserve Rome as much as anyone else," Ardaric said. He tapped Dietric on the shoulder. "Come along, we should be going back. Tacs, you will be here when I need you again?"

"Oh, yes," Tacs said, and gave him that smile again, full of teeth.

FOUR

⊂⊉

Tacs shared an aul in
the northeast part of the Hiung camp with his mother and his
brother and his brother's wives. Because his brother was rich
enough to keep three wives, and because Tacs was a bachelor,
he could find no comfort there; in the crowd and under the
constant pressure of their work, no one paid him any attention,
and of course he had no wife to see to his needs. Therefore he
spent most of the day either in the Kagan's stockade with his
friends, or in the aul of his friend Yaya, Marag's younger
brother.

Yaya had a wife, Ummake, but she was usually sick, and
there was no one to prod the friends into keeping their clothes
neat and themselves clean and fed. They spent the evenings
telling lies and stories and getting drunk on tea made from the
white-flowered herb the Hiung called The White Brother.

Several of the other unmarried young men of the palace
guard also gathered in Yaya's aul whenever they could. Since
long before the raid into Italy, they had made themselves a
nuisance to the people living in that neighborhood; because
there was no one to feed them, they found it necessary to steal,
and of course no one mended their clothes or made them keep
the aul and the horse pen clean, and they were lax in observing
taboo. Yaya's wife had given up trying to keep order and now
told stories and stole food and drank The White Brother along
with them, when she was not lying in the back of the aul
coughing and spitting blood.

After Tacs brought Marag back, Yaya went to his grand-mother's aul for the funeral. He did not come back until the day that Tacs first spoke with King Ardaric. The first sign Tacs had of his return was the sight of Yaya's skewbald horse in the pen behind the aul. He turned the black pony loose in the pen and went around the aul toward the door.

The aul, made of hides lashed to a dome-shaped frame of sticks, was sagging heavily on one side. Tacs stopped to run his fingers over the sunken hide. He could feel the broken sticks of the frame where they pressed outward. If they did not fix it before the first heavy snow the aul would collapse on their heads. He went around to the door and ducked inside, into a smoky, ruddy dimness full of half-seen people.

"Yaya?"

"Here," Yaya called. "I saw you talking to the Gepid King."

Tacs climbed over two people sprawled on the ground be-side the fire. Sitting down beside Yaya, he loosened his boot-laces and pulled off his boots. In the darkness behind him he could hear a low rasping cough: Ummake was sick again.

Tacs said, "I talked to Ardaric because Attila ordered me to. Do you think I love him? What has your father said about vengeance?"

"They asked a shaman," Yaya said, disgust in his voice. "There is no need for vengeance."

Monidiak leaned across the fire to hand Tacs a jug. "Who was the young one with King Ardaric?"

"I think it was his son. He never told me." The jug was half full of tea; he sipped it, rolling its sweetness around on his tongue. "Is there anything to eat?"

Yaya took the jug. "Ummake was too sick to go to the butchering, and no one bothered to bring us anything."

"It wasn't my fault," Ummake called, from the back of the aul. Yaya crept into the darkness toward her, speaking softly to her.

"Monidiak," Tacs said. "What about that spotted steer you killed?"

In the firelight Monidiak's round handsome face was copper-colored; his eyes glinted. "I had to give it to my mother. Don't worry. We have always eaten before."

Tacs got the jug back and drank several mouthfuls of tea. His head buzzed. Warmth spread slowly through his belly and up into his chest. He lay back to see around Yaya into the back of the aul. "Ummake? Do you want The White Brother?"

"No," Ummake said, in a faint, half-choked voice. "Thank you, Tacs."

Tacs sat up straight again. Yaya and Monidiak were staring at each other, frowning.

"There is one place where we can find meat and not make the people here angry at us," Monidiak said. "You know where that is."

Yaya shook his head. He crawled up closer to the fire. "What if we're caught?"

"Puh." Monidiak clapped his hands together. "What if we die tonight in our sleep?"

"Then we won't need meat," Yaya said.

Tacs said, "Monidiak, do you want to steal from the Germans?"

"Of course."

From beyond the fire, Bryak drew himself closer. "I hear plotting. Will you need help?"

"Four of us can do it," Monidiak said. "But if Yaya is afraid—"

"I'll go," Yaya said. "But if we are caught, the Kagan will find out, and you know what he might do to us."

Monidiak shrugged. "Better that than sitting around here getting drunk on an empty stomach." He reached for the jug, smiling.

THE SNOW BEGAN TO FALL
while they were riding along the river past the Gepids' camp.
Tacs could tell from the small, stinging flakes that it would be
a heavy storm. He pulled his fur hat down over his ears and
pressed the black pony up closer to Yaya's skewbald horse.
Yaya looked around; already his eyebrows and the ends of his
mustache were caked with snow. Tacs smiled at him.

"At least we won't leave any tracks."

Yaya grunted. He turned to Monidiak, riding on his other
side. "This was your idea. We could have begged some food
from the Kagan's kitchen. We could have stolen some from my
father. We could have waited until tomorrow. What if we get
lost in the snow?"

Bryak gave a short laugh like a dog yapping. He and Monidiak began to insult Yaya for his caution. Tacs looked around
them. They were crossing the edge of the marsh and the horses
were walking short-strided on the uneven brittle footing. Up
ahead of them, through the falling snow, he could just make
out the buildings on the top of the hill where the Gepids
camped. Beyond this place it was forbidden for Hiung to
travel except with the knowledge of the Kagan. Of course they
had all ridden through it dozens of times, but none of them
knew it well. Monidiak who was cousin to Edeco, the Chief
of the Kagan's Guard, often ran errands for him and claimed
he knew where the Gepids would be keeping their camp stock.
The snow blew straight into Tacs' face. His cheeks were stiff
from the cold.

They dropped into a single file to cross the ford. After the
first wild flurry of snow, the storm seemed to calm a little, and
Tacs could see farther across the plain. Holding his horse back
a little, he let Yaya catch up to him, and when the other man
came even with him, he unhooked the jug from Yaya's belt
and held it up. Yaya nodded and pushed it toward him. Tacs
took a long swallow and handed the jug on to Bryak.

Before them, Monidiak swung his horse to follow the river and settled frowning down into his saddle. Yaya took the jug from Tacs. "See him?" Yaya whispered. "He has forgotten. He is getting us lost."

"No," Tacs said. He knocked the snow off the shoulders of his new coat; he had won it from Monidiak at dice. Monidiak's mother had spent half the season covering it with designs in red and black thread and beads. Now Tacs wished he had worn his own coat to get soaked with snow. He looked unhappily up into the sky.

Monidiak said, "Whoa. Come here to me." He spoke crisply, like Edeco giving orders. They rode up around him, putting their horses head to head and their backs to the wind.

"Up to the north," Monidiak said, "there is a grove of willow trees. Yaya and Tacs must go there. The grove is along the river at the edge of the Gepids' pasture. In this storm, who can say, but they might have gathered up their herds over there, in the curve of the river, to get some shelter."

"There will be guards," Yaya said.

"Yes. I am not stupid. Bryak and I will go north of the grove of willows, and find us a steer. Leave the guards to us."

Tacs said, "Why must two of us wait in the willow grove? You will need help."

"You go," Yaya said. He drank again from the jug. "You will all be killed."

Monidiak picked up his reins. "This is my raid, I will do it my way. In this storm it is safer to go by twos, that's all. Go to the willow grove. Bryak, come with me."

He and Bryak cantered away. The snow enveloped them. Tacs looked toward the river to orient himself and tightened his calves around the black pony's barrel. Their horses carried them off at a trot; Yaya handed him the jug.

"Monidiak has no plan," Tacs said.

"We should not have come," Yaya answered. "You are always calling me a coward, and yet I am always right."

Tacs swept the snow off his shoulders. "Not always." Monidiak was quick-minded and would have time enough to think,
riding around above the herds. He squinted forward into the
snow, watching for the first sign of the willow grove.

DIETRIC SPREAD HIS HANDS
over the fire. Here inside the lean-to, it was warm enough almost to take off his coat, but his fingers and his feet were still
numb. The other herders crowded in around him, jostling him.
They spoke to one another over his head; none of them spoke
to him, except to apologize for knocking into him.

At the first sign of snow, he had come out to the pasture to
help them; he always did, although they never asked him to. At
first he had only gotten in their way, which they had borne
patiently enough. Now he was of use in their tedious, difficult
work.

The oldest of the herders squatted before the fire and
stretched his fingers toward it. Dietric cleared his throat, re-
hearsing in his mind what he would say.

"How long will the snow keep up, do you think?"

The old man looked quickly up at him and politely averted
his eyes. Dietric looked into the fire. "Two days, maybe," the
man said. "It will get heavier tonight." He peeped up at
Dietric again and rubbed his hands vigorously together to warm
them.

Dietric moved away from the fire to let another man get
warm. Sometimes he played the king's son over them and made
them give up things for his sake, to see how they would react.
Standing up in the eave of the lean-to, he watched the old man
clap his hands together and blow on them and put them almost
in the flames. He longed for them to admire him, although
they themselves bored him. They preferred Ardaric to him;
Ardaric hardly knew in what season the calves were sorted
and assigned.

Beyond the lean-to, the sheltered pasture inside the curve of the river was veiled in the falling snow. The nearest cattle stood under a tree with their backs to the wind and their bodies pressed together. Now at last his fingers were thawing out, and one of the herdsmen came to his side and quietly offered him a drink of beer. He smiled and the herder smiled and gave him a pat on the arm, like a mother. Dietric turned back to the snow.

The cattle were moving. Sometimes they moved before the wind, in a storm like this, hunting better shelter. He straightened up, alarmed; the cattle were breaking into a trot.

"Hey."

The other herders turned, saw, and shouted. Dietric took a step out of the lean-to, toward his horse, and the nearest herder stopped him.

"No—in this storm you will be lost. They won't go far. We can gather them after the storm." He drew Dietric back into the lean-to.

"Why would they do that?" Dietric said. "Something must have happened to scare them."

The herders shrugged. They passed their beer around without concern, chattering to each other and telling stories about their wives and the other women. Such talk always embarrassed Dietric; Ardaric never allowed loose words in his presence. Deep in their conversations, the herders ignored him. When their eyes happened to meet his they looked quickly away. He glanced out into the sky. If he left at once, he would reach the village by sundown, following the river all the way so that he wouldn't get lost. He backed away from the fire and pulled on his mittens.

He got his horse and rode off into the storm. At first his tall black gelding balked at going into the snow, but Dietric pried it away from the other horses and forced it three hundred feet through the grey, muffled landscape toward their own stable, and the horse realized where they were going and lengthened stride. The storm had laid down only a few inches of snow, which blew in swirls over the frozen ground. He swung the horse to keep the river on his right hand and gave it its head.

While he rode he thought about the sudden bolting of the cattle. If something—the wind, even the stinging snowflakes —had frightened only one of them, they would all have bolted, just to keep together. The herder was right, of course, and they would all be gathered together again in the morning when the snow had stopped. He rode in among trees, where the wind hushed and the snow lay deeper, and abruptly reined in.

At the same moment he saw them, the Huns saw him; there were two of them, bent over a dead steer, butchering it out. Dietric thought, They are stealing one of our steers. They stampeded the cattle. His heart seemed to have stopped beating. He looked hard at the nearer of the two Huns; it was Tacs.

He gathered up his reins and rode forward toward them, before they could attack him. "Wait," he said. "Listen to me."

The two Huns lunged toward him. One seized his horse's reins; the other, Tacs, in a gorgeous snow-covered coat, spoke quickly in his own tongue and shouted something. From behind Dietric and overhead, shouts answered—there were more of them, in the trees. He knew they would kill him for having caught them stealing. He said, "If you do what you are thinking of, we shall all get into trouble, but if you listen to me maybe we can find a way out of it."

Tacs turned his face up toward him. "What do you mean?" He looked at the other man and said something, his voice sharp.

Dietric looked down at the other man. His body stiffened; in the Hun's right hand was a long butcher's knife, already bloody.

"What do you mean?" Tacs said, pulling on his leg.

Dietric said, "You know what will happen if I am murdered. You know who I—who my father is." His lips were stiff with fear and cold and he could scarcely form the words. "These herds are mine, too. I will sell you the steer."

Another Hun appeared beside Tacs, spoke to him in Hunnish, and looked up at Dietric. "I am leader here. Talk to me."

It was the Hun with the red feather. Dietric repeated what he had said. He could not keep from glancing down at the Hun on his left, holding his long-bladed knife before him. The blade was pointed at his chest. They were all grown Huns, warriors, and killing would not seem so much to them as it did to him.

The leader said, "Yes, you are right, we would be in a lot of trouble if we killed you, if we were caught. But if we let you go, you will tell your father we have stolen a steer, and the Kagan will take us for punishment."

Dietric said, "If you give me something for the steer, you will have paid for it." He looked at Tacs, standing behind the leader, hoping to see something benign in his face. But Tacs was frowning at the Hun before him, obviously worried. It was Tacs he recognized.

The leader snorted. He spoke to Tacs; the third Hun, with the knife, tried to speak and was silenced by the other two in unison. Tacs shrugged. Wheeling toward Dietric, the leader said, "What will you take in trade for the steer?"

"Something of value," Dietric said. He looked them over, in a panic to find something rich. "His coat."

They both scowled at him, and the Hun with the knife laughed. The leader glanced over his shoulder at Tacs; they spoke a little, and the leader turned to face Dietric.

"It is too much."

Dietric thought, He is enjoying it, and wondered if that meant he was safe. Relaxing a little, he began to long for the coat. "What is a steer worth?"

"Your life," the leader said, in a comfortable voice. "We will give you the coat for the steer if you give us some gold back."

"No," Tacs called. "I will give him gold. Don't give him my coat."

"We have no gold," the leader said. "Not here."

Tacs hugged his arms over his coat; slowly he began to undo the clasps. Dietric said, "I will give you an emperor for the coat. And the steer."

"Two emperors," the leader said.

The Hun with the knife turned abruptly and walked over to the steer. Bending over it, he began to butcher it up, as they had been doing when Dietric came. Dietric said, "One emperor only." He only had one emperor; his father had given it to him for a charm. "I will have to bring it to you in the stockade."

Tacs came forward, holding the coat bundled in his arms. The leader stepped back, turning away. "We are already trusting you too much," he said, and went to help cut up the steer.

Tacs held up the coat. Bending down, Dietric lifted it out of the Hun's hands; the man's thin fingers stroked the coat, giving it up.

"I'll bring you one gold emperor at the stockade," Dietric 'said. "You are there often?"

"When you come, if I give you gold, will you give me back my coat?" Tacs rubbed his upper arms; without the coat he seemed smaller, almost frail. Dietric thought, He is cold, he will freeze, and nearly gave him back the coat. Straightening up, he reined his horse hurriedly around. "Maybe." It was such a beautiful coat and no other Gepid would have one like it. "Good-by." He rode away under the trees, following the river.

They did not come after him; he rode on, stuffing the Hun coat underneath his own sheepskin to keep the snow off it. He could hardly believe what had happened; he felt as if he had been outside his body, watching, while the whole thing went on below him. They would have killed him if he had not spoken out. Now he began to shiver. Ahead of him, the river wound out into the open, away from the trees. The snow was falling more thickly, wet and sharp on the edge of the wind. He thought of Ardaric, what he might possibly say, and sorted out his arguments in reply.

FIVE

⊂⊨

THE KAGAN ORDERED DEN-
gazich, his son by a princess of the Ostrogoths, to give judgment in the matter of Gundhar and Eidimir, and on the first
day after the snowstorm, Ardaric and Dietric went to the
Kagan's palace to hear the decision. Everybody knew that the
judgment was Attila's and not Dengazich's, who, Ardaric said,
was only a little older than Dietric and not as clever.

The snow that had been falling the day Dietric bargained
with the Huns had fallen for two days afterward, and Hungvar
was covered with snow as high as Dietric's girth. Except where
constant traffic had beaten deep paths into the snow, it was
impossible to tell what lay beneath, whether plain or marsh
or the river itself, frozen solid in its bed. The wind had whipped
the snow into fantastic drifts, crested like roosters' combs and
the manes of horses. But in the morning the wind had died
away and a dry cold settled over Hungvar.

Dietric wore his Hun coat, although he knew it made
Ardaric angry. He had told his father the whole story, without
mentioning that Tacs had been among the Huns; Ardaric had
raged awhile and threatened to throw the coat into the fire, but
Dietric patiently argued with him until Ardaric let him keep
it. Quilted and padded and lined with fur, it kept him much
warmer than his sheepskin, yet on the short ride to the palace,
the cold still reached his body.

The crisp air and the blazing blue of the sky exhilarated
him. They rode up the road to the stockade gate. Half a dozen

Hun women were sweeping the blown snow off the road before
the gate, using little bundles of twigs tied together into
brooms. Dietric smiled at them, but only one of the women
smiled back.

The Kagan's judgments were always given from the west
end of the porch. Today there were several judgments and a
crowd stood waiting in the open area between the porch and
the stockade wall, all stamping their feet and beating their
arms to warm themselves. On the porch, three of the Kagan's
sons and his Roman secretary, Constantius, sat encased in fur,
so that only their eyes and foreheads showed. Inside the stockade, the snow had been swept up into heaps along the fence.
Dietric could hear the screams and laughter of children from
another part of the stockade; he guessed from the noise that
they were sledding. For a moment his own childhood haunted
him.

Ardaric dismounted and a slave came up to hold his horse
and Dietric's. They walked over to the crowd waiting for the
judgments. As if their coming were the signal, a Hun guard
came forward with the Kagan's horsetail standard and planted
it in a heap of snow before the porch. The long black horsetails shone in the sunlight as if they had been brushed. One of
the four men sitting on the porch rose and came forward and
began to speak in Hunnish.

"Ellac," Ardaric said softly. "The Kagan's heir."

Dietric nodded. He had seen Ellac before—a true Hun,
flat-faced, and arrogant. Few of the people in the crowd listening understood what he was saying; they were mostly Germans,
who seldom bothered to learn Hunnish. Dietric looked around
behind the crowd, at the gate, where the palace guards usually
were.

There were four or five of them there, sitting on the ground
in a roofless shelter made of snow. Dietric squinted, trying to
make out their faces, but could not. Now Ellac was speaking
German, delivering judgment between two Germans not of the

same tribe, the kind of case that only the Kagan could settle.

"Stop fidgeting," Ardaric said.

Dietric stood straight and tried to concentrate on Ellac. After their judgment was spoken, Ardaric intended to go into the palace and complain about the Huns' stealing his cow. The previous afternoon, he and Dietric had gone out after the snow stopped falling and found what remained of the slaughtered beast, frozen hard as stone in the bloody snow. Tramping around the willow grove, Ardaric had at last admitted that Dietric's action had been proper. That was when he told Dietric he might keep the Hun coat.

"The Kagan wishes," Ellac said. "It will be." He looked over the crowd in a sweeping glance and stepped back.

Dengazich came forward, wrapped to the cheekbones in sleek black fur, taller and rangier than a full-blooded Hun. Of course he spoke Hunnish at first. Dietric shifted his weight from one foot to the other and back again, and his eyes strayed across the yard. From the Court of Women a little group of people was coming, carrying baskets: washing. No, the baskets were empty. Dietric frowned, wondering where they were going. He turned to watch them walk out the gate, and Ardaric jabbed him in the side with his elbow so that Dietric grunted and the people around them turned to look. Dietric stood straight, but through the corner of his eye followed the band of people carrying baskets.

Just before they reached the gate, which, as always during the day, stood wide open, a Hun on a black pony trotted in. Tacs. Dietric could not help but smile; he looked straight forward again, toward Dengazich.

At last Dengazich spoke the Hunnish words that Dietric knew meant the end of the speech, and without pausing started at the beginning again in German. Gundhar and Eidimir and their witnesses were there, near the front of the crowd; they stirred at the sound of their names, and Ardaric moved forward a few steps. Dietric realized that now Ardaric himself was a suppliant in this case. He frowned, not liking that; he preferred to think of his father as a king without kings over him. But of course the Kagan was over everybody. He glanced behind him and saw the black pony standing hipshot before the snow shelter where the Hun guardsmen were.

"Therefore," Dengazich was saying, in his clear, excellent German, "it is our judgment that Gundhar and Eidimir henceforth shall share equally in the profits of these herds and in their losses, each having them in his care for alternating years, and since Gundhar held them all the year that King Ardaric had the issue for judgment, Eidimir shall have them for the next year. The Kagan wishes. It will be."

Ardaric made a rumble of sound in his throat; his pale brows drew together over the high bridge of his nose. Dietric said, "But that's just what you said, isn't it, Papa?" and was startled that Ardaric swore at him. Gundhar and Eidimir turned back toward the gate. They looked unhappy as well.

"You fools," Ardaric called. He stepped out of the crowd to shout at them; neither man met his eyes or stopped to attend him. "If you had left it where I judged it, it would have been the same, and you would not have humiliated me. You fools, you mice-minded feather-assed greedy little men."

Gundhar and Eidimir walked quickly away, their heads down as if out of a high wind. On the porch, Dengazich laughed. Everybody was staring at Ardaric. Dietric drew away a little, embarrassed. Ardaric swore loudly at Dengazich, who laughed again, and strode away toward the north side of the porch and the door into the palace. The laugh disappeared from Dengazich's face as if washed away, and he followed Ardaric with his pale eyes. Something in the set of his jaw and the line of his body made Dietric nervous. He knew without knowing how that Dengazich hated his father. For a moment, Dietric waited to see if anything else would happen, but

Ardaric tramped up the steps and into the palace, and Dengazich sat down again, his long half-breed face sinking down into
the fringe of black fur.

Fat Constantius came forward to deliver a judgment, his
scanty hair greased down and his nose red from the cold.
Dietric backed out of the crowd and went across the yard toward the little snow shelter where the guards were. The black
pony was still standing before it, eating from a pile of hay.
When Dietric approached, it flung up its head and snorted and
moved quickly sideways; its lips wrinkled back from its long
yellow teeth. Dietric stopped, alarmed.

Tacs leaned out the door of the snow hut. "Oh," he said, in
an uncertain voice. "What are you doing here, king's son?"

Dietric took his eyes from the pony. "I have the emperor
I owe to you. May I—does he bite?"

"Yes." Tacs came out of the snow fort, holding out one hand
toward the pony, which pinned back its ears and backed off in
a rush. Tacs said something angrily in Hunnish. The pony
wheeled and trotted off around the hut, and Tacs followed a
few steps and stopped. He looked back over his shoulder at
Dietric.

"Sometimes he won't listen to me. Come inside."

Dietric went to the hut, watching for the pony, and stepped
through the space in the wall. There was no roof at all; the
walls came to his chest, two feet thick. When Tacs followed
him in, they were all packed together, nearly touching. The
three other Huns in the fort stared at him, blank-faced, through
their eyes like slots cut into the hide of their faces. Dietric could
feel himself blushing. Everyone else was sitting, even Tacs,
while he stood hovering over them.

"Sit down," Tacs said.

Dietric sat down on his heels. He had no room to stretch
his legs out. They were all staring at him. He cleared his
throat. Inside the fort, it was amazingly warm. The air smelled
of Hun and something else, something sweet. In the next

moment he recognized the two Huns sitting opposite him—
the man who had held the knife on him in the willow grove,
and the one who had named himself their leader.

They both stared rudely back at him, and one said something
to Tacs in Hunnish. Tacs put one hand out to stroke the sleeve
of Dietric's new coat.

"I have gold now," he said hopefully. "I will give you three
emperors and you can give me back my coat."

The man on Dietric's left said something in Hunnish.
Dietric glanced at him; he did not recognize him, but he knew
there had been a fourth man among the Huns in the willow
grove and he guessed this was he. When the man had finished
speaking, Dietric turned to Tacs.

"If I give you back your coat my father will know that you
were the one who traded it to me in the first place."

The Hun who had been the leader nodded. "So Bryak just
said. Tacs, leave off, you can get another coat." This man had
a round, good-natured face, quick to smile. "I am Monidiak.
Tacs you know, and that is Bryak, and that Yaya."

Bryak, on Dietric's left, smiled at him. Yaya, who had held
the knife on him in the willow grove, was a sour-looking man
with a wide, flat nose. Monidiak said, "We were all on the
raid against your father's herd."

"Oh," Dietric said, warily. "Well, it was very clever."

"It was stupid," Yaya said. His eyes were so bloodshot that
no white showed. With his squat nose, they made him look
brutal and coarse. He had a jug in his lap, and he sipped from
it. "All was stupid, very stupid." He passed the jug to Bryak.

"Here," Bryak said, holding the jug toward Dietric. He
looked at Tacs and asked something in Hunnish; his sparse
eyebrows rose. Dietric looked from one man to the other, surprised to find them all so different. He took the jug. Inside,
the liquid splashed. The sweet aroma filled his nose and mouth.
He expected it to taste as sweet but it was so bitter that he
gagged and spat the mouthful out across Monidiak and Yaya.

Yaya snorted; the others laughed. Tacs took the jug at once and drank some and handed it back. "Just little sips. When you get enough of it it is easy to drink it. Little sips at first."

Dietric put the mouth of the jug to his lips. For a moment he could not make himself drink it again. Even the memory of the taste made his throat constrict and his stomach clench, but he drank several times. They seemed to expect it, and they were watching him closely, all smiling. When he lowered the jug and they laughed again, it was pleasant laughter.

He had never been so close to Huns for so long, and to find them friendly startled him. He made himself meet their eyes. The lids of their eyes were perfectly smooth, without crease or fold, from corner to corner. His head was throbbing. Monidiak's eyes floated before him, narrowed with laughing. Astonished, Dietric took a deep breath, and the air in his throat seemed palpable as water.

"What is this?" he asked, looking at the jug in his hand, and the way he said it sounded stupid even to him. They all laughed again, and Bryak gave him a gentle friendly shove.

"The White Brother," Tacs said. "You take his leaves and some of his stems and blossoms and the root and seethe them in water. Do you like him?" He took the jug and drank; amazed, Dietric saw him swallow a whole mouthful.

"Am I drunk?" Dietric asked. His arms and hands felt warm. Reaching out to his right, he touched the wall of the snow fort and the packed ice warmed his fingertips.

"Is he drunk?" Yaya said, aping Dietric's voice, and snorted.

"No," Monidiak said. "Not really. Take some more."

"No." Dietric laughed. "No, I can't. I'll die."

Bryak said, "Let him alone. He isn't used to him. Tacs, see who is guarding the gate."

Tacs on all fours crept to the space in the snow wall and looked out. "Mikka. Here comes The Fluteplayer. I wonder what he wants." He shouted something in Hunnish out the door.

Dietric began to feel more in control of himself. The warmth in his hands and arms was spreading throughout his body. He looked at Monidiak, and Monidiak smiled and said, "He is very good to you, isn't he."

"You had a red feather before."

"Yes. I like red things." Monidiak held out his hand to Yaya, who was drinking from the jug, and Yaya took another gulp and handed the jug on. Tacs pulled back into the snow fort.

"Make room. Bryak, move over."

Between them and the sunlight, a man came through the space in the wall and crouched down among them. He was a Hun, but his eyes were pale and clear. He wore circles of gold wire threaded with small jewels and hung through holes in his ear lobes, and around his neck on a thong he carried a flat wooden flute. Tacs squeezed over to one side, practically sitting on Dietric, and The Fluteplayer made himself comfortable in the space opened for him. Monidiak offered him the jug but he waved it aside. His bright pale eyes turned on Dietric and he said something in Hunnish, smiling; he was leaner than the others, bony and angular, even in his smile.

"This is The Fluteplayer," Tacs said to Dietric. "A very great shaman. But he speaks no German. I'm sorry. You would like talking to him. He could tell you things."

"What things?"

But Tacs was back facing The Fluteplayer and talking to him in Hunnish. They sat so close together their knees touched. Tacs gestured furiously all the while he talked. To his surprise Dietric could tell by the gestures that he was talking about the raid on Ardaric's herds. Gradually he realized that the oddly familiar word he heard repeated over and over was Ardaric's name twisted into Hunnish. The Fluteplayer's eyes moved steadily from Tacs' face to Dietric's. He kept on smiling his lean half-smile. Dietric thought that he looked hungry.

Bryak said softly, "Drink more of The White Brother. He will make you wise."

Dietric took the jug, thanking him. Bryak laughed. "Or he will make you no longer care." He turned away. Dietric sipped from it. Now he found the taste less bitter, even pleasant in small amounts. His head pulsated again, and with it his vision, growing darker and lighter by turns. Yaya sat slumped down on his hams, his head sunken between his shoulders and his eyes all but closed. His mouth hung open. For an instant Dietric was disgusted and frightened. He wondered if he would become like that if he drank any more; he saw how his father would see it. But Monidiak and Bryak were handing the jug back and forth between them steadily and seemed no different. He wondered what they were saying—their gestures were as strange to him as the Hunnish words. Their voices were lively and occasionally they burst out laughing. With no one to talk to he felt lonely and suddenly sleepy, and he yawned.

"Dietric," his father said. "Come out of there."

Dietric's body jerked; he looked over The Fluteplayer's shoulder. Ardaric was standing there, scowling. The Huns were all staring at him, except for The Fluteplayer, who sat smiling at the ground; he clapped his hands together once and thrust them into his lap. Dietric with a burst of energy got himself into his coat and out to face his father.

"What were you doing in there?" Ardaric shouted. "I smelled that—did you eat anything? Drink anything?"

"No," Dietric said. On his feet, outside the shelter, he felt as if he had been drinking water. The cold air steadied him. Ardaric was staring at him suspiciously. Dietric said, "Don't shout at me. Why are you so angry?"

Ardaric started off. "Don't concern yourself. Come along. We are going home."

He strode toward the palace, where Dietric could see their

horses waiting. The porch was empty and the crowd that had been listening to the judgments was drifting off in different directions across the yard. A train of six donkeys, laden down with goods, stood to one side near the Court of Women; the drovers were setting up plank stalls to display whatever they were selling.

"What happened?" Dictric asked.

"The Kagan says that he can do nothing unless I know who it was who killed our cow. Did you see them well enough to recognize them if you saw them again?"

"Yes," Dietric said, solemn.

Ardaric grunted. Between his bleached eyebrows two deep creases formed; he jerked his reins out of the hand of the slave and turned to his cream-colored horse. "What good will that do? There are thousands of Huns in Hungvar, some leave and arrive every day."

Dietric said nothing. He knew he should tell his father all the truth. But they had stolen only a single cow. He realized that he had not given Tacs the gold emperor and slipped his hand into the pouch on his belt to touch it. The cool gold rubbed smooth on his fingertips. Throwing his reins over his horse's withers, he pulled himself up into the saddle.

Ardaric was staring at the men setting up the bazaar in the yard. Dietric nudged his horse up beside his father's and waited. Tacs and his friends were coming out of the snow fort; while Dietric watched, they walked single file toward the other end of the palace, talking back and forth over their shoulders to each other, climbed up onto the porch, and went inside. One of them—he thought Yaya—tripped over the doorsill.

"There must be a way for you to get into their village. Perhaps you would see one of them."

Surprised, Dietric looked up at him. "Are you still thinking of that? Why is it so important?"

Ardaric tugged furiously on his mustache. "I won't have

Huns able to say they robbed me without punishment." He kicked his horse into a trot toward the gate. Dietric followed, past the rows of stalls on which the merchants were displaying glass and Persian sugar, while the women of the Kagan gathered with their servants to buy.

W HY DID YOU SEE THE KA-gan?" Tacs asked. He settled himself comfortably near the fire in the middle of The Fluteplayer's aul and reached for the ewer warming on the flat stone in the middle of the coals.

The Fluteplayer slapped his hand aside. "Don't drink that, it isn't for you. Nor are my visits to the Kagan. You should stay away from King Ardaric's son. He looked very angry when he found his son with you." The Fluteplayer poured something from a small jar into a larger one and sealed it with a wax plug.

"I didn't go to him, he came to me. And why should I care what King Ardaric thinks? He isn't my king. If I can't drink that, what can I drink—I'm thirsty."

"There, on the lodgepole."

Hanging on the aul's master pole was a skin bag; Tacs went to it, pulled out the stopper, and drank. It was only water. While he drank, he looked around the aul, admiring the red-lacquered benches covered with furs, the woven rugs, and the gold and silver ornaments arranged on painted shelves on one side. The Fluteplayer had two wives but Tacs rarely saw them; they stayed out of sight whenever people came here, usually going into the little aul that The Fluteplayer kept behind this one. Even for a shaman he was very rich. He was also of Tacs' totem, and at one time Tacs knew that the shaman had considered taking him for a pupil. Now The Fluteplayer was mixing liquids together in a glass vessel. He wore no tunic, and the sharpness of his elbows and shoulderblades showed through his skin.

"So," The Fluteplayer said, and put a glass stopper in the jar and set it among several others on a little wooden bench against the wall. "I would stay away from Ardaric's son because he can do a Hiung nothing but harm."

"He knows we are the ones who stole the steer from his father, and he hasn't told, I don't think—"

The Fluteplayer turned around without standing up. "There is no way we can talk to them or they to us. Even meaning well they can only trouble us. I'm not sure if it flows in both directions. I hope so. Why do you want to talk to me?"

"Oh," Tacs said, wrenching his mind onto the new subject. "But it is still Ardaric. I told you that the Kagan has ordered me to tell him everything I can remember about Italy."

The Fluteplayer nodded.

"I have talked to him once, and he listened and asked good questions, but later we spoke a little of Rome—his son was there, it was before Monidiak's raid. Something Dietric said—" He waved his hands in front of him. "No, let me think of how to say it."

The Fluteplayer was smiling at him. He sat all in a heap, as if he had been dropped by the nape of the neck, his arms and legs all angles and his spine curved like a crane's. The door to the aul opened and one of his wives came in, carrying meat in a pot, and went quietly behind the painted screen across the back.

Tacs said, "The way Ardaric and Dietric spoke of Rome I wondered how they could want to attack it. They spoke of Rome as if they loved it."

"Ah." The Fluteplayer nodded. He laced his long fingers together and set his chin on his knuckles. "Go on."

"That's all."

"Why does it disturb you, then?"

Tacs looked from side to side, startled. "But—how can they be the Kagan's men and love Rome? Rome is the Kagan's enemy."

The Fluteplayer shrugged. "A variety of intentions can serve the same end, after all. They love Rome so much they want it for themselves. Don't let it trouble you. The Kagan knows of all these things and deals with them properly."

"It's still wrong," Tacs said stubbornly.

"Perhaps. Now let us speak of another thing."

His tone of voice alerted Tacs, who said warily, "Which?"

"Certain people have spoken to your brother Ras about you, Bryak, Monidiak, and Yaya."

"They hate us. They won't take one step to help us, can you blame us for—"

"Don't interrupt me. I understand your situation. I told Ras nothing could be done unless somebody took care of you, and Yaya's wife cannot. She may not live out this winter. Ras has agreed with me but he is unwilling to put himself to any trouble over you. All he would say is that you should get married."

"I don't want to get married."

"If you did, I suppose you would only drag your wife into that situation in Yaya's aul. Actually, I can see no easy solution. But I told Ras that I would do what I could. Therefore I am telling you that you are not to steal or fight or play tricks on the people around you, or on the Goths—the Kagan is angry about your raid on Ardaric. Fortunately for you and your friends he is also amused."

Tacs put his head to one side. "If we don't steal, how can we—"

"You can get your own food and cook it yourselves and mend your own clothes and take care of your own aul. Or you can go back to live with your brother and his wives, where you will make no one but yourself miserable. I'm not suggesting to you. I'm telling you what will be. Do you understand me?"

"Fluteplayer, you don't—"

"I understand perfectly."

"But how can we get food and cook it? We don't—"

"You can learn how. Every day, one of you will come here, to my aul, and get meat and grain for the day for the five of you. Learn to cook it. And keep your aul reasonably neat. Clean up your horse pen—all the people around you complain of the stink. And keep your horses in the pen. Especially your pony."

"He won't stay inside the fence."

"Teach him to stay there."

"But—"

"He is small enough to get into people's auls, and he does. And he bites the children."

"They tease him."

"Would you rather let him go loose and have someone kill him?"

"No."

"Also if you are going to ignore the taboos against washing in stagnant water and against not washing at all, don't let other people see."

Tacs mumbled something down at his hands. He could not meet The Fluteplayer's eyes; he burned with embarrassment.

"Don't worry," The Fluteplayer said, in a kinder voice. "I'll see that nobody else bothers you and that you have sufficient of everything to keep you from hunger and cold. It would be much better if you would learn to care for yourselves but for the sake of your neighbors someone has to take control of you."

"Yes," Tacs said, still looking down.

"When Ummake is well enough, tell her to come to me."

"What for?"

"Don't ask me questions."

"Can't you make her better?"

The Fluteplayer grunted, and his wide, thin-lipped mouth curved down at the corners. "I've tried. I'll try again. Go away, now. I have things to think about."

Tacs got up. The Fluteplayer was staring across the aul, his face still warped into the grimace, and his bony fingers wound together. Tacs knew he was thinking of Ummake. Picking up his coat, he opened the door and went out into the bright, windy winter day.

SIX

⊂⊨

IN THE BAZAAR RED AND
yellow awnings flapped over the stalls of the rich merchants—
the poor ones sat on the ground with their wares spread out in
front of them on mats woven of straw. Riding through the
gate, Dietric looked curiously down the double row of stalls.
But Tacs wasn't there, and Ardaric would be impatient. He
turned to look back at the snow fort. It was empty, one wall
caved in. Dismounting, Dietric looked up at the top of the
gate, hoping to see Tacs on guard there, but he knew neither
of the two Huns sitting on the platform beside the gate-winch.
He had no idea where to look next. Tacs could even be in the
Hun village. Or he could be inside the palace, on duty there,
but Dietric had been inside the palace only once in his life.
Leading his horse, he walked slowly toward the front door.

With a lance tilted up against the wall beside him, the Hun
on duty beside the door squatted on the porch working a strip
of leather with the tip of a small knife. When Dietric approached him, he glanced up. His expression never changed,
and Dietric did not recognize him, but the Hun turned and
shoved open the door and shouted through it in Hunnish into
the entry chamber. Without looking at Dietric again he bent
over the piece of leather.

The door opened wide, and Yaya came out. "You want?"
he said, in his cold voice.

"My father King Ardaric sent me to bring Tacs back with

63

me for another meeting." It made Dietric angry that Yaya could hardly speak German; all Huns spoke German.

Yaya's eyes widened. "Back to—there? You home?" He jabbed his chin toward the Gepid village.

"The Kagan has ordered—"

"Tacs not go."

"The Kagan has said that he must obey my father's orders."

Yaya stared at him a moment, clapped his hands together, and said something in Hunnish to the sentry. Putting down his leather, the other man answered. Yaya came forward to the edge of the porch.

"Tacs there." He pointed around the side of the palace. "Around back there. He not go. You listen." Turning, he marched back through the door into the entry chamber. The door slammed shut behind him.

Dietric led his horse toward the corner. The Kagan's palace covered as much ground as his father's whole stockade; a Hun would have mounted and ridden around it. Rounding the corner, he came into a yard where three oak trees stood. A number of children were playing with a ball in the shade, but Tacs was nowhere in sight. Keeping to the side of the palace, out of the way of the children, he walked to the back and turned the corner.

Here, between the stockade and the rear of the palace, there was a small forge. He could hear the creaking of the bellows, and smoke rose in a thin stream above the fire. A group of men stood around the forge; among them was Tacs. Dietric hurried forward, dragging his horse after him by the reins.

"Tacs!"

Tacs turned around to face him and waved. Dietric flung his arm up in answer. He dropped his reins and walked up to the little group of men, smiling at Tacs. "My father says—" Suddenly he realized that he was in the presence of the Kagan. His throat seized shut. He stared into the Kagan's narrow eyes, unable to think. The Kagan was exactly his height, but vast, bulky, like an oak tree. Dietric tore his gaze away and looked down at the ground.

"Continue," the Kagan said, in German. Dietric looked up cautiously, saw that they were all looking elsewhere, and drew closer to look.

Besides the Kagan and Tacs, there were four others—a young boy who stood beside the Kagan, a German man, and two Huns. While Dietric watched, the Kagan put his arm around the boy's shoulders, and the child leaned his cheek affectionately against the Kagan's side. Clearly this was one of the princes. The boy's cheeks were smooth, without the ritual scar. Perhaps the Kagan's sons were not treated so roughly. He sneaked a look at the Kagan and saw on his cheek the deep, puckered ridges of the scars. Abruptly he was looking again into the Kagan's small black eyes.

"Tacs," the Kagan said. "It is the son of Ardaric. Am I right?"

"Yes, Attila," Tacs said.

"You resemble your father very little," the Kagan said. He swung his head toward the Hun at the forge. "Why are you not ready yet?"

The Hun answered him in their own language. Dietric craned his neck to see. The Hun was working the bellows with one hand, keeping a wide bed of coals bright as winter berries. With the other hand he was turning a sword blade over and over in the heat. Dietric thought, If he heats it too far, it will break, and was pleased with his knowledge; he wished he dared say it out loud. The Hun took the sword from the fire and spat on the blade. The spittle disappeared with a crack, and the Hun lifted his eyes to the Kagan's.

"Now, Hrold, you are watching?"

The German nodded, impassive. The Kagan gave him a sharp look, and he twitched. "I am watching, my Kagan." He bowed.

"Good." The Kagan laid his hand on the shoulder of the second Hun, who had stood silent all the while between him and Tacs.

That man stepped toward the forge, and Dietric realized that this was a punishment. The silent Hun had stolen something from the German Hrold. His stomach tightened. He looked quickly at the boy beside the Kagan; he was pressing his cheek against his father's coat; one hand was knotted in the coat's skirt. Dietric looked back toward the forge. The guilty man laid his right arm down on the oak table before them. Taking the sword in both fists, the Hun smith hacked off his hand. It required several strokes. With each stroke the smith laid the hot blade against the wound. Dietric coughed. The smell hurt his nose.

The smith chopped down hard, and the hand flew off and fell into the dirt at the Kagan's feet. For a moment longer, while the smith cleaned the sword, the Hun leaned against the table, his head bowed, and the charred stump of his arm stretched out across the wood. Dietric crossed himself. The Hun straightened up and turned to the Kagan. His face was the color of dust; his eyelids fluttered as if he were about to faint. He knelt down awkwardly in the dirt and lowered his head down to press his cheek against the Kagan's fur boot. Standing up slowly, he walked away, staggering every few strides.

In Hunnish, the Kagan spoke crisply to his son, pointing down at his feet. The boy bent down, picked up the hand, and trotted after the crippled man. Dietric twisted his head to watch him; the boy called out, and the man turned and stopped. Catching up with him, the boy gave him back his hand, and when the man started off, went with him. Dietric straightened and found the Kagan's eyes staring at him again.

"You are looking for Tacs?"

"My father wants to talk to him, my Kagan."

"Go." He waved Tacs away.

Tacs said, "To your camp? But, I—Attila, must I go to his camp?"

The Kagan looked around. "Yes, if he wishes. Oh. I see." He had turned toward the smith; now his body swung massively back toward Dietric. "Go to the crossroads before your camp and have your father meet him there. Hrold, you may go." The boy was coming back; the Kagan turned toward him, smiling, and when the boy jogged into their midst he stretched out his hand to stroke the boy's smooth cheek.

"Can you do as he says?" Tacs asked, coming toward Dietric.

"What?"

They started back the way Dietric had come. Dietric veered over to collect his horse, grazing in the sun beside the stockade wall. He took the emperor from his belt pouch, rubbed it between his thumb and forefinger, and handed it to Tacs when he reached his side again.

"I forgot to give this to you the other day."

"Thank you," Tacs said; his voice was full of surprise. "Thank you." The coin disappeared into his tunic of matted grey fur. "Can you get Ardaric so that I don't have to go to his camp?"

Dietric said stiffly, "You think it's a trap, don't you? You think I told my father and he wants you to come to our village so that he can capture you."

"Well—" They rounded the corner of the palace. Tacs looked up at him. "You know what happens if a German catches a Hiung stealing something. Hrold caught that other man himself, and so the Kagan had to punish him according to the law. What would you think if you were me?"

"If I had told him, he would want the others, too, not only you. I know their names too, you know."

Tacs was looking around the front yard; presently he put two fingers to his lips and whistled. "If you say it isn't a trap, I will believe you. But why should you not have told him?" He sat down on the edge of the porch and pulled the soft folded tops of his boots up to his knees. "But if you say so I will believe you."

Yaya came out the door to the palace entryway and walked along the porch toward Tacs. His feet boomed on the plank floor of the porch. Tacs looked around. Yaya said something, and Tacs answered in a monosyllable. Taking Tacs' lance from him, Yaya jumped down from the porch and sauntered around the palace toward the Kagan.

"How long have you guarded the Kagan?" Dietric asked.

Tacs cocked his head to one side. "One of my brothers was a guard and he died and I took his place." He looked at Dietric's black horse and sidled around to see better. "Is this yours?"

"Yes," Dietric said. "What do you think of him?"

Tacs bent down to run his hand along the horse's black foreleg. His pony was trotting toward them, holding its head unnaturally high to keep from stepping on its trailing reins. Tacs stood up, approached the pony cautiously, and mounted it. Dietric climbed into his saddle and rode over.

"What do you think of my horse?" he asked, again.

Tacs said, "You shouldn't ride him in the snow." His voice was reproachful. "He may go lame. But he will outgrow that splint. All big horses get them. I don't understand why German horses are so big."

Dietric said, "All the Huns who can, ride German horses, I've noticed."

"That is why the rich Hiung have more lame horses than the poor Hiung." Tacs' eyes slid toward Dietric's horse. "Also the rich Hiung just have more horses. You paid me that emperor when you didn't have to; I will do you a favor: if you want we can trade horses."

"Trade horses." Dietric licked his lip. He wondered how he could get out of this without offending Tacs. They rode out the gate and passed beneath the oak tree outside. The snow lay thick over everything, blue in the shadows, scratched by a thousand bird tracks. They rode down the hill toward the ford. Down by the marsh where the willows shaded the snow and kept it soft, the children had made forts for snowball fights.

Dietric glanced uncertainly at Tacs. "Your splendid little horse is much too fine to trade for my rotten old nag. How could I accept it?"

Tacs turned his eyes toward him and laughed. Suddenly Dietric realized that he was teasing him. His ears burned, but he forced himself to smile. Tacs reined his pony back and held out his hand, palm up.

"I am a poor Hiung with four horses and two of them are lame and the lame ones are both crossbreeds. You Germans have made me a beggar. You owe me your horse. If you are good to me I won't even make you take the pony."

Straightfaced, Dietric said, "If German horses all go lame, the favor is that I don't give you another useless horse to feed."

Tacs' smile spread from ear to ear. "I told you—rich Hiung have many lame horses. I need more horses to go lame so that I will be rich."

He began to laugh even before he stopped talking. Dietric eventually had to laugh along with him; when he did, Tacs punched him lightly in the arm.

"Was that the Kagan's son?" Dietric asked. "The boy with him."

"That was Ernach," Tacs said. "The brother of Ellac, the Kagan's heir."

"He is very handsome, he does not look like the Kagan."

Tacs put his head back and laughed. Dietric felt suddenly as if he and Tacs had been friends for a long time. He noticed the deep scars on Tacs' cheeks.

"Ernach has no . . ." His courage vanished; he began to think the question unseemly. But Tacs was watching him and waiting. "Scars," Dietric said. "I thought all Huns had scars on their cheeks?"

"Who? Ernach?" Tacs looked around at him, his head cocked. "He is not a man yet, he is only a child. They cut your cheeks when you become a man, there is a long ceremony, three days, and on each day the shaman slashes you. When you are a man you must know how to receive hurt without hurting back. Something like that." He lifted one hand to his cheek. "They give you The White Brother so that it doesn't hurt so much. I screamed very hard. They like that, the old people, they like the shaman to do a good job. And then everyone gives you presents."

"Oh," Dietric said. He thought, How have we lived so close together and misunderstood that? They had come to the ford; the snow had been swept away, and planks and gràvel laid down over the bare ice. He said, "I'll bring Papa to the crossroads near the foot of our hill."

Tacs nodded. "Good. He may bring his soldiers but I can see them long before they can catch me."

"I know he will bring no soldiers."

"Maybe someday I can go to your camp, though. I have never been there."

Dietric looked down at him. "I've always wanted to see your village. If you come to my camp, can I visit yours?"

Tacs nodded, excited. "Yes. Good. We can be . . . companions." He sounded uncertain about the word; his eyes lifted to Dietric's. "If you come to trouble in my camp, I will help you, and so with me and you in your camp."

"Good," Dietric said. They had almost reached the crossroads. On the icy hill above them, Ardaric's little stockade stood like a parody of the Kagan's. Two Gepids rode down toward them; they eyed Tacs suspiciously, and although one answered Dietric's wave, the other didn't even notice him.

SEVEN

⊂╪

THE HUN VILLAGE SPRAWLED
in no order along the north and west walls of the Kagan's
stockade. Walking his horse along behind Tacs' pony down
the bank that marked the south edge of the camp, Dietric
looked out from a height over the rounded huts and piles of
trash, racks of drying meat, the children, the dogs, the loose
horses, and the adults at their work or their leisure, and wondered how any of them found their way around. Tacs kicked his
pony down the bank and Dietric followed, keeping his tall
horse close to the pony, although he felt ridiculous looming
head and shoulders over Tacs.

On its own level the village seemed impenetrable as a thorn
thicket, without lanes or paths. The strong reek of curing hides
and horse dung mixed with odors from the cooking pots
hanging over every fire they passed. Dietric let his reins slide
through his fingers. His horse would follow the pony, and he
wanted to look around. In between the huts were pens made of
withies; most of them held two or three horses. The huts themselves were shaped like upside-down bowls, their wooden doors
and even their leather covers painted with Hunnish devices.

In his own village, the men would have all left at sunrise to
work; here, the men sat or stood or even lay on the ground
before their huts, doing nothing. They were all staring at him.
He could feel their curious eyes on his back and he met their
stares and they did not look away, as a German would have. He

wondered what would have happened if he had not been with Tacs. His skin felt hot and cold at the same time.

Tacs called out to someone passing and was answered. They rode on through the village. Dogs barked and snarled at them and darted at the horses' heels. Some of the women he saw— the old women—were making bread, patting out flat loaves no larger than their hands. A baby, wrapped in a blanket and bound with string, hung from a pole in front of a hut. Its black eyes followed Dietric without expression, like the eyes of the adults and children. Somewhere someone was playing strange tuneless music on an instrument Dietric did not recognize, all twangs and whines.

"Ho," Tacs called, and Dietric looked around and braced himself, and his horse slid down another embankment into the lower village. Here the huts were farther apart. Children dangled by their knees from a little tree; a boy shouted the Hun word for German and laughed, derisive. When Tacs called a greeting, a man sitting before a hut lifted one hand in answer but said nothing. A heap of bear pelts lay on the ground before a fire. On them lay an old person. Dietric could not tell if it were a man or a woman, but it was so bent that its chin almost touched its knees and its hands twitched aimlessly in its lap and yet its black eyes followed Dietric, unwinking.

Tacs reined up and held out one hand to stop Dietric. "Watch out—you could get lost around here, if you don't watch where you are going. Come inside."

Tacs had brought him to a hut whose door was painted with a red and yellow marking. Dietric dismounted, looked for something to tie his reins to, and finally dropped them. Tacs went through the door and bending his knees and his back Dietric followed.

They crawled into warmth and a darkness barely lit by a little red lamp. Dietric was instantly aware of the presence of half a dozen other people, although no one spoke or moved. Something came between him and the red lamp, and he started, but it was only Tacs, bent over the lamp, the red light brushing his forehead, his nose, and his cheekbones. He trimmed the lamp up higher and drew back to Dietric's side.

"Sit here." Tacs pulled him backward, and Dietric's outstretched hands sank into fur deep as a bed. He sat down on it, straining to adjust his eyes to the light.

"You know them," Tacs said, gesturing to one side. "Yaya, Monidiak, and Bryak."

From beyond the lamp came a general mutter. They did not want him here. Dietric stirred, suddenly depressed. He had thought it would be fun to come here, and Tacs had been happy to bring him. Stories came back to his memory about what happened to strangers among Huns.

Out of the dimness to his right came a jar, outlined in the red light, and a low Hun voice said, "Here, have something to drink. Tacs, where have you been?"

Between the moment he took the jar and the moment it reached his lips, Dietric realized that it was a girl who spoke. Tacs leaned around him to answer her. "I went to the camp of the Gepids to see King Ardaric again. Ah. It was very exciting. I thought once or twice I might not come back. Dietric, are you taking that home with you?"

"Oh." Dietric quickly handed him the jar. "I'm sorry." He had taken only a sip, wary of the bitter taste, but he found it surprisingly pleasant, and the warmth spread through him and the red light seemed kinder to his eyes.

"I wish you had told me," the girl said. "It was your turn to go to The Fluteplayer's, and I had to go instead. He frightens me, he asks so many questions. What happened in the Gepid camp? You didn't go alone, did you?"

"Dietric took me. They just stared at me. I could tell how much they hated me, and there were so many big dogs— Dietric, this is Ummake, she is Yaya's wife."

"Hello," Dietric said.

"Is it really so much different from our camp?" Ummake

hardly even glanced at Dietric; he thought she was con-
temptuous of him, and slid back away from her.

"Oh, much different. I couldn't have found my way alone.
All the houses are alike."

Startled, Dietric said, "But how can you find your way here?
There are no paths, everything seems so random."

Ummake laughed. Tacs said, "But it's easy to find your way
here—just look at the markings on the aul doors."

"Easy enough, if you know what they mean," Ummake said.
Something touched Dietric's hand, soft and warm; in the dark,
the light pressure almost made him gasp. Ummake had touched
him. "Tacs doesn't think of such things. Are you frightened
here?"

"Not here," Dietric said. "Outside."

"Oh," she said, "don't be afraid. No one would hurt you
here. It would be too much trouble. Why did you come?"

"I've always wanted to see your village."

She laughed again, and again she touched his hand, but in
the red dark she drew away and a moment later he heard her
talking to Yaya. He wondered what she looked like—her voice
was quiet and deeper than an ordinary woman's. He longed for
her to touch him again, to speak to him again. But she was
talking to Yaya, whose harsh, drunken voice drowned hers.
An unreasoning anger made him warm.

"Here," Tacs said, and handed him the jar of The White
Brother. "Treat him well. Are you hungry? Do you want
something to eat?"

"No, thank you."

"Your father gave me food. Here. Just a little."

Dietric started to refuse again and remembered what his
father had said of Hun customs in offering food; he wondered
if Tacs would be insulted if he refused again. He took the slab
of bread on the palm of his hand. It was warm and there was
meat on it. He crammed it into his mouth. Blood flowed over
his tongue and down his throat. The meat was barely warm.

They ate their meat half-cooked. His stomach heaved, but he choked down the mouthful, and someone gave him a cup of wine and he drank it all to wipe out the sweet taste in his mouth.

Monidiak and Tacs were talking in Hunnish; Dietric heard Tacs say his name, and he thought he heard the word Sirmium. His ears strained to catch anything more. On his right, Ummake laughed, laughter as low and rich as her voice, that made Dietric's skin tingle. On his left hand, Tacs said his name again to Monidiak.

"Are you talking about me?"

Tacs was lying back on his elbows, his feet toward the red lamp. The ruddy light lay on the bones of his face like paint. "The Kagan is sending Yaya and me and some other people to Sirmium, to meet Edeco there—Edeco our chief, the master of the Guard, who has been in New Rome talking to the Emperor. We are to bring him home. He has some Romans with him. I thought maybe you would want to come with us."

Dietric's heart jumped. "To Sirmium? But—could I go? Would the Kagan let me?" In his mind he saw the Kagan's narrow dark eyes, stony as an eagle's.

"Yes, of course. Why wouldn't he? Will your father let you go?"

"I—" He would not. A deadening weight pressed against his chest. "I'll ask him." But Ardaric would say no. A wild longing filled him, as if he would die if he could not see Sirmium.

"If he doesn't," Monidiak said, "come anyway. Or don't ask him at all. I did that when I was young and when I came back my father thought it was a great joke."

Tacs struck Monidiak in the chest with his open hand. "Your father was Tssa. His father is Ardaric."

Soft and rich, Ummake's voice on Dietric's right said, "You are a Gepid? What are your totems?"

"I—we—the Gepids have no totems any more, we are Christian men now."

"No totems?" she said, as if he had told her they had no eyes.

He would have to ask Ardaric's permission to go to Sirmium, there was no way to avoid it. Sirmium was Roman, once it had even been a capital of the Empire; Tacs had said there would be Romans in the party they were to meet. Surely Ardaric would see that it was an honor. Ardaric would let him go. The Kagan—

The jar of The White Brother came back to him again, and he drank. In the dark red light, colors moved before his eyes, aimless swirls of red and blue. The name Sirmium fell again and again on his ears. Tacs and Monidiak were laughing and talking, and Yaya was speaking to Ummake in his harsh, ugly voice. How could she endure him? The occasional sound of her voice and her rich laughter filled him with longing. An instant later he thought of Sirmium and the longing doubled. He lay back on the furs, running his hands idly over their softness; Ummake's laughter stroked him like soft fur. In Sirmium, he would surely find . . . something. The sweet aroma of The White Brother reached him and his mouth ran with water. He drank the last of the sweet tea in the jar. But almost at once another jar was passing among them, full. He shut his eyes, dizzy and full of desires.

"Dietric," Tacs said.

"Ah."

"I will take you to the edge of the camp. You might not find your way in the dark."

"Dark." He sat up straight, wondering if he had slept. "Is it dark?" Dazed, he looked around, but in here, of course, it was always dark.

"Yes. Come on."

Ardaric would be angry. Dietric got to his feet. He smelled meat cooking, and Ummake was gone. Stumbling on the loose rugs on the floor, he followed Tacs outside.

The sunset still colored the western sky, but in the east and overhead stars shone. Dietric's horse still stood in front of the aul, its reins trailing. All around them, the Huns were gathering up their equipment and moving inside for the night. Yaya walked past them, leading two mares, one with a new foal skittering at her heels. Dietric picked up his reins.

"I'll ask my father if I may go to Sirmium. Thank you."

Tacs nodded. "We will make a good trip out of it if you come. Tell him the Kagan allows it."

Dietric vaulted up onto his horse's back, and Tacs went to his pony. In the dark the wind was coming up. All around him, in the neighboring auls, he could hear the sounds of people gathering for the night.

"Wait," Ummake called, and came from the aul. "Here, take this, you will be hungry on the way." She held up a bit of bread. Now, at last, he could see her, and she was ugly as any other Hun, flat-faced, her eyes without fold, her nose only a bump. Mumbling something, he took the bread and turned his horse away, unable to meet her eyes.

W HEN ARDARIC RODE INTO the Kagan's stockade, he saw the Kagan at once, with Constantius and a few of his palace guard around him, standing before a stall in the little bazaar. In spite of the cold and the bitter wind, Attila wore no coat. Half a dozen of his women were also shopping, each with her attendants, but they stayed well apart from him and his party. The women looked constantly over their shoulders at him and spoke in whispers among themselves. The Kagan ignored them.

Ardaric left his horse with a slave and walked over. The Kagan was picking through a collection of precious stones and talking to Constantius about the weather. One of the guardsmen around him was Tacs, carrying an armful of fur; Tacs saw Ardaric and backed away to give him room near the Kagan, and sunlight flashed on a bit of gold in the heap of black fur— the clasp of the cloak. Attila lifted his head and smiled.

"You came right away. I am pleased. See these stones. Constantius likes the red ones. What do you think?"

"My Kagan," Ardaric said. The edge of the awning was flapping almost against his ear, and he moved away from it, annoyed. "You should see goods like these in your reception room. Why trouble yourself to come outdoors in the cold?"

"I enjoy the cold. Every winter I sit inside day after day and get fatter. Which do you like?"

On the heels of his words, a door banged open in the Court of Women. Everybody swung to look in that direction. Kreka, the Kagan's favorite wife, was coming out, a fringed parasol held above her head by two of her slaves, and five other maids trailing behind. Seeing the Kagan, Kreka feigned surprise and in deference to him made as if to go back into the Court of Women. The Kagan lifted one hand to keep her still and sent one of the guards to her to give her permission to stay.

Kreka was a Hun, short, fat, and middle-aged; she was the mother of Ellac and Ernach. She wore a scarlet tunic that warmed her sallow skin. When the guardsman had given her the Kagan's message, she flung up her hand in a rakish salute and strutted off into the bazaar, walking away from Attila.

Ardaric looked sourly after her. He had long since ceased being shocked by Hun women and their crudeness. They lacked everything seemly in a woman. He had even heard that they told each other bawdy gossip and delighted in stories of adulteries and other crimes. The Kagan was watching him; Ardaric looked down obediently at the silver tray the Medish jewel merchant was holding before him.

"What do you wish them for, my Kagan?" he asked.

"I like them."

Ardaric ran his fingertips through the stones. Their hard, smooth surfaces scratched against his skin. In the shade of the awning they caught no light and seemed dull. The Mede was standing just the other side of the counter, smiling all over his long brown face. Ardaric could see him adding up the Kagan's money as if it were already in his hand.

"I have found the men who raided your camp, Ardaric," the Kagan said.

"You have." Ardaric straightened, excited.

"I will punish them and repay you for the cow. They will be sent away for a while to learn honesty. For your injured pride and your son's, I can offer only the balm of knowing that the guilty men will suffer worse than either of you have."

Ardaric looked down at the jewels. He had wanted to punish the thieves himself, but he was afraid to insist because it might offend the Kagan. He smiled. "I think I like the emeralds best, my Kagan."

"You have excellent taste. So do I." Attila gave the silver dish of jewels a little shove and started away. His party moved off around him. Ardaric lingered, watching the Mede. The merchant's face collapsed, the smile fallen; for an instant he seemed about to call after the Kagan. Ardaric laughed at him, and the Mede flushed.

"He said he liked them," Ardaric said. "He never said he would buy them." The Kagan was already out of the bazaar, and Ardaric ran after him, delighted with Attila's joke.

In the yard, going toward his palace, the Kagan stopped and let Tacs, on tiptoe, throw his cloak around his shoulders, and Ardaric caught up with them. Constantius, his neck creased into fat rolls, was looking down at his feet and frowning. The bright sun shone on his shining bald head.

"You mistake me, Constantius," the Kagan was saying. "Why should I spend my money on jewels? They will spend it all for me." He gestured toward the stall, clasped his cloak over his shoulder, and gave a roar of laughter. With the guardsmen around him he went on toward the palace.

Ardaric looked back at the stall of the Mede jewel merchant. It was surrounded by women. Their shrill voices rose, quarreling over the jewels. In their midst the tasseled parasol of the Khatun Kreka bounced and swayed.

Constantius was staring at them, his eyebrows drawn up into round arches. "What are they doing?" Ardaric asked.

"They are asking which the Kagan preferred." Constantius let out a squeal of feminine laughter. "He is a man of thrift, the Kagan—he never spends his own gold if he can use someone else's." Turning, he started at a jog after his master, the skirts of his gown caught up in one hand.

EIGHT

⊏⊨

IN THE COLD, WATERY DAWN
light, Dietric shivered uncontrollably. All around him the
auls lay covered with new snow. Over the smokehole of Yaya's
aul, the snow had melted and frozen again into a little dome
of ice. No one seemed to be awake yet, except for Tacs and Yaya
saddling up their horses, Ummake who sat on a rug in the
doorway of the aul with her hands tucked into her lap, and
Dietric himself.

Ardaric would know where Dietric was as soon as he found
him missing. Tacs was sure that Dietric had escaped success-
fully but Dietric expected at any moment to see his father
charging through the Hun village, starting trouble that might
lead anywhere. He had a sudden fanciful vision of the snow-
covered auls as eggs, the people tucked snugly inside, and of
Ardaric breaking the shells and spilling the Huns out un-
finished. He shivered, wishing he had never come.

He wore his sheepskin over his Hun coat; the others had
helped him pack his boots with straw, and yet the cold drove
to his bones. Tacs' black pony, shaggy as a herder's dog, stood
hipshot before the aul eating snow. Yaya came out of the aul
with a long narrow pack and flung it across the pony's saddle,
and the pony pinned back its ears and lifted one hoof to kick.
But Yaya moved away toward his own horse. His breath steaming, Tacs came around the aul and lashed his pack fast behind
his saddle.

When Dietric asked his father if he could go, Ardaric had

81

refused him angrily, adding a warning that the Huns wanted something of him and were trying to put him in their debt. Dietric half-believed it. But even if it were true, he refused to miss a chance to go to Sirmium, to see Romans, to ride with the Huns. Even when the Kagan took his army off to fight, very few Germans actually rode with the Huns. Usually the Huns took the vanguard, reconnaissance, and the rearguard, and the Germans were the main body of the army, used only after Huns had done all the exciting work.

Tacs and Yaya mounted up. Ummake rose from her rug and came forward, her face uplifted into the clear light. She went first to Yaya and spoke to him, smiling. He put his hand briefly on her coarse black hair. She raised her hand in a salute to Tacs, and when he had answered her she walked back through the snow toward Dietric, lifting the hems of her wide-legged trousers up out of the wet.

"Dietric," she called. "Keep watch on them for me—let them not be seduced." Her white teeth flashed, and she went back to Yaya for a moment before going into the aul.

Tacs and Yaya started off, single file. Following, Dietric wondered what Ummake had meant. But it was surely a joke, with no meaning. He was beginning to see how different the Huns were from the Gepids and the differences seemed to him magical and important. The dawn light was growing stronger. Now the cries of children and dogs broke the silence of the night just past. Already tracks wound in and out of the clusters of auls. Gradually, while they rode through, the camp noise increased, until, when they reached the south edge of the village, the racket of people talking and shouting, cooking food, getting horses, and going for water was as loud as at midday, and the village was choked with Huns.

Beyond the last aul, Tacs fell back to ride beside Dietric. "Ardaric won't catch you, don't worry. Be careful with that horse, I told you, he will pop a splint in the snow if you push him."

"I've been putting packs on his leg," Dietric said.

Tacs frowned. "That won't do much good until he goes lame. But it does no harm."

Ahead of them, waiting in a pack on the snow-covered plain, were a dozen Huns on horseback. Dietric had expected more; he would have thought an envoy from Constantinople worth a larger escort than that. Ahead of him, Yaya squeezed his horse into a trot, and the men waiting for them wheeled their mounts and started off, spreading out, so that their tracks fanned out over the snow. Dietric's horse without a command broke into a jog. Beside him, Tacs was fastening the clasps on the front of his coat, his rein laid down on the pony's neck.

Now that they were moving, Dietric could barely feel the cold. Before them lay the rolling plain, buried in snow. His father had not caught him. Dietric looked back. The Kagan's hill with its stockade already lay well behind them. Ardaric would never stop him now. He turned forward, clenching his reins in his fist, and laughed.

THE SUN ROSE INTO THE GREY sky, and behind them Hungvar sank into the distance and disappeared. For a while they rode parallel with the river. The line of trees along its banks stood out dark against the white plain and the light grey sky. But by noon they had left the river behind them as well. Dietric thought they were traveling due south. Pale silver, the sun glided through the sky, too weak even to keep them from looking straight at it. Dietric thought of the tales of his childhood, the Snow Giant, the Snow Maids, the stories of deep cold and dark locked tight against the warmth of the sun. No one told them very much now because they belonged to the time before Christ came to the Germans and they were saved, and no one wanted to think of how they had been damned, before Christ came to them. Perhaps that was what the stories meant, after all: the cold and dark of the time before Christ.

"When will we reach Sirmium?" he asked Tacs.

"Who knows? Three days. Four."

Dietric had thought it farther than that. He studied Tacs' profile; the little Hun was smiling, his eyes bright, obviously happy. Dietric thought of the story that Tacs had come back alone from Italy, after the army left him behind. For the first time, riding over the plain, he realized why his father refused to believe it.

"When you were in Italy—"

Tacs looked up at him. Dietric could think of no way to ask what he wanted to know. He wet his lips with his tongue, looking ahead; the other Huns were riding in a wide, ragged rank over the snow, some talking, some riding apart from the others, silent.

"Weren't you afraid?" Dietric asked, finally. "Being alone."

Tacs thrust out his lower lip, like a child pouting. "I am not afraid of anything."

"I mean—weren't you lonely?"

Now Tacs was refusing to look at him. Dietric cast around for a way to make up for suggesting he might have been frightened. "I would have been so lonely I would have died. I don't think I could have done it."

Tacs glanced at him through the corner of his eye; the look on his face said he was sure that Dietric could not have done it. But his mouth relaxed, and he began to smile again. "I wasn't alone until the very last—Marag was with me. Yaya's brother."

Dietric looked quickly around for Yaya. "I didn't know that."

"He died in the mountains. It was hardest in the mountains, we didn't understand them, we could find no food and nothing was in the same places, and it was cold and there was nothing for the horses to eat."

Yaya was holding his horse back, so that they could catch up with him. When they reached him, he said something rapidly in Hunnish, gesturing behind them. Tacs nodded and answered him definitely. Yaya looked at Dietric as if he weren't seeing him; his eyes made Dietric suddenly uneasy.

"We should teach him to speak Hiung," Tacs said, in German, pointing toward Dietric with his chin.

"Why?" Yaya asked. "He too much friend already."

Tacs' eyes widened. "Why are you angry?"

"No angry." Yaya looked off, aloof.

With a shrug, Tacs looked up at Dietric. "Yaya has a very bad temper. And he is worried about Ummake, too."

"Who will take care of her?" Dietric asked.

"The Fluteplayer. She—"

Yaya said, "No say him. Ummake is mine!"

"I never thought—" Dietric started, but Tacs cut him off.

"Leave him alone. If you didn't want him to come along, why didn't you say something before?"

Yaya was still looking off across the plain before them. His jaw thrust out belligerently from his dished face. "I not care."

His head to one side, Tacs stared at him quizzically. After a moment, he spoke tentatively to Yaya in Hunnish. Yaya never answered; his horse broke into a canter and he raced away from them, toward a little group of men riding together off to their right. Tacs looked after him longingly.

"I wish I could ride like that," Dietric said, pleased that Yaya was gone.

"Yaya has a great magic for horses," Tacs said.

"What? But all Huns ride well."

"Of course, we are Hiung." Tacs straightened up, no longer looking toward the other men. Dietric knew he was angry with Yaya.

"Could you teach me?"

The little Hun leaned back in his saddle and looked critically at Dietric and his horse. At last he slid back down again into his saddle. "No."

For a moment Dietric could say nothing; tears stung in his eyes. He was ashamed and looked away.

"You have to learn it when you are a baby," Tacs said. "Before you are even born. I can show you but you are too old, I think, you are too used to walking, and your legs and back aren't made right. You know there are things Hiung are no use for, because we have not learned it the right way. Growing food, and making excellent camps such as yours." His voice wavered, as if he were unsure such things were worth a Hun's doing. "You ride well enough for a German, anyway," he said. "You ride much better than your father does."

"Oh," Dietric's chest swelled. "Do I?"

"But you have to go more with your horse. Here. Watch."

The black pony shot forward at a gallop, charged across the snow for a dozen strides, wheeled, and loped back diagonally across its track, throwing snow in chunks into the air. It swerved again, and raced back toward Dietric, circled Dietric's horse, and came up beside it again at a trot. "You see?" Tacs said.

Dietric brushed at the chips of snow that had pelted him and his horse. "What was I supposed to see?"

Tacs wrinkled up his nose; he looked so funny Dietric almost laughed at him. A surge of affection rushed through him. At last Tacs made a flipping gesture with his hand. "I can't explain. Maybe if you watch us all for a long while you can see. It's all in the way you go with the horse. The horse doesn't know what you wish of him from your hands and legs but from how you sit on him." Tacs put his hand on the small of his back. "Everything goes from here. Do you see?"

"No," Dietric said. "I'm sorry."

"I can't explain. Watch us. Watch Yaya, he has an old magic for all such matters. Watch how Germans ride, it's much different."

"Do you really think Yaya rides better than you do?"

Tacs looked at him solemnly, nodding; his voice was even

reverent. "All the men of that family have it. Marag could ride any horse. They loved him. He talked to his horses. Yaya is the same. I have heard the magic is buried in the skull of a horse out on the steppe somewhere and until the skull of the horse turns to dust they will all own that magic."

Dietric said, straightfaced, "I understand." Something Ardaric had mentioned came back to him. "Where is your magic buried?"

Tacs jerked his head around, startled. "What?"

"My father said that you had a . . . that the Kagan had said you had some sort of strong magic."

"You should never talk about a man's own magic in front of him," Tacs said. "You are a German and therefore don't know that but never do it again. Now you do know. Remember." He shook his head at Dietric's bad manners. But an instant later he was leaning toward Dietric, grinning. "Actually, it isn't so. I have no magic at all. But for some reason everybody thinks so and I let them. It makes them kinder to me if they believe it. But I have no magic."

Before Dietric could speak, one of the Huns ahead of them called out in a sharp voice, and they all wheeled toward the east. Tacs murmured something under his breath and started at a gallop toward the man who had called out. Dietric followed him. He realized that someone had seen something in the east but he could make out nothing on the snowy plain. He tried to use the small of his back to guide his horse but could feel no difference.

All the Huns rode together into a little knot, nervously facing the east. Now Dietric saw the plume of windblown snow rising along the horizon. A few moments later he saw a column of horsemen coming toward them at a gallop under the flying snow. Tacs gripped his arm above the elbow.

"They are Germans—Gepids. Aren't they? Do you know them?"

Dietric blinked. He couldn't even count the riders yet. While he watched, the oncoming band of men swept up to within a few hundred yards of them and stopped. One of them came forward a little way. They were Gepids; they wore their yellow hair in braids and their beards were as long as Ardaric's. Dietric recognized none of them, but he knew who they had to be: men of a community that lived along one fork of the river south of Hungvar.

"You—Huns," the leader of the band shouted. "Where are you going? Who sent you?"

Tacs clapped Dietric urgently on the shoulder. "Tell them that we are on a mission for the Kagan. Hurry."

"Why must I—"

Tacs gave him a little shove. Dietric rode up out of the group of Huns and flung up one arm in salute to the other Gepid. "I'm Dietric, King Ardaric's son. These men and I are going on a special mission to Sirmium, in the name of the Kagan."

The other Gepid trotted his horse closer. His long, snow-burnt face was full of surprise. He craned his body forward to stare into Dietric's face. "The son of the King? How do I know you aren't lying?"

"I swear it by Jesus Christ," Dietric said. "Why would I lie?"

The other man looked beyond him at the Huns and, settling down into his saddle, directed his gaze back to Dietric. "On the Kagan's business?"

"Yes."

With a nod, the other man lifted his reins. "Make sure they don't steal anything. The faster they are gone the happier we shall all be." Turning his horse, he cantered back to his fellows. Watching him, Dietric for the first time saw how stiff he was through the back, how he banged into his saddle with each stride of his horse. What the man had said left a distaste in his mouth. He reined around and returned to the Huns.

All but Yaya cheered him, and when the Gepids started

away, cheered him again. Their hands reached out to pat him and stroke him in thanks. Bundling him into their midst, they swung off again on their way. Tacs came up beside Dietric.

"They believed you. They would not have believed us, they would have made trouble until we fought them. The Kagan—" Tacs shook his head. "He was very angry about our raid on your father's house, you know. He says whenever we do anything like that to Germans the Germans get him a little more in their power. Ayya. He would have been more angry if we had made any trouble with the Gepids. If you had not been with us maybe we would all be in bad trouble now."

All the other Huns were talking excitedly, still clumped together in a pack. Dietric said, in mock seriousness, "Maybe I have magic for such things."

"If you do it will be of much use to you when you are the King," Tacs said. "But still, you should not talk about it, even to me."

A<small>LL</small> DAY LONG, WHILE THEY rode across the unending snow-covered plain, the sun floated like a ghost through the packed clouds; the afternoon drew on, and the sun drifted slowly down the sky in the west, and gradually it disappeared into heavier, darker clouds moving up before the north wind. The air turned abruptly colder. The sky darkened. Dietric had packed a heavy cloak lined with wool behind his saddle, and he began to long for it. But until the Huns put on their cloaks he refused to wear his. He looked overhead, into the lowering arch of the sky. In his ears, the wind hissed and whined.

"Snow," Tacs said. "It's going to storm. I hope it doesn't last long."

He looked worried, too, and Dietric felt better about his own fears. "Where will we spend the night?"

Tacs lifted one shoulder and let it drop again. Lifting him-

self a little in his saddle, he shouted ahead of them in Hunnish. The other Huns had been trotting along abreast in a wide,
uneven line. When Tacs called they promptly turned and rode
together into a knot. Tacs wedged his pony into the circle
of horses, but Dietric hung back, unsure, and the circle closed
without him.

Packed together, the Huns began to argue in Hunnish.
Dietric moved to one side so that he could watch Tacs. The
argument divided itself in half: some of them were gesturing
forcefully south and some were pointing up at the sky, to the
north, and to the ground. Their voices rose. Tacs and a few
others said nothing. Yaya was one of those who wanted to keep
on riding; he leaned in front of another man and tugged insistently at Tacs' sleeve, shouting. Tacs smiled at him but said
nothing and looked down at the pony's withers. Gradually, the
Huns who wanted to stop were shouting down the others. Two
men who had begun with those who wanted to go on abruptly
switched sides. Now Tacs and the others started talking—three
of them fell in on the side that wanted to go on, but Tacs
wanted to stop, and suddenly nearly all the Huns joined him,
leaving the other side only the three or four who had spoken
up last. Disgruntled, they quieted down, and the knot of
horsemen broke up.

At a trot, Tacs came toward Dietric, smiled at him cheerfully,
and kept on going. Confused, Dietric followed. At first he
thought Tacs was going back the way they had come and he
wondered if they had decided to go back to Hungvar and wait
out the storm. But the black pony swerved. Dietric rode up
alongside Tacs, and the pony leaned toward his horse and kept
him circling at a quick trot around the trampled patch of snow
where the Huns had held their council.

Half the others were also riding in circles around and around
in the snow; the rest were trotting away. Before Dietric and
Tacs had gone three times around the circle, the horses had
beaten down a great patch of snow. Tacs stopped. To Dietric

he said, "I hope it snows just tonight. I wouldn't like to be snowed in here. Let's go find something to burn."

He started off across the circle. Before they reached the other edge, Yaya joined them. He and Dietric looked angrily at each other and tore their glances away. Tacs seemed not to notice. With Yaya on one side and Dietric on the other, he led them into the deep old snow and across the plain.

Dietric wondered where on the featureless plain Tacs meant to find firewood. The air smelled almost bitter with the oncoming storm. Beneath the clouds the light turned a dirty yellow. Tacs led them in a wide circle toward the east. Suddenly he gave a sharp, barking cry and his pony burst into a lope, bounding forward through the snow. Following him, the others saw that he was leading them up to a ravine.

The ravine was only a crack in the steppe, nowhere deeper than the height of a man, choked with brush. Tacs rode straight into it, and Yaya forced his way after him, ahead of Dietric. Dietric hung back. He was afraid that Yaya would lead him into some harm. The ravine walls rose up on either side, hemming him in so that he could not escape. He could hear Tacs crashing through the brush up ahead; in the darkness in the ravine he could not see him.

Suddenly, from one side of the ravine between Tacs and Yaya, there came a terrible snorting sound. Dietric yanked his horse to a stop. He expected a bear to come hurtling out of the tangled brush against the ravine wall, but Tacs and Yaya whooped. Tacs galloped back toward Dietric, forcing the pony up the ravine wall.

"Yaya!" he shouted, and exploded into a long string of Hunnish. Yaya leapt down from his horse and waded into the brush. He had his lance out and was jabbing it into the crackling black net of branches. Dietric's horse began to fret. The enraged thunderous snorting doubled.

Yaya gave a yell. From the brush under him a small squat animal burst. For an instant Yaya with his lance poised could have killed it; the beast on its short legs slipped on the steep slope and had to scramble for its footing. But Yaya held back. "Dietric," he shouted. "Dietric, kill it." Yaya laughed. The little beast shot toward Dietric, snorting, its striped fur standing on end. Dietric could not move. He thought he saw its curved eyeteeth bared. His horse whinnied and reared. The black animal dashed almost under the horse's hoofs, and the horse whirled and bolted. Dietric lost his seat, clung for a moment, and fell off. His elbow struck a buried rock and he cried out. Against his face the snow was burning cold.

Yaya was laughing at him. Dietric sat up, wiping the snow out of his eyes. Tacs rode down the ravine toward him. "What happened?" He looked at Yaya; when his eyes returned to Dietric, his face was expressionless. "We have to catch your horse." He rode past Dietric and picked his horse up into a lope. Laughing, Yaya rode past him. Dietric got to his feet. His rage boiled around inside him; for the first time, he hated Yaya.

Wₕₑₙ THEY HAD CAUGHT Dietric's horse, they went back to the ravine and gathered all the dead wood and branches they could find, bound them in bundles, and dragged the bundles behind the horses back to the camp. By that time it was completely dark. The other Huns had made a snow wall to shelter them against the wind. They built a fire inside it and cooked dinner in a skin pot. While the broth simmered they sat packed together like a litter of puppies. Everything stank of wet fur and sweat and the peculiar sweetish odor of the Huns. The snow blew steadily across the light from the fire, a stream of tiny white flakes laid out slanting on the wind, and the fire popped and spat when the snow fell into it. But in the shelter of the wall, with Tacs pressed against one shoulder and another Hun against the other, with Huns before him and behind him, Dietric was comfortably warm.

They ate a gruel made of grain and melted snow and dried meat and drank melted snow and the tea made of The White Brother. To save wood they let the fire burn low. Beyond the little puddle of light the vast darkness shook with the night wind. The horses drifted up to the fire and came inside the wall and dozed. Dietric was groggy with fatigue. Twice he slept, jerking awake when his head slumped forward. The second time, when he opened his eyes, someone was talking and everyone else was quiet.

In the dark he could see nothing except the faintest outline of the bodies packed around him; the voice came out of the darkness, speaking Hunnish in a storyteller's voice. He understood a few of the words, but not enough to know what the story was about—just the words for horse, for water, and for storm. But the voice with its changes of tone and rising and falling pitch fascinated him and filled him with strange emotions. Although he could not understand the story he knew when there was danger by the voice, and when the danger had been defeated, and when the happy ending came.

A little silence followed. Beyond the wall that sheltered them and the fire, the wind screamed across the darkness. Through its roar Dietric thought he heard the howling of wolves. He lifted his head; he strained his ears to hear.

"What are you listening to?" Tacs said softly.

"Wolves."

"Only wolves?"

The Hun in front of Dietric looked around—he was younger than the others, solemn-eyed. Dietric, wondering how old he was, almost forgot to listen to the storm.

His hair prickled up; he lifted his head again with a jerk. Beside him, Tacs said, "Do you hear them now?"

"What is it?" Even in the midst of the Huns, Dietric felt cold and unprotected. He wondered how he had not heard it before. It sounded like laughter—like the chuckling of madmen, strangely soft inside the roar of the storm wind. Now it rose to a woman's wail. "What is it?" He gathered his feet under him to stand up, but none of the others was rising, and he settled down again.

Tacs spoke a Hunnish word. "I don't know what Germans call them. The spirits of people who have died at night, in the snow. All they can do is try to lure people out into the storm. If you went out you would freeze to death. Your spirit would take the place of the one that lured you out and that spirit would rest forever but you would have to go on calling until you found someone to take your place."

"But what did they do?" Dietric said.

"They died in the snow, at night, alone. And their spirits got caught in the wind. It moves so fast they can't come down out of the storm, they are blown along and along forever, until they can catch someone and pull themselves down out of the wind."

"But what did they do? Did they sin? Why are they punished like that?"

Tacs' eyebrows rose and lowered again. "They died at night, in the snow."

Dietric hunched his shoulders. His mind was numb with the possibility that people could be condemned for nothing but accident. He had always assumed that only bad people were punished. Sinking his head down between his shoulders, he burrowed closer into the packed humanity around him, down out of the wind.

NINE

⊂≡

THE FOLLOWING NIGHT, THEY
slept in the camp of a Hiung family going north from the
mountains to Hungvar. The camp stood on a stony hilltop
at the edge of a valley that cut south into the mountains, toward Sirmium, and the next day they followed the valley to
the cliff at its southern end and slept there in the shelter of the
overhang. The day after that, in the late afternoon, they rode
out onto the high plain where Sirmium was. Covered with
snow, the mountains stood all around like a wall. In spite of the
cold, Sirmium's river still ran, carrying chunks of snow and
blue ice along in its course.

Most of the plain was swept clear of snow by the wind.
Drifts lay up against the walls of the city; the snow was filthy
with the garbage thrown over the walls. Tacs glanced at
Dietric, riding beside him. Dietric's mouth hung open and his
eyes moved hungrily over the city. Jerking his gaze around
toward Tacs, he asked, "How many people live there?"

Tacs lifted one shoulder. "I don't know. Edeco might know,
I shall ask, if you want. Many." He smiled. "Do you like it?"
He was as pleased as if he had built it solely to show Dietric.

"I've never seen a stone city before. Only Hungvar. That's
completely different."

Tacs grunted. "Hungvar isn't a city. Cities are wicked
places."

They rode up to the gate. Some of the city's people were
outside, because the gate stood open, and Tacs knew that

Romans kept their gates closed during the day if they possibly could. He wondered what city people could do in the snow. The mountains all around them awed him and made him restless, but going into the city filled him with unhappiness. They rode under the arch of the gate, and the shadow fell on them, colder than the sunlight, like a piece of iron.

Once inside the gate, the Hiung reined in and grouped together in a circle, heading their horses in. Tacs made sure that there was room for Dietric. Immediately everybody began to talk at once. The Kagan had ordered each of them to go to Sirmium to meet Edeco but he had appointed no one to lead them and all the ride south they had suffered of it. Tacs looked at Dietric again; the boy, pale among the dark faces of the Hiung, was staring hard at the men talking and his lips moved, silent, forming Hiung words.

"Tacs," Yaya said. "Do you remember where the palace of the proconsul is?"

Tacs straightened up, looking around to get his bearings. "Ayya. Yes. Down this street there is a square with a fountain of stone children, and streets go off from it. Two streets go to the south, one uphill and one flat, and in the flat street is the proconsul's house."

"That's where Edeco will be," another man called. "Shall we meet him there? Does anyone know where we will sleep?"

Yaya shouted, "In the barracks of the Roman garrison. I know where that is."

Tacs gathered his reins. "Dietric. Let's go. They will stay here until the sun sets talking it all over." He backed the pony out of the circle.

"Where are we going?" Dietric asked. He kicked his horse up beside Tacs', and at a walk they rode down the street into the city.

"To see what happens."

Dietric glanced behind them. "Maybe we should stay with the others. Will we really sleep in the barracks?"

"Yes. Don't you want to see what the city is like? If we stay with them we'll see nothing."

Dietric settled down into his saddle. "It is nothing like what I expected."

Tacs laughed. They were riding down the center of the street; on either side walked the people of Sirmium. Their clothes were made of woven cloth and their shoes of leather, and they stared at Tacs and Dietric as if they had never seen such people. All around them were houses made of blocks of stone, and Tacs shook his muscles loose, trying to keep his mind light—it frightened him that he could see no more than a few hundred feet from his face.

"It's so closed in," Dietric said. "They are staring at us. I'm so ashamed. I look like a barbarian."

Tacs sneaked a look at him through the tail of his eye but said nothing. They rode down another street. Ahead of them, screaming and laughing, children played with hoops in the street. The hoofbeats of the horses echoed off the stone walls around them, so that they sounded like four horses instead of two. At the sound the children stopped playing. Under the grime and dirt their faces were white; they had long thin noses, like Germans'.

"Watch out," Tacs said.

"What?" Dietric looked down at him.

Tacs gestured toward the children, who were watching them approach, and turned up the hood of his cloak so that it protected his neck and head.

Silent, intent, the children like cats had drawn back against the walls to let them pass. Tacs pretended he didn't see them. He kept the black pony close to Dietric for shelter. They rode past the first of the children; ahead the street narrowed between high vine-covered walls.

Abruptly the children whooped, and snowballs and rocks and pieces of roofing tile sailed past the two riders from behind. Dietric let out a yelp. Jerking his hand up to his temple, he brought it down bloody and twisted angrily to shout at the children. Tacs kept his eyes forward. With each stride something struck him in the back. The pony shied and kicked out, and Tacs squeezed his calves together and the pony moved sullenly back into line. The children were chasing them. Dietric shouted furious insults at them in German but the children were shouting Latin and knew no German. At last they reached the edge of the square with the fountain of children. The voices of the children behind them faded away. A rock glanced off Tacs' shoulder and a rotten fruit flew past him and smashed into pulp on the pavingstones.

"Brats," Dietric said. "Don't their parents have any control over them?"

"They always do that," Tacs said. "Come on."

"But I am a Christian, like them," Dietric said.

Tacs grunted. The square was wide and sunny and filled with Romans. In the middle stood the wide basin of the fountain and above it the fake rock with its three marble boys, two kneeling, one standing, all with marble shells in their hands. Because of the cold no water came from the shells; but Tacs had been there when the fountain was running, and it was beautiful. He wished Dietric could see it. Vendors had put up their stalls around it and under the bare branches of the trees along one side of the square. Tacs could smell oranges and apples. He began to think of eating.

"Hiung!"

"Hiung," Tacs shouted, and threw his arm out. Dietric beside him started and his horse shied toward the fountain. A man on a black horse pushed toward them through the crowd of people waiting in front of the orange-seller's stall. An old woman in a shawl swore at him and shook her walking stick at his back, but he ignored her. Tacs reined the pony around to meet him. The man wore the heavy armor of a cataphract in the Roman army, and his horse although only a hand taller than the pony was hundreds of pounds heavier. He reined up his horse right shoulder to right shoulder with the pony and took off his helmet.

"Arrun of the Khatrigur Hiung, the snake and the spring rain."

"Tacs of the Mishni Hiung, the frog and the willow tree." Tacs took a jug of The White Brother from his saddle and held it out.

"Any news of the Kagan?"

"He thrives and his enemies wither."

Arrun held the jug to his lips and drank deeply. Lowering it, he smacked his lips together. "Ah. Very good. Who is he?" He gestured toward Dietric.

"Just a German. Are they putting Hiung soldiers into this province now?"

"No, I am just unlucky." Arrun had a thick-boned, humorous face full of laughter. Now he smiled. "Until the spring I have to take the place of an Isaurian I killed. He deserved killing but my commander thought he would make himself look clever if he loaned me to the army here. All my friends are in Antioch and I am left alone. You are the first Hiung I have seen since the snow came, except for the envoy going home from Constantinople. Are you with them?"

"The Kagan sent a band of us to meet Edeco and take him home."

Arrun's eyebrows arched up. "You come from Hungvar itself?"

"The guards of the Kagan."

"Hunh. I would rather be there than here."

"So would I. But if I'm here I can make something good out of it. Can we find something to do tonight, my friend and I?"

"Pleasure?" Arrun thrust out his lower lip. "They sell wine in that street there, in a house called Fortuna, and they have dicing too and sometimes cock fights and dog fights."

"Do they get angry if Hiung join them?"

Arrun broke out laughing. "Oh, they used to, now and then, when I did, but you know any Hiung can make his way through five or six city people."

Tacs made a face. "I don't want to get into a brawl. Somebody would get killed. Anyhow, I don't think my friend knows much close fighting. What about women?"

"Oh. The church porch after dark."

"Good." Tacs spat, pleased. He had been to Sirmium twice before without finding out where the whores paraded. With his fist he bumped the cataphract in the chest. "Thank you. I think we are staying in your barracks. Maybe we can go to the wineseller's together and you can tell them not to fight with us."

"Sometimes it's more fun to fight than not to."

Tacs socked him again, laughing. "If you think so you should come back to the Kagan. What fighting do you get with the Roman army?"

"With the Roman army." The cataphract let out a shout of laughter. He turned his horse with the rein against its thick neck, raised his arm, and rode off, still laughing.

Looking at Dietric, Tacs surprised him with longing on his face; he said, "Why do you look so strange?"

"Nothing." Dietric straightened his face up. "Who was that?" They started off again through the crowd.

"Some soldier of the Emperor."

"Where did you know him before? Is he from Hungvar?"

Tacs shook his head. "He is of the Snake Clan of the Khatrigur Hiung, they come from far, far down the Long River, near the sea."

Dietric sighed. "I have no friends here."

"What? I am here. Am I not your friend?"

"You aren't a Gepid."

"Why must I be a Gepid to be your friend?"

"I'm sorry. But you were as friendly with that man, whom you had never met before, as you are with me."

Tacs could think of no answer. He did not understand what Dietric meant or why he would say such things. The air of cities poisoned everything. He cast around him, hoping to find something to show Dietric and make him happy again.

"There. Is that a shrine to your Ancestor?"

Dietric lifted his head. Bending down, Tacs grabbed his rein and led his horse at a trot along the side street. The shrine was small, but its covered porch ran the whole length of the front of the building. Through the double doors Tacs could see faces painted on the walls, and on the doors themselves were crosses. The roof sloped up to a peak, and down the roof and along the eave of the porch an old vine grew, silver-grey, heavy with buds.

"This is a church," Dietric said.

"That cataphract said we could get women there tonight."

Dietric looked down again; his throat and cheeks turned slowly red. He cleared his throat. Exasperated, Tacs shook his head. "Do you have any coins with you?"

"No," Dietric said loudly. "No, I never thought of it."

"I will give you some. They won't take anything but money. Yaya once tried to buy a whore with a saddle and she threw him out of her house without his clothes on." Tacs laughed, remembering how Yaya had run down the street trying to cover himself with his hands. "They make sure you have enough money before they do anything. A saddle is worth too much, anyway, whores only cost a copper or two. Only it isn't for very long. Sometimes they make you pay more to do anything but lie on their backs. Whores are lazy. If you find a good one sometimes you should give them more, after, to show them that you appreciate what they do."

The flush had drained out of Dietric's cheeks, and he looked down quickly into Tacs' eyes.

"Would your father be angry?"

"Yes, probably," Dietric said. His voice was relaxed again, and, relieved, Tacs settled back and let his legs dangle.

"Your father is a strange man. Maybe Yaya will come with us, and a couple of the others."

"You mean—" Dietric's voice broke with a squeak. "All of us? At once?"

Tacs looked hard at him, suspicious. "No, one at a time, but. . . ." He said nothing for a moment, thinking. It had never occurred to him that Dietric might be a virgin. Their horses carried them to the end of the church-street and down to the south. "Or just the two of us could go," he said; tentatively.

"Oh," Dietric said. "That's better." He lowered his eyes and the red flush climbed up his throat again and into his face.

"After we meet the Romans."

A T THE BARRACKS, THE Hiung were given one of the three sleeping rooms all to themselves. The room was made of stone, except for the wooden wall that separated it from the rest of the barracks and the roof, also of wood. Four times longer than it was wide, the room had only one window, which let in only the indirect light from the shaded courtyard. Hard wooden benches for sleeping lined the walls.

Until supper, the Hiung amused themselves shouting insults through the wall and out the window to the soldiers of the garrison, who shouted back. Since the Hiung used their own language and the Roman soldiers spoke camp Latin nobody took offense. Tacs sat on one of the benches and stretched out his legs. The stable was at the far end of the compound and the long walk, carrying his gear, had started cramps in the muscles of his calves. While he was peeling off his boots, Yaya came over and sat down next to him.

"Where is your boy?" Yaya asked, and his lip curled.

"Dietric? He's coming. Why are you so angry?"

"He thinks he is better than we are."

Tacs let out a yelp of laughter. "No—he wants to be like us. Are we to eat with the Romans?"

"I think so. With the soldiers." Yaya jerked his shoulder toward the yard behind them.

"Oh." Tacs dropped his boots on the floor and kneaded his leg muscles between his palms. Yaya hitched himself forward and took Tacs' right leg and began to massage it. Tacs sighed and relaxed. "I thought maybe we would eat with the real Romans, the ones from New Rome. I told Dietric—"

Yaya drove his fingers into Tacs' calves. "Don't talk about him."

"You are wrong about him, he—"

"I said not to talk about him." Yaya's fingers unknotted the kink in his muscle. "Is that good?"

"Yes. Better."

Yaya started with the other leg. Dietric came through the door on the far side of the room, carrying his saddle over his shoulder; he stood a moment and looked around, and when he saw Tacs started toward him. But seeing Yaya he hesitated and finally went over to another part of the room. Tacs looked down at the bench he sat on—the soldiers who had stayed there had cut signs and pictures into the wood.

"You should not have brought him," Yaya said. "You should not have anything to do with him."

A T SUNDOWN ALL THE GAR-rison of the Romans went out into the yard to get their dinner, but the Huns had to wait until the garrison had finished. Finally the Huns were called out into the dark. In the middle of the yard, between two torch standards, stood a great basket and an iron cauldron. A slave gave each of the Huns a dish like the ones the Roman soldiers ate out of. At first they all tried to get to the cauldron at once, but after a while, with the slaves shouting and striking at them with their long spoons, they understood and made a line and walked past the torches.

Dietric got into line near the front and looked around for Tacs to let him in. Tacs was standing in the middle of the yard, watching; suddenly he threw down his dish and walked back toward the barracks, moving so fast on his short bowed legs that he waddled from side to side.

Astonished, Dietric stood staring after him until the man behind him poked him and he had to move forward again. The slave behind the cauldron dumped a spoonful of stew onto his plate and another slave, standing beside the basket, dropped a chunk of bread on top of the stew. A third with a dipper thrust a measure of wine into his hand.

Dietric looked around to see what the others were doing. Most of them were sitting on the flagstones of the yard eating with their fingers, their plates inches from their faces, stuffing in the food. Grease ran down their chins and covered their hands. Outside the light of the torches, in the soft darkness along the walls of the barracks, there was laughter—the Roman garrison, laughing at the Huns.

They would laugh at him, too, if he sat down like the Huns and ate the way they did. He carried his plate far across the yard, into the darkness. It was colder there but he felt safer, and sitting down cross-legged he used the bread to get his food from the plate to his mouth and drank his wine in small sips, like a Christian man.

The Huns were finished long before he was. They left their plates lying on the flagstones and went inside. Cursing, the slaves moved around the yard gathering up the plates and cups and throwing them into the iron cauldron to be washed. Dietric got up and carried his plate to the cauldron and dropped it in. One of the slaves was close by. Dietric smiled at him but the slave only stared at him sourly.

He went inside; most of the Huns were sitting in the middle of the barracks room, in a circle, playing some kind of slapping game. Just after Dietric came in they all roared with laughter at something. Tacs wasn't with them, and Dietric finally came on him sitting off to one side, with Yaya behind him combing Tacs' hair through his fingers and braiding it.

Dietric sat down cross-legged beside Tacs. "You said we would go to see the Romans."

"We will." Tacs had his head cocked to one side against the pull of Yaya's fingers.

"But it's dark   they will all be asleep."

Over Tacs' head Yaya gave Dietric an icy stare. He said something in Hunnish. Dietric caught the word for Roman. Tacs answered him in the same language.

"What did you say?" Dietric said, spiteful. "It isn't polite to speak in another language in front of people."

Yaya spat and said something harsh. For a moment Tacs simply sat there, his arms draped across his raised knees, and studied Dietric, expressionless. Dietric said softly, "I'm sorry."

"I just said that you were a German and all Germans love Romans—Yaya wanted to know why you wanted to go there."

"I don't love Romans. I'm just curious."

"Maybe they have some wine."

"The wine at dinner was very bad," Dietric said. That reminded him that Tacs had not eaten. "Why did you go? I was holding a place in line for you."

Yaya muttered something. His fingers wove Tacs' long black hair deftly into a tight braid. Tacs' eyes rested on Dietric but he said nothing. Yaya bound a piece of purple cloth around the end of the braid and let go and slapped Tacs' shoulder, and Tacs ran his hands over his hair. Yaya had plaited a hank from each side of his head above his ears in with the long hair at the back.

"Ayya," Tacs said. He looked back at Dietric and switched to German. "I can never do it right." His eyes looked steadily through Dietric. He had his feet under him already, and he rocked his body forward and stood up. "Now we go to see the Romans."

Dietric bit his lower lip. Tacs was angry with him and he did not understand why. Yaya smirked at him from the shadow by the wall, obviously pleased. It must have been something that Yaya said. He rose to follow Tacs, and Yaya got up and went toward the door, on a similar course but separated from him.

Outside, Yaya and Tacs stopped a moment to argue about whether they should take the horses, and finally Yaya shrugged and said, "You legs are hurtful. I walk good." He started off, striding as long as any Hun ever could.

Arguing, Tacs went after him. They crossed the yard to the gate and walked out into the street. In the darkness, the streets looked narrow and dangerous. So level during the day, the pavements now were rough and full of obstacles. Dietric found it hard to stride out, although the two Huns seemed to have no trouble. They turned a corner and the stink of burning garbage reached Dietric's nostrils. Voices sounded, muffled, beyond walls on either side. His ears hurt from straining to overhear. One of the Huns was singing under his breath, a whisper of sound so low he could not tell which one of them it was. They walked out of the narrow alleyway and into a square, picked out with torches. Dietric sniffed, amazed to find a warm, soft scent of earth in the air. It was almost spring; his first awareness of it was this tinge in the air.

They walked diagonally across the square, past the dry fountain. Roman soldiers sat on the stone rim of the fountain pool, Goths and Vandals, their helmets on their knees. Yaya called something sneering in Hunnish and the soldiers answered in Latin in the same tone.

"Why are there no Romans in the Roman armies?" Yaya asked, while they walked on.

"They are too good for it," Dietric said. "They leave that work to men with no craft for better things."

Tacs let out a burst of laughter and said something to Yaya. Dietric felt like reminding them again how impolite it was to speak Hunnish in front of him. But before he could gather the courage they had started into a southward street, also filled with torchlight, and he realized that the huge white building before them was the proconsul's residence. Excited, he strode forward toward the shallow steps. The two Huns broke into a trot to keep up with him. They climbed up toward the open porch. At the door stood two sentries in Roman armor. Tacs spoke to them in Latin and they stepped aside and let the three of them go in.

They walked into a hall as wide as Ardaric's whole house; the floor was made of shining black and white squares set into an even pattern—three black, one white, one black, three white, repeating itself endlessly down into the far wall. On a little pedestal beside the wall was a naked man made of gold. On the other side of the hall, on another pedestal, there was the stone head and shoulders of an older man with a leafy branch wound around his head.

Dietric thought that was a representation of the Emperor; but before he could ask, a door opened before them, and a Roman soldier came out—a high-ranking officer, in armor chased with silver and a helmet whose fluffy feather plume bobbed with each stride. Behind the cheekpieces of the helmet was the face of a Vandal. Seeing them, he stopped and called out sharply in Latin and then in German, "Who are you? Where do you think you are going?"

"To see the Romans," Tacs said, in German, and smiled, showing his eyeteeth. "Where are you going? What a pretty hat you have."

Yaya snickered. The Vandal's nostrils flared; around his mouth a line of white appeared. Backing up, he shouted through the door in Latin, his eyes remaining on Tacs. Tacs knocked Yaya in the ribs with his elbow, and Yaya whispered and glanced quickly at Dietric. The Vandal said, "He wants to know your name, pig."

Tacs started toward the door. The Vandal took a long stride sideways to block his way, and Tacs dropped his head down between his shoulders and put his hand on his belt near his knife. The Vandal stood head and shoulders over him and in his armor looked twice as broad. Dietric took a step forward. Yaya shoved him.

"Stay back, little boy."

Through the door, Dietric could hear voices rising with questions, and now footsteps slapped on the tile floor. Tacs and the Vandal were circling, slowly as dogs getting ready to fight, Tacs to the left and the Vandal to the right. A shadow stretched out across the floor between them, coming from the door.

"Tacs," said the man in the door. Turning his head, he called, "Edeco, it's Tacs."

The Vandal relaxed. His arms went to his sides, and he glanced through the door and without a word paced off down the corridor. The man in the doorway—a Hun, he was—called them in, smiling, and he stood to one side to let them by; they went into a room brilliant with lights.

Dietric had never seen such a room. Even the palace of the Kagan was rough and without luxury compared to this. There was no way of comparing that to this at all. Scenes of men fighting covered the shining walls, each figure slightly larger than life; masses of candles hung from the ceiling in metal frames. There was a long table in the middle of the room, covered with a cloth embroidered in red and gold; the plates and pitchers were of chased silver, and in a vase in the middle of the table was a great burst of flowers—flowers, in the depth of winter. The Romans sat along one side of the table on low chairs and couches. They were real Romans, not the Romanized

Goths and Vandals of the garrison—men whose skin seemed fine as glass, who sat with the grace of gentlemen.

On the other side of the table sat two Huns, one of them the man who had summoned them in, and a man not a Hun: Orestes, the Kagan's Roman-bred counselor. Slaves passed back and forth around the table, tall goose-necked ewers in their hands, and while Dietric watched, one raised the ewer above a cup and poured a stream of red wine into it. Everybody was watching him and Tacs, even a benchful of servants waiting along the wall. Dietric lowered his eyes.

"Tacs," one of the Huns said. "Sit down. Who are—oh, Yaya. Of course. But. . . . "

Tacs pulled Dietric forward by the arm. "This is the son of Ardaric the King of the Gepids. Dietric. This is Edeco." He gave Dietric a little shake.

Edeco was young, handsome in the round-faced way of some Huns, and dressed in a scarlet tunic. He was frowning. "King Ardaric is known to me very well. Sit down. Tacs, are you in command of this escort the Kagan has sent me?"

Tacs slid onto a bench on Edeco's side of the table; Dietric sat down next to him, and a slave quietly brought them silver cups and filled them with wine. Yaya sat down between Edeco and Tacs. Dietric lifted his cup and across its edge studied the Romans.

Their robes were white as salt, the hemlines embroidered with gold thread, and on their wrists and fingers they wore rings that clicked like little bells. They even smelled different from Germans or Huns, like soap, as all clean, rich things must smell. Like their garments their skin and their features seemed more finely made than Germans' or Huns'. They sat with their feet together and their knees spread under their robes, their arms folded, and although they turned their heads and occasionally lifted their hands to take food or to drink, Dietric had the impression that they never moved at all.

They were speaking Latin, which Dietric did not understand, and when the Roman who had been speaking when they entered stopped talking, Edeco answered in the same tongue, harsh-voiced as Yaya. He seemed impatient and restless and he clearly disliked the Roman he spoke to. Tacs and Yaya were arguing softly over the quality of the wine, whether it was better or worse than the wine that the Kagan had had of the Romans of New Rome the year before. Dietric could not keep their voices out of his ears; they distracted him, and he grew irritated.

When Edeco finished talking, one of the Romans said something in a careless voice. He spoke through his nose and his voice was thin and unpleasant. Another Roman, younger and with more hair, frowned and spoke to him as if reproving him. Dietric glanced up at Edeco, startled; the Hun, scowling, was staring at the Romans and his hands pressed violently against the table in front of him.

Softly, Tacs said, "The Roman said that we should not compare our Kagan, who is a man, with their Emperor, who is a god."

Edeco stood up. His voice was choked with rage. The Roman with the nasal voice began to talk, but the younger man put one hand on his arm and stopped him. Beside Dietric, Tacs was looking quizzically up at Edeco. Edeco kicked back precisely, knocked his chair out of the way, and turned on his heel and walked out the door.

Tacs said, "If their Emperor were a man and a Hiung, he wouldn't pay gold to the Kagan." He looked into his wine cup and twisted to call a slave.

The Hun who had let them in laughed and glanced over at the Romans, and Yaya gave a drunken giggle. Tacs held up his cup to a slave. One of the Romans—the younger one—turned toward the bench of servants and called, "Vigilas." A Goth sitting on the bench came up and bent and spoke to him. Across the Roman's patient, weary face a smile worked; his eyes turned piercing on Tacs.

At the far end of the table, on the Hun side, Orestes leaned forward and spoke to the Romans, his face creased with his smile. Yaya knocked his elbow into Tacs' arm, slopping wine out of the cup. "What are they saying?"

Tacs lifted his head and listened. "That if the Emperor were a Hiung he would be Attila." He shook his head. "They should not say such things—it is an insult to the Kagan."

The Roman with the nasal voice said something in a careless tone and lifted his hand. Orestes smiled the way Tacs sometimes smiled, all teeth. Looking at him unsettled Dietric: Orestes had the face and the hands of a Roman but many of the mannerisms of a Hun, as if two souls lived in him. Ardaric had said once that Orestes had forsaken Christ and now practiced outrageous and disgusting rites in his house at Hungvar. Tacs said, "Now the Roman is making nothing of what he said and asking will someone get Edeco back. If we are to go to Hungvar he says we should try to keep friends." Tacs lifted his head and called to Orestes, who replied one word, and Tacs said, "This Roman's name is Maximinus."

At the sound of his name the nasal Roman looked away. Orestes spoke in Hunnish to Tacs, who got up and went out of the room, apparently to fetch back Edeco. Turning toward the Romans, his forearms lying on the table before him and his head thrust forward over his interlaced fingers, Orestes said something through his eternal sneering smile.

Maximinus, the Roman with the nasal voice, jerked his head back, reddening, but the younger man drew him firmly down, and spoke mild-voiced to Orestes with a polite bow at the end of it. The Goth sitting among the Romans grunted. Orestes leaned back; his eyes flickered toward the door. Yaya's gaze had been swiveling back and forth between the Romans and Orestes, but now he looked over at Dietric.

"You understand?" he said, hopefully.

Dietric shook his head. "Where did Tacs go?" Through the corner of his eye he saw the Goth Vigilas interpreting.

"Edeco," Yaya answered. He turned his eyes back on the Romans.

Dietric drank more wine. Neither Orestes nor the other Hun, sitting now between Yaya and the end of the table, was looking at the Romans. Maximinus tapped his fingernails impatiently on the table. Beside him the younger man had taken a wax tablet from his sleeve and was marking it with a slender gold tool. Dietric thought, All these men have come so far together but there is nothing between them except boredom. Suddenly all such doings became in his mind filmed over with grey, nerve-wracking but meaningless.

He drank more wine. The only sound in the room was the slap-slap of the feet of the slaves carrying the ewers of wine endlessly around the table and the minute clicking of Maximinus' fingernails on the marble tabletop. Vigilas had slouched down on the end of Maximinus' couch, his shoulders stooped. He was a man of middle-age, with a heavy, shrewd face.

Dietric remembered that Tacs had said they would go to find a whore when they were done here, and his mouth grew dry at the thought. He wondered whether Yaya would come. If Yaya came Dietric knew he himself would fail. A slave was waiting beside him to fill his cup again, and he set the cup down. The sound of the wine running into the cup was like the roaring of a waterfall. Dietric wondered if Tacs knew he was a virgin, recalled the strange look Tacs had given him when they first spoke of whores, and was ashamed to be innocent.

Someone was running in the hall, coming nearer. The light footsteps rattled up to the doorway and through, and Tacs came over to the table. He put one hand on it, taking his weight slightly off his legs, and spoke to Orestes. Orestes nodded and said something, amused, and gestured with his forefinger to Tacs to go. Dietric stood up. Yaya said, "I stay.

Warm here, and wine." He planted his elbows on the table. Dietric went after Tacs toward the door.

Outside, Tacs looked up at him and laughed. "Edeco would not even let me in. He said through the door that he will stay alone tonight and not have to look at Romans again until tomorrow but he means no ill will. I was to tell that to Orestes but I didn't. Edeco was tired of the Romans and they should know it. Do you remember the way to that shrine?"

"Yes," Dietric said, and they went down the corridor toward the door.

Moonlight flooded the square before the church, but the porch lay deep in shadow. The tall double doors were shut. Tacs and Dietric climbed the wide steps to the porch and Tacs led the way along it. Dietric could hear the blood beating in his ears and in spite of the intense cold his palms were sweating. Along the building wall, in the shadow of the porch roof, the whores were lined up like horses waiting to be sold. When Tacs and Dietric came toward them they called out in soft voices full of a forced and unpleasant femaleness. One jumped out and pulled open the front of her dress. In the darkness Dietric could barely see her white breasts. She snatched his hand up and pressed it against her flesh, and he jerked it back, horrified.

Tacs said something, and the whore answered in Latin. Dietric could not see her face, only the white breast she had left hanging casually out of her dress. Against the palm of his hand the memory of her nipple burned. She and Tacs argued about something, and finally Tacs with a little shrug seemed to give in. He gestured to her, and she pulled her dress closed over her breast and walked off the porch. Tacs followed her, and Dietric fell in step beside him.

"She wants three coppers each," Tacs said. "But she has a house. That's better than the orchard when it's cold out."

"Yes," Dietric said, hoarse.

"Let me go first, and you keep watch outside. In case something happens. Sometimes they are friends with thieves. When you have your clothes off they come in and try to rob you. It's hard to fight back with your clothes off."

Dietric could say nothing. They were crossing the square toward a narrow street. The whore walked before them as if she were not with them. Her body fascinated him. She was only a girl, younger than he was, too thin to be pretty, but her long black hair swayed when she moved, disturbing him. They walked into the narrow street. Dogs barked from behind a high fence to Dietric's left. He smelled garbage. Something touched his wrist, and he jumped, but it was Tacs, giving him money.

"I will repay you," Dietric said softly. "I promise."

Tacs laughed.

The whore stopped in front of the house beside the one with the dogs. It was a small stone house with a wooden door. A lamp burned over the lintel. The girl knocked on the door and called out sharply in a strange language. A man answered in a drowsy voice. The girl stood to one side of the door and turned and smiled at Tacs and Dietric, a meaningless, uninterested smile, to keep them happy. In his memory Dietric saw her breast hanging out of her dress, blue-white in the darkness. The door opened, and a short man, covered with wooly black hair, came out pulling a tunic closed around him. He looked incuriously at Tacs and went by Dietric without glancing at him, yawning, off down the street.

The girl spoke, and Tacs said, "She says that's her brother." He smiled at Dietric and winked. The girl said something else —Dietric could see her face clearly, in the lamplight; she had small sharp features and a pouting mouth. Tacs answered her and she went through the door, and Tacs following pulled the door shut behind him. Dietric leaned up against it, his legs wobbly with excitement.

Beyond the door, the girl's voice sounded briefly, and Tacs spoke to her. Metal rang on metal. That was the money falling into her cup. Tacs had said he was to pay her before he—they —did anything. He could smell the bitter odor of his own sweat. Beyond the door, wood creaked. Her couch. They were doing it. Her breast had been soft against his fingers, yielding and soft. He leaned his weight heavily against the door, but it was shut fast.

There were no more edifying noises. Dietric's ears strained. He looked around; the street was empty. He noticed light shining on the fence next door, and went toward it—it was the light coming through the shutter over the girl's window, around the corner in the alley. Dietric leaned against the corner of the house, looking at the window. What were they doing in there? He knew, his wild imagination knew, having seen dogs and cattle and now and then people. He slid down the wall to the window and pressed his eye to a crack in the shutter. All he could see was the front of the room, lit by another oil lamp on the table, beside a brass bowl. It was wrong to spy. It was evil and sinful. He bent his knees and moved his eye against the crack, trying to see more, and silently the shutter swung open as wide as the palm of his hand.

He backed up, sure they would see and call to him to shut it, and his scalp heated with embarrassment, but no shout came. He heard harsh breathing—two heavy breathings. The soft crunch of straw. The lamplight wavered along the walls of the room. His throat closed, and he moved sideways until he could see them.

The girl was on her hands and knees on the couch; her head hung down, and all her long black hair spilled over her naked shoulders and her arms. The lamplight shone on her hips and thighs and on Tacs' hands that lay on her hips, the fingers spread, his knees between hers, and his hips thrust and his hands on her hips drew her back to meet each thrust. Dietric could not breathe. Tacs' body glistened with sweat. He moved one hand to the middle of the girl's back and pressed, and obediently she lowered her shoulders to the bed. Tacs' head rose, mouth open, eyes squeezed shut, the scarred skin of his cheeks golden, like an idol's, and his hair falling tangled over his back. The rasp of his breathing grew heavier and faster. Dietric clasped his hands together, trembling. He himself was twitching as if he already penetrated the girl. His tunic was propped out in front of him like a tent on a pole. Tacs shuddered. The rhythm of his breathing broke sharply, and he folded forward over the girl's back. Immediately she wiggled out from under him and went off into a corner of the room. Tacs fell on his side and curled up on the couch like a dog.

Dietric backed away from the window, embarrassed again. He pushed at the front of his tunic until his pole sank down, half limp, and went quickly to the door. Voices sounded behind it, and more coins rang in the girl's bowl. The door opened. Tacs' face, bleary and sated, shone in the lamplight. "Go on." Dietric went into the room. His hand shook, and when he dropped his coins into the bowl one missed and fell to the floor. The girl sat on the bed, watching him. He started toward her, pulling off his belt, but before he went to her he crossed to the window and shut the shutter tight across it and fastened it with the bolt.

PALE FROM HIS SEASON IN New Rome, Edeco sat at a table, eating; he looked up and gestured with his right hand that Tacs should come closer. At first he was more interested in the meat in his hands than in Tacs. Tacs came up to the little marble table and stood across from Edeco, waiting. Edeco looked up and set down his food. As always he was frowning.

"Last night, at first, I thought they had the name wrong. When I left Hungvar everyone was very sadly saying you and Marag were dead. How did you come home? Sit down. They overcook their meat here but there is certainly a lot of it."

"Thank you," Tacs said. He looked around the room for something to sit on. In the dimness of an alcove, a slave was waiting, and he came out and put a short wooden bench up to the table opposite Edeco. Edeco took chunks of meat and put them down on the marble tabletop in front of Tacs, where they lay in a pool of juice. The slave came back with a plate, but Edeco waved him off impatiently.

"Go away. All the way out."

The slave padded to the door. Edeco stared after him.

"They have spied on me three months now. The customs a man falls into under watch aren't fit for Hiung."

There was a basket of bread on the table, circular flat loaves still warm. Tacs tore one in half and made a dam on the table against the juice, which was running down toward the edge. He had not eaten yet in Sirmium; that morning they had again tried to make him stand in line for his food, like a slave. "Marag is dead. I came back to Hungvar in the fall, before the snow started. I should have done it before. Everybody treats me very well now, the Kagan also. Tell me about New Rome."

"You have been to New Rome. Tell me about the old one."

"The City? We never went past the gate."

"Ardaric ordered you there. Did you see it?"

"Yes. We stayed there watching three days."

"Could we take it? If Visigoths could take it, Hiung can. How high are the walls? Is it as big as New Rome? Is the harbor as good?"

Tacs took a bite of meat. Rich juices filled his mouth. He swallowed enough so that he could talk and said, "It's scattered all over hills and marshes and there is no harbor at all, only a river with marshes on either bank. The river can be guarded so that no food is smuggled along it into the City. I don't think there is much to plunder. The Goths must have taken it all. I heard owls in the city at night and the wolves go right up to the walls looking for food. Why should we take it?"

"Ah. You never heard the old man. He says if we take Rome curses will fall on us and we shall all die miserably, screaming."

"What old man?"

Edeco spat out a lump of gristle. Picking up the ewer on the table beside the basket of bread, he poured wine into his cup and drank and handed the cup to Tacs.

"Last summer when we were in Italy, an old man brought us the tribute money from Rome, to make us go back. You left the day before he came, I think. He was a high priest, and along with the gold he gave the Kagan a stern lecture about Rome and how it is protected by spirits and the demon Christ and his powers. You know that the Kagan is always tolerant of old men. Since we were all starving and sick, he decided to take the gold and go home, but first he listened to the high priest, very patient."

Meat fibers were stuck between Tacs' teeth. He worried them loose with his tongue and his thumbnail. "Why do you want to take Rome, then?"

"To show that our magic is stronger than theirs."

Tacs drank the last of the wine and set the cup down. "I'm not sure. It is a strange place. I had trouble sleeping there. Maybe there Hiung magic won't work. It is full of spirits. The old man could be right."

Edeco shrugged one shoulder. "Perhaps. The Kagan did not believe him." He looked away, frowning again. Tacs wiped his greasy fingers on his thighs. He could tell that something was worrying Edeco; out of curiosity he almost asked, but he knew if it were important he would know it eventually anyway.

"Are we going back to Hungvar tomorrow?" he asked.

Edeco jerked his gaze back to him. "Oh. Not for a few days. These Romans say they won't go until they've had a chance to rest. We came very slowly. I don't know why they're tired. Probably it's treachery. How is the road north?"

"It's open," Tacs said. "But you know how the rivers run to flood when the spring comes, if you wait that long."

"Just a few more days," Edeco said. He looked off again, absently, frowning, and after a moment turned back to Tacs and stared at him hard. Tacs smiled at him. Edeco grunted and lowered his eyes.

"Who commands the Kagan's guard, with me gone?"

"Monidiak, I think."

Edeco nodded and sank into silence again, his eyes on his hands before him on the tabletop. Tacs ate more bread.

"Do you know Vigilas?" Edeco asked.

Tacs shook his head.

"He came to Hungvar once, on an embassy from the old Emperor."

"I don't remember."

"Perhaps you weren't there. He is this embassy's interpreter, a Goth. He was there last night."

"I remember him," Tacs said. He waited for Edeco to go on, but Edeco only poured more wine and drank and handed the cup across the table. Whatever worried him lay in his eyes like his habitual frown.

"Well," Tacs said, uncertain; he thought he should go, and he stood up.

"Tacs," Edeco said suddenly. "Is it better to honor an oath or to keep trust with the Kagan?"

Tacs sat back down again. "What?"

Edeco rose and went around the table. Although he wore a tunic of fine red cloth and even the gold armbands that the Romans favored, he had on Hunnish leggings and boots of silver fox fur. He went toward the door and looked out, to make sure no one was listening, and said, "I have sworn an

oath not to tell something, but if I tell none, a certain wickedness will be done, or rather will go unpunished for not being
known, and the Kagan will be ill-served."

"What oath?"

"According to certain spirits of the Romans, but an oath
nonetheless."

"Why did you swear it?"

"At the time I didn't realize what it was they would tell
me. You know how a man can be curious, and when people
offer something in secret he'll chafe to know it, even if he
would refuse it."

Tacs had no idea what Edeco was talking about. He sat
still, waiting.

"So I must break the oath and I am afraid that something
bad will come of that. What shall I do to guard myself?"

Tacs laughed. "I am no shaman. Ask The Fluteplayer when
you get back to Hungvar."

"I have heard it said often that you have certain kinds of
magic."

"Talk to The Fluteplayer. Which spirits did you swear the
oath on?"

"The demon Christ and some of his attendants."

"Oh." Tacs frowned. "I could ask Dietric, he is a Christian."

"No. Don't mention any of this to a German, they are all
half Roman. I'll talk to The Fluteplayer, but you must promise
to do something for me. You must go back to Hungvar now,
ahead of the rest of us, and tell the Kagan that when I was
in New Rome, the Romans took me aside and had me swear
an oath not to reveal this and then asked me to murder the
Kagan for gold."

Tacs started. Edeco was watching him closely; deep lines
that had not been there before marked the corners of his
mouth.

"I agreed to it and they gave me some gold. I was afraid
to turn them down for fear they would kill me on some pretext,

but I never meant to do it. I should have turned them down, shouldn't I?"

"To kill the Kagan?" Tacs swallowed. "Who asked it? This Vigilas?"

"He was there, but it was one of the counselors, a gelding, Chrysaphius. I should have turned them down."

"How can they call their Emperor a god who would command such a thing—to steal the magic of a whole people?"

"I doubt the Emperor knew of it. You know I will not do it, frog, leave off. But I must tell the Kagan so that he will punish them."

Tacs nodded once. He felt as if the shadow of a lance had passed over him.

"Will you go ahead of us to Hungvar and tell him?"

"I will."

"You must say I never meant to do it and that I only pretended to accept it to lure them here to be punished."

"I will. Let me tell Dietric. He has a deep respect for the Romans and should know that they are wicked."

"He would make excuses and stay as he is. Why have you become such friends with a Gepid, anyway? He would not defend you to his people as you defend him to me."

"Don't say that. You don't know him. I like him."

"He is Ardaric's son. I have known Ardaric and worked with him since my father's death. It is possible to be wise without being good, and Ardaric is the proof of it."

"Dietric is not like Ardaric," Tacs said stubbornly.

"Aaaah." Edeco clapped his hands together. "Don't tell him. Sometimes I think you are too simple to bother with."

Offended, Tacs said, "I never said that I was clever."

"At least you don't lie."

Tacs rocked back and forth on the bench, glaring at Edeco. The other man got up and walked across the room. All the furniture here was carved of dark wood and polished with oil, and the lines of the tables and benches drew the eye to see the room as one thing, balanced between the tiles of the floor and the ceiling and the shapes of the walls and windows. It was airy and full of light even in winter but like everything Roman it seemed at its best without people in it. Suddenly Tacs yearned to leap up and knock over the furniture and splash offal and garbage across the walls and floor. Edeco came back and sat down again opposite him.

"I'm sorry. It is I who am simple, to speak to you like that. But I have been with the Romans so long there is no peace in my mind any more."

"Why should you be sorry? Everybody else thinks I'm stupid, too."

"Puh." Edeco put one hand on Tacs' chest and shoved him. "Go away. I haven't got the leisure to cope with your pride. But don't tell anybody why you are leaving, and go tomorrow back to Hungvar."

"Can I take Dietric with me?"

"Yes," Edeco said. "He would suffer, alone with the rest of us."

Tacs got up and went out of the room.

TEN

The KAGAN THRUST OUT HIS
lower lip. He sat slouched in his high seat, his left shoulder
hunched up and his right arm stretched along the arm of the
chair. To his right sat his sons Ellac and Dengazich. They had
listened without a word to Tacs and not once had they looked
at him. The Kagan had not looked away from him. For the
first time Tacs felt uneasy about carrying such news.

The silence stretched on and grew heavy and awkward. The
Kagan scratched idly at the wispy hairs of his beard, his eyes
steadily on Tacs'. Tacs' legs began to ache, starting at the
ankles and spreading up into his knees and thighs, and he
shifted his weight to his toes, uncertain whether he should ask
to sit down. The Kagan watching him smiled and said, "Sit,
little frog. You weren't made to stand."

Staring at the blank wall opposite, Dengazich made a face
and quickly pulled it straight. Tacs sighed and squatted on his
heels.

"So," the Kagan said, in a mild voice. "Edeco confided in
you because the oath he had sworn troubled him and you are
the friend of a shaman, The Fluteplayer. What did you say to
him concerning the oath?"

Tacs had expected questions about the plot. He had no
answer ready for other questions, and he had to think to remember. At last he shrugged. "Nothing. I told him to talk to
The Fluteplayer. I don't remember saying anything else."

"Unh." The Kagan smiled. His face smoothed out and he

glanced at his sons. Dengazich's quick smile passed over his face but Ellac's face showed nothing.

"How did Edeco look?" the Kagan asked. "When he spoke of this plot to murder me, did he seem . . . upset?"

"Naturally." Tacs lifted his hands, palms up. "Even to think of such a murder—"

"Sssh. I prefer short answers, you know that. Did he seem as upset about the plot as the oath and breaking the oath?"

"Well," Tacs said, "he had known of the plot longer than I." He did not understand this questioning; he was impatient for the Kagan to come back to the subject of the plotters and the embassy coming to Hungvar, so that Tacs could tell him his plan for their punishment. The Kagan's keen interest in Edeco he did not understand.

But the Kagan only sat back, relaxed. "Did you bring King Ardaric's son back with you?"

"Dietric? Yes."

"I am pleased. Ardaric has been nagging me about him like an old woman. You should not have taken him, he had asked Ardaric if he could go, and Ardaric had refused. Did you know that?"

"He never told me," Tacs said.

"But you knew."

"He is old enough to do as he pleases, and not as his father wants."

The Kagan shouted with laughter. His head jerked toward the two young men sitting beside his high seat. When he could control his laughter he said, "Don't talk like that in front of my children. You see Dengazich—he is scarcely the age of Ardaric's son and you will inspire him. Thank you for telling me all this. You may leave. See that—Dietric goes back to his familial hearth." For an instant, speaking of Dietric's home, the Kagan's voice sharpened with contempt. But a moment later he was smiling and mild again. "You may see that there is a place made ready for the Romans and their people, when they get here."

Tacs' eyes popped open. "Attila. Do you mean you will let them come, even now?"

The Kagan rubbed his chest. "I think to make much of this plot would be to make the Romans too important. They are unimportant. Do as I say, frog."

"Oh, well," Tacs said. "I don't understand you." He got up, stretching his legs carefully, and went out of the room.

"Why do you let a mere warrior talk to you that way?" Ellac said.

The Kagan rose from his chair. He pressed his hand tightly against his side. "He can talk to me as he wishes. You will talk to me with respect. Go away."

Ellac rose and marched away. Across the room, on the table where the drink stood in ewers, was the amulet the shamans had given him. Attila started toward it. He gestured to Dengazich to go with Ellac. Nausea filled up his belly. He knew if he could pour honeyed milk over the amulet and drink it before the pain started he would not collapse. But the pain like the stab of a knife struck him in the belly, and he lurched another step toward the table and fell to his knees. Darkness covered his eyes. His mind was paralyzed. A moment later he was looking up into the face of Dengazich.

"What is it?" Dengazich cried. "My father, my Kagan—"

Attila became aware that he was on his knees and his son was holding him up. He straightened his body, taking his weight out of Dengazich's arms, and got heavily onto his feet. He went to the table for his amulet and the honeyed milk. Dengazich followed him, like a hawk on a hare.

"What happened to you? I saw you fall, what happened?"

"I tripped," Attila said. The amulet was in a small box of opaque Eastern stone. He opened it and dropped the amulet into his cup. "Where is Ellac?"

"Gone. He left before you . . . fell."

The Kagan drank. The sweet mare's milk disguised the taste of the amulet. In his belly the pain stabbed again, much softer, and faded away.

"Has it happened before?" Dengazich asked.

Attila filled his cup again. "I tripped." When the first pain began, in his panic he had suspected even Dengazich of cursing him. He understood the seizures better now and no longer watched his sons, but he thought it dangerous that the young man should know of his weakness. He went back to his high seat and sat down. Dengazich moved around before him, rest-less, and at last hunkered down on his heels and looked up at Attila.

"Ellac does not know. What have the shamans said of this?"

"I tripped," Attila said again. "If you say anything more of it, to me or to anyone else, I shall know and you will suffer." He sipped the sweet milk. "Do you doubt me?"

Dengazich looked up at him, his Gothic eyes like the eyes of a lynx. Attila made his own eyes round. Suddenly the boy dropped forward onto his hands and knees and knocked his forehead on the floor. "My Kagan." Leaping up he ran out of the room.

Attila drank milk. Each attack of pain left him weak, and each time it took him longer to recover. Twice he had vomited blood. That frightened him, and it shamed him to be afraid. He sat slack-muscled, willing his body to gather strength.

The shamans all agreed that it was an old spell. Against a Kagan many enchantments must always lie, such men had many enemies, and now Attila's strength was going, he was aging, and the enchantments weighed on him. So all the shamans had said.

Two of them—one The Fluteplayer whose magic was an-cient and strong and who had several demons—had said that there was something else, and to this Attila himself agreed, that certain spells laid against the Hiung when the animals became men were coming to flower, and of course such spells affected him as Kagan especially.

Although he could not remember it himself he had heard thousands of times how the Hiung had followed the white stag through the swamps into Europe, and how then they had covered the plains, hordes of warriors, each clan with its own king, and women, children, young men, old people, as numerous then as the Ostrogoths or the Franks now. Since that time something had happened to them. Gradually the Hiung were dying. Sickness that left Germans healthy as before killed Hiung, and Hiung women bore children and the children lived a year or two years and died. The young men went on raids and into wars and to join the armies of the Romans and were killed, or they married the women of Germans and their children were Germans, not Hiung.

Dengazich was no Hiung, but a German, like Ardaric, and Ellac's mind was dull. Only Ernach of all his sons had any heart or craft to lead, and Ernach would not receive the cicatrice until the following midwinter. None of Attila's children knew the incantations to be said over a dead father. He should have taught them, they should have learned it when he said it over his own father, every year in the season of Mundzuk's death, but Attila had not said it now for ten years, not since the year he killed Bleda, his brother and Mundzuk's eldest son.

In that same season when he should have prayed over his father's spirit, each totem and clan of the Hiung had been used to come together and hold kurultais for the working of hunting magic and go out to hunt for meat for the winter, but for many years there had been no such Great Hunt. The Hiung sat idly in their camps and waited for the Germans to bring them their food, and no one remembered the rituals of meeting, and the men who owned the hunting magic were dying off without sons. No one remembered the songs and rituals for protecting their flocks and herds, because few Hiung kept herds any more, the Germans tended them, they were the herds of the Germans now.

His birth-name was not Attila, nor the hidden name he had taken with his cicatrice when he became a man; he had received the name Attila as a willing gift, because he had brought his people together and made them powerful over all others. Now it seemed to him that soon after his own death, the Hiung themselves would be gone. In his belly the pain nestled, soft, in the honeyed milk, and with an effort of will, he turned his brooding mind to other things.

Dietric stayed with Tacs on the porch of the Kagan's stockade until after dark. When he had run away with the Huns, he had never considered that he would someday have to face Ardaric over it. He spoke of this to Tacs, but his friend brushed him off. "He'll be so happy to have you back he'll just shout a little and send you away to think on your wickedness. You worry too much."

"You don't know my father very well."

"Don't go back at all. Stay with us."

Dietric grunted. He sat back down against the wall. Monidiak, Bryak, and Tacs were playing sticks, punching and slapping at each other with each move, their voices raised like those of women arguing. Dietric watched them, wishing that he could stay with them. Their lives seemed so much easier than his.

Tacs had never even hinted to Dietric why they had left Sirmium so abruptly. In the morning, before he went to see Edeco, he spoke of seeking out a cock fight and had described to Dietric at great length how to choose a cock to bet on. At noon he saw Edeco and by midafternoon he and Dietric were riding back to Hungvar.

The trip back had been bitter, grinding work, riding from darkness to darkness. They had eaten only a few handfuls of

parched grain and drunk melted snow and The White Brother.
Nearly all the while he had been awake he had been drunk. In
his mind the whole journey was a white radiance of snow and
sky violated occasionally by the black angles of a tree.

Now while he thought of his father the memory of riding
home filled him with a warming triumph. Watching Tacs re-
arrange his sticks, he tried to think of some casual way of
mentioning the ride.

"Tacs, why did we come back so suddenly?"

Tacs looked back at him, smiled, and turned to Monidiak.
"He is the best rider of the Germans. He never once asked to
slow down, even."

Monidiak and Bryak laughed and leaned out to touch Dietric's arm. Dietric looked down, pleased, unable to meet their
eyes. He wondered if Tacs had told them why he had left
Sirmium. He looked out toward the gate. The sun had gone
down but there was still light left in the sky. A troop of
women was walking in through the gate, single file, carrying
baskets of snow to cool the Khatun Kreka's wine. Hun guardsmen waited beside the wooden winch for the last of the women
to come in so that they could close the gate. Against the fading
sky the stiff extended branches of the oak tree stretched like
a net.

"Well," Dietric said. "I guess I have to go."

"Come stay with us," Tacs said, looking over his shoulder
at him. "Why should you go back ever?"

Monidiak said, "You are a man, Dietric, not a little boy—
come live with us."

"I wish . . ." He tried to imagine himself living with the
Huns, but he could not. "I have to go back. I'll come to see
you tomorrow, Tacs. Maybe." He bent and slapped Tacs on
the shoulder. Picking up his Hun coat from the porch rail, he
went around the corner of the palace for his horse. Behind him
Monidiak shouted to the guards to keep the gate open for him.

With the setting of the sun the air had turned cold. He

rode out the gate and down the deserted road to the ford and crossed the river. The night wind swept across the snow-covered plain and slapped him in the face, raw and rich with the smell of the coming thaw. He rode along the river bank, listening to the trees creaking in the wind. Everyone else was inside for the night.

The ride back from Sirmium stayed in his mind, growing as he thought of it. One night when they had stopped to rest Tacs had told him of how he and his friend Marag had crossed the Alps from Italy in the face of a screaming autumn blizzard. When he spoke of Marag's death, Tacs' voice was full of a hopeless longing. So even Huns died in the snow, and to survive such a journey was surely a sign of strength. With his father's house growing large on the hill before him, Dietric took the memory as a kind of armor; no matter what Ardaric said, he knew better.

Nonetheless, he went in to the stockade through the little back door, which he knew how to force, and took his horse to the stable and stayed there until he was sure everybody was busy at dinner. If he managed to get to the sleeping loft and spend the night uncaught, Ardaric would look silly raging at him. The familiar smells and sounds of his home worked on him. Suddenly the ride from Sirmium seemed to have happened years before, and to another man. Of Sirmium itself he remembered only a jumble of details.

Opening the stable door, he looked out across the slushy yard toward the hall. Torchlight spilled out through the cracks in the shutters and he could hear the laughter and chatter of the people inside. He could smell the meat and bread and even the beer. Tears came to his eyes. This was the real, the true life; the life of the Huns was a ghost. He started toward the back of the hall, where there was a window he could sneak through.

"Stop there—you dog! Stop!"

Dietric stopped. His arms broke out in gooseflesh; his mouth dried up. Ardaric walked out of the lee of the hall, his fists swinging at the ends of his arms, and his chin thrust out.

"Where have you been?" Ardaric shouted, taking a stride for each word. "Where did you go, when I ordered you—I *ordered* you not to go with them—"

"Please—" Dietric looked around to see who might be listening. "Please."

"Please," Ardaric said. "Please." He strode up to Dietric and struck him across the ear. "Please!" With the other fist he hit him on the other ear. "Please!"

Dietric lifted his forearms to protect himself. "Father—"

Ardaric's great fists flew around him, pounding his arms and glancing off the top of his head. Dietric bent over, trying to get down out of the way. Tears of humiliation ran down his face. He thought of running. Instead, he straightened up and hit Ardaric in the face.

The skin split across his knuckles; his arm went numb to the elbow. Ardaric wobbled back, his arms flailing, and sat down hard in the wet, filthy snow. Startled, Dietric laughed.

Ardaric heaved himself up out of the snow and came stiffly toward him. Dietric whirled and ran. His feet skidded on the slush and he had to work to keep his balance. A giant weight struck him in the back. He fell on his face in the snow and slid across the ground, Ardaric on his back. When he came to rest his father leapt up and seized him by the arms and dragged him to his feet.

"Strike me, will you—" Ardaric began to beat him over the shoulders. "Strike your poor father—pray to God for forgiveness, you wretched dog—"

Dietric folded his arms over his head and stood, crouched, while Ardaric slapped and punched him. He became gradually aware that half the population of the stockade was watching and laughing; the windows of the hall were mobbed with faces. But he had no more embarrassment left; he waited patiently for Ardaric to tire or get bored and stop, and at last the force of the blows lessened.

"Apologize," Ardaric shouted.

"I'm sorry." Dietric shook the front of his coat to knock the caked slush off it. "What for?"

Ardaric was staring at him, his wide chest rising in hard breaths. "You went to Sirmium? What did you do there?"

"Let's go inside," Dietric said. "I'm cold."

Ardaric took him by the arm. "You should be, you are a disobedient cur of a worthless son." His arms encircled Dietric in a painful hug. "The Lord chastiseth whom He loveth." His voice broke; Dietric, amazed, felt his father's wet clumsy kiss press against his cheek.

TACS' BROTHER RAS KEPT A dozen mares on the plain west of Hungvar, and every evening he went out himself and brought them in to be milked. The day after he had come back to Hungvar, Tacs rode out to the pasture to get his own horses, which he had left in his brother's care. He had ridden halfway to the pasturage when he heard a shout behind him; Ras himself galloped up to him. Ras was six years older than Tacs, his only living full brother, and although they had never been close to one another Tacs liked to talk to Ras, who had many strange and unsettling ideas.

Ras galloped up on his black horse and jerked it down to a walk. Being tall and long in the face, he resembled their mother more than their father Resak whom Tacs favored. "I did not know that you were back again from Sirmium, brother," he said.

"I came back yesterday," Tacs said. "Edeco sent me back before the others."

The two brothers rode forward, side by side, at a walk. Ras carried his leadline coiled on his shoulder. Tacs had always admired him more than he would admit even to himself; Ras was very rich and had the respect of all the important men. While they rode Tacs kept glancing at Ras through the corner of his eye.

Suddenly Ras said, "What was there to see in Sirmium?"

Tacs lifted one shoulder. "Only what is always there—many buildings, people, the things the Romans make. I met a Hiung in the service of the Emperor, I saw the house of the proconsul, I had a whore, all the same things."

"You should be careful of whores, you might be robbed."

"I took my friend with me to stand guard."

Ras gave him a sharp look. "That Yaya? He is of no value."

"No—Dietric, the son of the Gepids' King."

"The Gepids' King. Ardaric? I thought Yaya was your friend."

"He is, but Dietric is my special friend. Like Marag."

Ras turned his gaze forward again. They rode under the branches of the trees that marked the edge of the pasture. On the naked grey twigs fat green buds showed, ready to burst. In the shadows snow lay in patches on the ground, pocked and watery.

"They still speak of that," Ras said. "How you brought Marag's body back to his family to be buried. His father brought me three colts and salt and iron, and he wept and swore that you are a great man."

Tacs said nothing. He wondered why Marag's father would bring such useful gifts to Ras and not to him, except of course Ras was the head of Tacs' family. It startled him to hear admiration for him in Ras' voice, and he cleared his throat and looked elsewhere. The plain before them dipped to the frozen stream and rose again on the far side. Hundreds of horses grazed across the brown mud their hoofs had made of the snow. Most of them were moving slowly across the plain toward the places where their masters would be gathering them. Ras' horses already stood waiting under a dead oak tree, their heads together, their tails to the unceasing wind; patches of shedding hair clung to their flanks.

"So Dietric is your special friend now," Ras said. "That is something to think about. That black mare of yours is a bad one. She never stays with the others. Do you see her anywhere? Yesterday I found her all the way across the stream, down in the ravine."

Tacs craned his neck to look among the horses wandering slowly across the plain. The black mare loved to stray. When he did not see her, he put his fingers to his mouth and whistled. The black pony threw up its head, and among Ras' horses the sorrel mare and the grey gelding that belonged to Tacs started toward him, shouldering their way through Ras' horses.

Ras went off to hitch his horses to his leadline. Tacs' horses were coming to him, their heads low, and their long snarled manes drifting out on the wind. The black mare appeared at the edge of the trees; she stood a moment, her head raised into the wind, and Tacs whistled again. His black pony neighed. With her head high, the mare galloped over the slush toward them. Although she was heavy with foal she ran with a smooth easy stride that Tacs liked to watch. He thought that she wandered to find a place to have her baby in safety. Like the pony she came of pure Hiung stock—the pony was her child. She came up beside the sorrel mare and nipped her in the neck, and the sorrel kicked at her. All three horses ambled toward him and stopped, their noses almost touching the black pony's muzzle.

Tacs dismounted and neck-roped the three horses together, talking to them quietly and patting them. The black mare licked his hands; all three horses sniffed at his clothes in search of the presents he sometimes brought them. After he had pulled the burrs and tangles out of their manes he scrubbed some of the long winter hair off their flanks. The black mare's barrel had a bump in it that he decided was the foal's heel, and he touched it and said a charm for swiftness. When he was finished, he stood looking into the sorrel mare's eye. Horses' eyes were unlike human eyes, there was something cold and unfriendly about them. All his horses hitched to his leadline, Ras came riding back, and Tacs mounted and they started home, side by side.

"So the Gepids' King's son is your friend," Ras said. "A German and a Hiung. That is very strange."

"Everybody says I shouldn't be his friend."

"Do they? Perhaps they are right. I couldn't say. It seems odd to me, but I have no friends who are not Hiung. In fact I have no friends who are not exactly like me, with young children and several wives and the same cast of mind. You are as strange to me as a Gepid."

"What?" It pleased Tacs to think his brother found him strange. They passed under the bud-heavy branches of the trees and up the little slope toward the Kagan's stockade. To the north, the Gepid camp with its trim wooden houses came into view, and in the south he could see Orestes' house and the stone Roman bath.

"My friends and I," Ras said, "often disagree with the Kagan and his doings but we obey him because that is the correct way to act. I don't understand why a young man like you, with no responsibilities, should cling so close to Hungvar, taking orders and wasting your youth. If I were you, I would go out and see what there is to be done in the world, what adventure I might find. But you just stay here and get drunk and play stupid games and tricks and get into trouble. You have always been frivolous, even The Fluteplayer agrees with me on that, and he is very fond of you."

"What adventures could I have if I went off alone?" Tacs cried, angry. "I have to have my friends with me, or what fun is there?"

Ras' long face drew longer with thought. "I don't know. But I would find out, if I were you. There seems to be so much to do that you will not do."

"What should I do? What have you ever done?"

They were coming up to the ford over the river. It was crowded with people—Gepids returning to their camp, Hiung going to the stockade, merchants moving in both directions. Ras and Tacs pulled off to one side to wait until the crowd thinned enough to let them cross with their horses.

"Don't listen to me," Ras said. "I meant nothing by it, it is all dreaming."

"Then why did you say it?"

Ras moved his shoulders irritably. "What is the Kagan planning? Do you know if he wants to ride to Rome again?"

On the ford, the traffic momentarily ceased, and they rode across, scattering a little herd of goats a Gepid boy was trying to bring over the river.

"Yes," Tacs said. He was unsure if he should be telling Ras, but he knew of no way to evade it. "Of course he is."

Ras shook his head. He wore his hair long and unbraided on one side to cover his ear; he had lost the lower half of it in a fight when he was younger. "Sometimes I think we would be more comfortable with a lesser man to rule us—as it was in the old days, when there were many chiefs and not just one."

Tacs stiffened; the black pony broke into a lope from the pressure of his legs, and he reined him down. When he looked at Ras again his brother was staring at him thoughtfully. Tacs jerked his eyes away.

"Do you know why I say that?" Ras asked.

"Because you are stupid," Tacs said. "Even more stupid than I am. You should love the Kagan."

"Maybe. But listen to me. A Hiung—because we are Hiung we believe in certain things—in the power of our ancestors, the old way of life, several other complicated beliefs. If a man believes in something more, he is no longer a Hiung. But what is he?"

"What do you mean? My mother was a Hiung, my father was a Hiung, what would I be, a Roman? A German?" Tacs shook his head. "A mare doesn't drop calves. What do you mean?"

Ras smiled at him, smooth as oil, "Did I upset you?"

"Yes," Tacs said. "You should not speak slightingly of the Kagan. You would not say it to him if he were here."

They were riding around the base of the Kagan's hill toward the Hiung camp. The thick smells of the evening cooking fires reached them. In the sky the colors of the sunset were dimming to grey.

Ras said, "Why did you do that—bring Marag's body home? It could not have been easy."

"Why—what else could I have done?"

They rode in among the auls; Tacs had to draw rein to follow Ras' string of horses. He could not imagine how anyone would say the things Ras had implied about the Kagan. It was as if Ras had spoken against Tacs himself. He rode along behind his brother toward the center of the camp, planning sharp retorts to give him when Ras left himself open.

When they came to the place where they would have to separate, Ras called out to him and waved to him. Tacs dropped his leadrope and rode around his horses toward his brother. His throat burned with the clever things he had thought up to say.

"Come share food with us," Ras said. "You have been gone and we should see you more, anyway."

"Yaya will—"

"Come along," Ras said. He smiled; he touched Tacs' arm. "You will have a chance to tell me what you think of me."

Tacs could not help but smile. He nodded. "If you have enough."

"We always have enough," Ras said, and started off toward
his aul, his mares in a jumbled herd trotting along behind
him; up ahead, Tacs could already see his brother's youngest
wife, waiting with a jar of water to pour over his hands when
he dismounted.

ELEVEN

⊂╪

SEVERAL DAYS LATER, THE Romans came to Hungvar. No one was allowed to greet them except the few men assigned to watch over them, but many curious people came anyway, pretending to be merely passing by. Dietric was among them; after Tacs had seen to the Romans and been dismissed, they met and went together into the Hun camp.

Ummake had fallen sick again, sick enough, Tacs said, to die, and The Fluteplayer was to cure her that afternoon. Dietric and Tacs went to the aul of the shaman. A little group of people was milling around it, staring curiously in through the door whenever it opened. Tacs had said that The Fluteplayer wanted him to assist him. It seemed to fill him with pride. Dietric hung back at first, wondering how The Fluteplayer would react to an unexpected visitor, but Tacs pulled him inside.

They sat down in the middle of the aul; the shaman was working in the back, his profile to them. He ignored them. Dietric looked around, amazed. He had never seen a German home as rich as this. He had seen nothing so fine since they left the Roman house in Sirmium.

"Ummake has been sick all her life," Tacs said; he shifted his weight on his hams and his fingertips stroked the pattern of the carpet. "Her mother ate snake before Ummake was born and that made the baby's blood all cold. Fluteplayer, where did this thing come from?"

"New Rome."

"Why would having cold blood make her cough up blood?" Dietric asked. "Do you really think that's why she is sick?"

"Certainly." Tacs spat to the right for emphasis. The Fluteplayer gave him an evil look and hastily Tacs rubbed the white spittle into the nap of the carpet. "Everybody knows that coughing blood is a mark of coldness."

Dietric watched The Fluteplayer pound berries on a flat stone. They three were alone in the aul; Tacs had said that the shaman was married but Dietric had seen nothing of his wife. The aul was dark and except for the muffled grating of the grindstone utterly quiet. In the dimness beyond the light of the small oil lamps, goldwork glistened, on the lacquered benches, on the lodgepole, on the hundreds of little jars placed everywhere, full of herbs and medicines. Even the air smelled exotic.

"I was in New Rome once," Tacs said. His hand traced the dark red pattern in the carpet, moving in slow swirls over the black. "They piss into gold pots there, even the dogs wear gold."

"If they weren't rich we would starve," The Fluteplayer said. "Be quiet, let me think."

Tacs put his hands on his thighs, the fingers curling, and sat absolutely still. Dietric glanced at him, amused. The Fluteplayer put a bowl down on the carpet and scraped the pounded berries into it. He took a jar from the many beside him and tipped powder from it into the palm of his hand and held the hand out over the bowl, an arm's length above it, and let the powder run down into the bowl in a thin stream. Dietric admired the man's show-craft. Ardaric had said once that certain of the Huns had a refinement and understanding that elevated them above the common ruck of their people.

The Fluteplayer lowered his hands and sat still, his gaze resting on the bowl, unwinking. The perfect silence hung around him like a shield. The lamplight picked out the small white pebbles bound into his greased hair; the cords on his neck stood out with effort. It was all very excellent flummery and Dietric let himself admire the shaman's cunning. He felt wiser than Tacs who obviously believed it all. A moment later the mess in the bowl gave off smoke.

The hair on Dietric's forearms prickled up. The Fluteplayer had not touched the bowl, nor moved, nor even spoken; only his eyes stared straight into it, but from the glassy surface of the liquid thin smoke rose. Dietric's tongue was dry; he swallowed with difficulty. He was afraid to speak. Through the corner of his eye he looked at Tacs, who had not moved at all, except that now the corners of his mouth smiled.

"Ho!"

Dietric jumped. The Fluteplayer stood up, uncoiling like a snake into the air, shaking his head and flopping his hands around on the wrists. "Now. Come with me. Tacs, carry the rattles, the feather-stick, and that brazier over there. Be careful, it is hot. Tell your friend to stay behind you and not to breathe the air around me." He picked up the steaming bowl and went out the door of the aul.

Tacs grabbed up two gourd rattles and a long pole strung with dyed eagle feathers. Dietric reached for the brazier, to pass it to him, but Tacs struck at his arm. "Don't. Let me do it, it's important to do exactly as he says." He took the brazier and went out, and Dietric followed him, empty-handed.

The crowd around the aul had doubled. The children were hiding behind their parents and a lean grey dog whined and slunk away when The Fluteplayer came out. It was an unusually hot day for early spring. The bright sunlight dazzled Dietric and made him blink.

The shaman led Tacs and Dietric single file through the crowd to the little aul behind his own, where Yaya had taken Ummake when she fell sick. The crowd followed. Dietric heard someone say, in Hunnish, "It is done by sunset." Immediately someone else began to argue.

Holding the steaming bowl out in front of him, The Fluteplayer started to chant, and the crowd hushed. Dietric thought
The Fluteplayer to be a young man still—certainly younger
than Ardaric—but the voice he chanted in quavered and
wheezed like an old man's voice. Some of it was in Hunnish
words but some was in hisses and strange soft whistles. Dietric
would have thought it flummery; he wanted to think it nothing
else, but the bowl was exhaling clouds of steam, and he could
smell the strong hot odor of the boiling stuff inside, and yet
no fire had touched it and The Fluteplayer held it in his bare
hands. Finally The Fluteplayer stamped his left foot twice
and stopped chanting and went into the little aul.

Tacs went forward again. Before he could reach the door
The Fluteplayer came out again and stopped him. Taking
the feather-stick the shaman turned to the crowd and shouting
in Hunnish Dietric could not follow raised the feather-stick
over his head and jabbed it down like a lance into the ground.

The crowd gave up a general sigh. The Fluteplayer went
back into the hut. Tacs shifted his weight from one foot to the
other; Dietric knew he was wondering whether to follow,
and almost at once the shaman called from within the hut,
"Well, come in, I need the brazier." Tacs ducked through the
door and Dietric went after him.

This aul was far smaller than the other. Piles of furs, fancy
clay pots, and sticks decorated with feathers, bits of shell, horn
and wood and berries crowded the walls. There was no furniture. It was very hot although there was no sign of a fire;
Dietric could smell stale smoke. Ummake lay on her back
on the floor in the middle of the aul. Her head touched the
far wall and her feet nearly reached the door. Beyond her, in
the dark, her husband Yaya sat. His eyes never left The
Fluteplayer.

Ummake's breathing came harsh and slow through her open
mouth. Even from here Dietric could see how rough her skin
was, parched and scaly. Bending over her, The Fluteplayer put

his ear down to her lips and listened. With his left hand he motioned to Tacs and Dietric to stay back.

Tacs settled down, his feet flat on the ground and his knees to his chest, with the brazier and the rattles in front of him. The only light came from the smokehole of the hut, which was open, and the hut was uncomfortably warm. The Fluteplayer took the brazier and put it down beside Ummake's head.

"Shut the smokehole."

Tacs bounded up and looked around for the pole, found it leaning against the wall, and with the hook on its end mancuvered the cover over the hole in the top of the aul. The dark and the wet heat closed down around them. Dietric blinked. Gradually his eyes adjusted to the dimness. His ears strained; he heard the others shifting back and forth and The Fluteplayer muttering and Tacs putting down the pole. Someone cleared his throat.

When Dietric could see again, The Fluteplayer was scooping glowing coals from a pot into the brazier with a long-handled shovel made of brass. He hung the shovel on the lodgepole and Dietric saw that it was formed in the shape of a serpent with a yawning mouth and arched fangs to keep the coals from rolling out. The coals gave off a faint red glow; in that light Dietric saw Yaya's face, rigid as a mask of wood, and realized that Yaya was afraid for his wife's sake. Dietric had not thought him capable of that.

With the brazier full of hot coals The Fluteplayer set it down near the sick woman's head. The pot of boiling medicine he set on top of the brazier, careful not to smother out the coals. Gesturing with his hand he brought Tacs forward to fan the coals and keep them burning hot. At first Tacs used his hands but after a moment The Fluteplayer, groping along the floor, found him a piece of bark, painted with symbols, and Tacs used it as a fan.

The Fluteplayer sat back on his heels and watched Ummake impassively. With each stroke the bark fan made a soft whirring sound and the steam washed across the woman's face. Dietric could feel the sluggish air move against his cheeks. In the brazier the coals glowed a deep orange-red. The medicine began to bubble. Torrents of steam flooded from its surface and billowed into the air, driven by the strokes of the bark fan. Tacs' face dribbled sweat. The Fluteplayer took his rattles in his hands and started to shake them.

Dietric wished himself away from here. The steam clogged his nostrils and seemed to penetrate behind his eyes into his mind. His skin streamed with sweat and his clothes were drenched. The hot, thick air was impossible to breathe. He had to force his lungs to take in the air. Lights danced before his eyes. The man hunched over the brazier fanning the coals seemed to him like a creature from hell, foul and crooked with his sins.

The Fluteplayer with the rattles shaking in his hands swayed back and forth, his eyes fastened on the sick woman's face. His lips writhed and his head bobbed loosely up and down. The sound of the rattles filled Dietric's ears: dry, sibilant, like snakes hissing. He saw sinuous curved shapes in the air, coiling languidly toward the ceiling. Each stroke of the fan seemed stronger than the last, each shake of the rattles louder, until the noise packed his ears. The air was too thick to draw into his lungs. Ummake lay in a puddle of sweat the shape of her body, two fingers wider than her body all around. Beyond her, Yaya was swaying wildly back and forth, his head wobbling.

The Fluteplayer bounded to his feet and fell forward across Ummake, braced up on his hands and knees. The rattles sailed across the aul. He lowered his face toward Ummake's and pressed his mouth against her mouth. Dietric gave a low cry. He wanted to look away, but the scene held his eyes fast. He thought at first that The Fluteplayer would crawl into her mouth and down her throat. The shaman hovered over Ummake like a demon. The woman's body lay caged inside his spraddled arms and legs; they were attached by their mouths, as if they grew together at the lips. It was a sin even to watch such wickedness. Dietric's head pounded. The hiss of the bark fan and the harsh breathing of the three Huns hurt inside his mind. The Fluteplayer was rising, drawing Ummake up with him. She came up almost to a sitting position, mouth to mouth with The Fluteplayer. At last he let her lie down again, and turning his head he spat something into the palm of his hand.

Dietric thought that it wiggled and tried to escape—a bloody worm, as long as a man's finger, lying on The Fluteplayer's palm. The Fluteplayer flung the worm into the bowl of medicine, and a great cloud of smoke rose and the medicine foamed over the lip of the bowl and splattered sizzling on the heated sides of the brazier. Tacs backed away. With short, jerky motions the shaman closed the brazier, beckoned Tacs to open the smokehole, and tipped the last little trickle of medicine from the bowl into a jar.

He looked up at Dietric and Dietric hastily lowered his eyes, but his gaze strayed back to The Fluteplayer almost at once. The shaman was staring at him, unblinking. Dietric mumbled something, got up, and went out into the open. He felt sick and drunken. The cooler air outside the aul struck his overheated body and sodden clothes, and he trembled, nauseated. The crowd watched him silently. The Fluteplayer came out behind him and walked away.

Fascinated, Dietric went after him around the curve of the shaman's living-aul. In sight of the door, he stopped, afraid to go farther. The Fluteplayer looked over his shoulder at him, stooped, and went inside his aul. Dietric sighed. He felt limp and enfeebled but his mind leapt with hope. He began to see how it could have been done: on The Fluteplayer's lower lip there was a swelling, as if he had bitten his lip there to draw blood.

BUT THE NEXT DAY, WHEN
he came to see Tacs, Ummake was sitting in Yaya's aul trading
lies with the others and eating boiled meat. Dietric sat down
opposite her, stunned; when she looked at him he stammered
a greeting and just barely managed to keep on meeting her
eyes. He could see at once that she was weak—her hands
trembled and she was propped up against a frame of wood—
but color glowed in her cheeks and her eyes were bright with
health.

"Ummake," he said. "I am glad to see you happy again."
He did not know the Hunnish word for well.

Her shining dark eyes widened with good humor. "It makes
me happy that you should speak to me in my mother's speech,
Dietric."

Tacs came over to him, bringing a little jar of The White
Brother. For a moment they sat together without talking and
passed the jar back and forth. Finally, Tacs said, "The Romans
are still camped on the plain, did you see them?"

Dietric nodded. Everybody knew that the Kagan had refused to see the Romans or even to let them come into the
stockade. "My father went there last night."

"Oh? Why didn't you go with him?"

Dietric lay back on one elbow. "He didn't ask me. I don't
think anybody was supposed to know. The Kagan must have
sent him to make secret arrangements." He glanced over his
shoulder at Ummake—Yaya was beside her, feeding her tidbits
of meat with his fingers. "What did Yaya give The Fluteplayer
for that little spectacle yesterday?"

"He has promised him half of the foals his mares will drop
this spring."

Dietric laughed. The White Brother was flowing through
him, warming and relaxing him. "No wonder he is rich, The
Fluteplayer."

"The Fluteplayer is a very great shaman," Tacs said. "You saw how he sucked the evil out of Ummake."

Dietric handed him the jar. His mouth was full of the sweet taste of the tea. "I saw him put on a great dumb show of curing and then he spat out something bloody. Did that cure Ummake?"

"Look at her—she is better now, isn't she? Of course it cured her. You saw that thing that came out of her—that bloody thing."

"Tacs," Dietric said. He glanced around to see if anyone was listening. "How do you know that The Fluteplayer didn't have it in his mouth all the while?"

Tacs shook the jar to raise the sediment and drank. He wiped his mouth on his forearm. "What do you mean?"

"When I think about it, it seems to me that he only spat out something that he had been holding in his mouth all the while. I saw a cut on his lip afterward. Maybe he bit his lip to make blood to cover something he had put in his mouth—a bit of rope, maybe. I don't think it came from Ummake."

Tacs was watching him obliquely. His reaction puzzled Dietric, who had expected disbelief or outrage. "He cured Ummake by sucking the bad thing out of her," Tacs said. "You saw it. Now Ummake is getting better."

"But I'm positive that the thing he spat out was a fake."

"Here." Tacs bent away to pick up a handful of little fruit-filled cakes. "Have something to eat. I don't understand you. Ummake is well, isn't she? Monidiak's mother made this, they are very good."

Dietric bit into one of the cakes; they were just large enough for two bites. Inside the warm crust there was a thick paste of apples. "She isn't well yet." It was frustrating to know himself clever as The Fluteplayer and yet be unable to convince Tacs of it. He finished that cake and took another.

"She will be."

"Maybe she would have gotten well in the normal course of

things." But when he thought of that, doubt overtook him; Ummake had been very sick. He shook his head. "I'm sure that The Fluteplayer is a fraud."

"He has a great power in him. Perhaps, as you say, the bloody worm he spat out did not come from Ummake. But the thing that it was meant to be came from her, and now that it is gone she is well. That isn't faking, that is real. None of us could cure her, but he did. You worry about things because you don't understand them, which is silly. The cakes are good, aren't they?"

"Delicious," Dietric said, chewing.

TWELVE

⊂⋣

THE KAGAN THRUST OPEN
the window shutters and leaned out into the air. Beyond his
stockade wall, the oak tree was a mass of pale green buds,
opening to the warm wash of sunlight, turning and turning in
the spring wind. He could smell the tree, and the new grass
and the river; the smells filled even him with coltish energy.
That amused him, to think of himself as a colt, and with his
vast belly dented by the windowsill and his head and shoulders
cramped into the windowframe, he burst out laughing.

The door behind him opened and sandals padded on the
wooden floor: Constantius. "My Kagan."

"Not today," Attila said, still leaning out the window. "My
mind is on other affairs." Ardaric was to come today and de-
scribe his plans for the new assault on Rome. Attila shut
his eyes and inhaled the spring wind.

"My Kagan," Constantius said stubbornly. "I beg that you
hear my opinion."

The Kagan opened his eyes. Far out there on the plain,
hidden from his eyes by the Gepids' hill, lay the Roman camp.
They had been there now for five days, and each day their messenger had appeared to ask for an audience; the day before, the
messenger had come twice. Attila heaved himself straight and
turned to go back into the room. "I am listening."

Round and butter-fat, Constantius as usual wore immaculate
white cotton, hemmed with blue and green. After ten years
among the Hiung he still wore Roman clothes, brought every
six months with the caravan from Italy. He cleared his throat,

looked around him, and went to the backless chair beside the throne. "May I sit, my Kagan?"

"Sit."

Constantius lowered himself onto the chair, pulling up the hem of his gown out of the dust. Attila walked across the room to his throne. Constantius scratched his nose.

"Well, Constantius?"

"Yes." The other man sighed. "My Kagan, you cannot keep the Romans waiting there too much longer, or they will go back to New Rome. That would give the Emperor an opportunity to stop sending you the annual gift."

"We can force him to renew it."

"Only by diverting energy and time from the Italian campaign. Nor can you keep up this pretext of anger that they should have tried to bribe Edeco to kill you, since—"

"It is hardly a pretext," Attila said. "No one hears of attempts against his life with an even mind."

Constantius rolled himself around in the chair so that he faced the throne, his short legs slewed over to one side. "My Kagan, everybody knows now that Edeco sent a rider back to tell you what had happened in New Rome, that you knew of the bribery long before the Romans came, and yet you had preparations made for them and allowed them to camp near Hungvar. My Kagan, people will think you a tyrant, arbitrary, and small-minded."

"I am," Attila said. "I enjoy it." But Constantius was right; the game had its limitations. "I could allow them to—Yes?"

Edeco came into the room, his lance in his hand. "Attila, King Ardaric is waiting to see you."

"Have him wait."

Edeco nodded; his eyes remained on Attila's a trifle longer than necessary before he turned and went out. Attila settled back into the throne, folding his hands across his belly. "Bring me a cup of milk, Constantius."

"My Kagan." Constantius levered himself up from the chair and went across the room to the table.

The night before, the Romans had sent a messenger secretly to Ardaric and taken him to the Roman camp, where he had stayed almost until dawn. When he returned to his own house he had been the richer by many little presents and a lot of gold. All this Edeco had discovered. There was always the possibility that Ardaric had not allowed himself to be seduced, and of course Attila had to remember that Edeco hated Ardaric. Constantius waddled back across the room with the ivywood cup in one hand and another cup in the other. Giving the one to Attila he sat down again to sip his wine.

The Kagan drank some milk and set the cup down carefully on the arm of the throne.

"Constantius," Attila said, "when the Romans' messenger comes today, tell him that the envoy may come to Hungvar— see that they are given the four rooms in the rear of the palace, the ones facing the stockade wall."

Constantius looked up at him. "There are far too many of them to be comfortable in those rooms, my Kagan. There are twenty of the Romans, and those rooms are very small."

Attila grunted. "I don't wish them to be comfortable."

"And the rooms are now in use—we are storing lumber there."

"Move the wood."

"Where shall I put the wood, my Kagan? If I put it outside, what if it rains? There are no rooms indoors, not with so many important men coming to Hungvar."

"Where would you suggest we put the Romans?"

Constantius stood. "In the empty house behind the Court of Women, my Kagan. Also, that will give them less honor than installing them within the palace itself. I shall have slaves make it ready."

"Constantius."

Halfway to the door, Constantius turned, his face wrapped in smiles.

"Put the lumber in the empty building behind the Court of Women. Put the Romans in the four rooms in the back of the palace."

Constantius' smile stiffened. "My Kagan." He walked briskly out the door; Edeco came in.

Attila drank his milk. His mood had soured. The Romans might have been eager to get the empty building behind the Court of Women so that they could sneak in and out unobserved. It could have been Constantius' idea, but Attila thought not: the request came too soon after Ardaric visited the Romans.

"Attila," Edeco said.

"Stop nudging me, Edeco. I might nudge you back. Shut the door and come here."

Edeco pushed the door shut and walked around in front of the throne. Attila finished his milk and set the cup down. "Is Tacs still so much in the company of Ardaric's son?"

"Yes, every day."

"Send him to me. Tell Ardaric that I will not see him today, he is to go back to his house and wait until I call for him. Is Tacs inside the stockade?"

"Yes, my Kagan—he is standing gate watch."

"Get him."

"Yes, Attila."

Edeco went out. The Kagan swung his feet up onto the table in front of him. His curiosity piqued him: he wanted to hear Ardaric's plan, and even if the Gepid King had been giving the Romans his ear, he could be brought back in hand with no trouble. But it was an entertainment to devise a way to frighten him. It would be interesting to see how frightened Ardaric would be. Attila picked up his cup and took it across the room for more milk, pleased with himself.

Dietric said, "Tacs was or-
dered to tell me to tell you that the Kagan knows of your
visit to the Romans last night and will know if you go there
again."

Ardaric started. To hide his dismay he turned his face toward the map spread out on the table before him. His knees
were quivering, and he sat down heavily.

"Papa," Dietric said. He touched Ardaric's arm; his voice
was much younger than before. "Is there something wrong?"

"Yes," Ardaric said. "Did you tell him anything—anything
at all—did you know that I had—"

"No! Papa, I didn't tell anybody anything, I would have said
nothing that might be wrong."

By his voice Ardaric knew he was lying. Furious, he lashed
out at Dietric, open-handed. "Leave me. Don't let me see you
the rest of this day."

"Please, Father."

Dietric was frightened, too. Ardaric felt a twinge of satisfaction. "Now you see what your friendship with that dirty Hun
has brought on us. Get away! Go!"

Dietric ran out of the room. Ardaric, breathing hard, stared
at the door. For a moment his rage at Dietric sustained him. He
turned his eyes back to the map. His fear rose again like a
tide. He marshaled all his defenses—he had told the Romans
very little, listened without comment to most of their talk—
he had known their flattery for bait, and he had not fallen. Not
really.

Gradually, the distant sounds of his household pierced
through to his whirling mind. He raised his head and looked
around the little room. They had built it only that spring; long
flat slivers of wood hung from the fresh planks, and it smelled
of sap. He should have known that morning, when the Kagan
abruptly sent him away, that something bad had happened. He

got up from his chair, but there was nowhere to go, and he finally sat down again.

Outside, someone was chopping wood. People walked past his window, talking; a knock sounded on his door and when he did not answer footsteps hurried away. Geese cackled. Inside the room it was quiet. He stared at the edge of the map, pegged down to the table. All that hard loving work for nothing. The careful making up of plans, the assembling of information, the weighing of choices—he wondered what the Kagan would do to him.

Yet he had done nothing. He had taken their gifts and given so little in return—the description of the stockade and its buildings they could have got from anyone, a merchant, another visitor, anyone. They had asked other things, mostly concerning the Kagan's relationships with other German kings, about which Ardaric actually knew almost nothing. Edeco had accepted a bribe to do far more, and there Edeco was now, standing guard over the Kagan again, commanding the antechamber of the throneroom. It was unfair, it was cruel. If he had been a Hun they would have treated him better.

All afternoon he sat in the room and stared at the map; at supper he could hardly choke down a mouthful. He went to bed at once but could not sleep, so that when the dawn came and everyone else spilled out of bed and hurried off to work, he lay groaning under the covers and pretended to be sick, up there in the dark where no one would see how frightened he was.

In the midmorning, a messenger came from the Kagan, and he had to pull on his clothes and climb down the ladder to hear him. The Kagan wished to see him at once. The messenger would ride back with him. The messenger was one of the guards, a tall, round-cheeked Hun whom Ardaric had seen in Tacs' company. Ardaric ordered beer brought to him and went into the new room to gather up his maps and his pieces of chalk and charcoal.

THE DEATH OF ATTILA

For a while, taking down the maps on the walls, he thought of refusing to go—of ordering his people to pack their belongings and leave Hungvar. Even rolling the maps up and tying them, he savored that—the Kagan's certain shock, his rage at Ardaric's defiance, and of course his secret admiration. Ardaric knew that he would not do it, it was too dangerous; Attila had hundreds of warriors idle and aching for blood. The whole people would suffer. He took the maps under his arm and went out into the hall.

Dietric was there, talking to the messenger. When he came near enough to overhear, Ardaric realized that his son was speaking Hunnish, halting now and again, but actually conversing with a Hun in his own tongue. Seeing Ardaric, Dietric stepped back, and the messenger stood up, a pleasant smile on his face.

"Your beer is very excellent, King Ardaric. Is there anything I am to help you carry?"

"No," Ardaric said, "thank you."

Dietric said, "Father, may I come?"

"No." Ardaric would not look at him; he followed the messenger through the door.

His white stallion was waiting for him, saddled and bridled in the red leather he had gotten in the Italian campaign the year before. The Hun messenger's horse stood a few strides beyond the stallion, but the messenger went to the stallion's head and held his bridle while Ardaric mounted. Dietric had come out with them; Ardaric gave him the maps to hold, while he climbed into his saddle.

The Hun went to his horse. Dietric handed up the maps. "Monidiak is always full of courtesy," he said.

Ardaric tucked the maps under his arm. "You speak Hunnish now."

"A little." Dietric stood back. Lifting his reins, Ardaric rode toward the gate.

Monidiak said nothing to him all the way to the Kagan's

stockade. Ardaric was arranging his arguments in his mind. There was no sense in denying that he had gone to visit the Romans. If the Kagan searched his house he would find the gold and the cloth, the Roman jewelry, the beautiful little silver crucifix. He would say that he had done what Edeco had done—or claimed to have done: listened and accepted the bribes so that he could find out what was in the minds of the Romans for the Kagan's use. But his hands were cold, his cheeks felt cold, and he knew that they would not believe him.

In the stockade yard, Monidiak held his horse again. The sentries at the door stepped back and let him enter without a word from him. He walked down the corridor to the stairway, shifted the maps to the other arm so that he could hold onto the railing, and climbed up to the second floor of the palace.

Edeco sat in the antechamber with his feet braced up against the wall, throwing date stones out the window and arguing with Constantius in Latin. Ardaric shut the door behind him and Edeco came lazily to his feet. For the moment, Ardaric's hatred of Edeco armored him against his fear. He looked the Hun hard in the eye and bit his words off crisply.

"The Kagan sent for me."

"Yes. You seem to be a busy man, now, traveling here and there." Edeco's wide nostrils flared. "What is that? What are you carrying?"

"That is not for your knowing. Tell the Kagan I am here."

Edeco drew a deep breath. Turning his head, he spat a date stone out the window, clapped his hands together, and went through the door behind him. Ardaric heard him speak to the Kagan in Hunnish; for the first time he longed to know that language. He heard Attila's deep, pleasant voice in answer. Edeco returned.

"Go in."

Ardaric reached to one side and took a date from the bowl on the table. Popping it into his mouth, he went through the door of the throneroom.

When the door shut behind him, all his pride vanished. He could not meet the Kagan's eyes. A shameful, rabbit cowardice possessed him. He saw only Attila's boots, the fur matted by the leather laces, propped up against the edge of the table. Unrolling his maps, he spread out the first one on the table; he knew he would have no use for it, but it was his.

"Ardaric," the Kagan said easily. "What have you for me today? Let me see."

The boots came down, and Attila swung himself onto his feet and walked around to Ardaric's side of the table. "Ah. You made use of the Roman map. Very good. Explain the notation to me."

Ardaric raised his eyes to meet the Kagan's. With their faces only a few feet apart Attila smiled at him. Ardaric's mouth was gummed with the date he had eaten; when he began to speak, his lips would hardly move. He translated the symbols he had used on the map, pointing out each one.

Attila made only a few comments. Every time Ardaric looked at him, he was smiling. They bent over the maps together and Ardaric began to sketch out his plan for the assault. The Kagan was in a superlative humor, his face vivid with good nature. Once he made a small joke. Slowly Ardaric understood that the Kagan would not mention his visit to the Romans. But even in the rush of relief, he was angry, even disappointed, that the Kagan did not think him important enough to punish.

THIRTEEN

⊏⊨

Aeaten and the plates were taken away, they brought in the dwarf. Even among Huns he was tiny and misshapen, and he danced and spoke gibberish and made such faces that everyone laughed, even the Romans, sprawling elegantly in chairs to the Kagan's right. The Kagan alone did not laugh. Dietric watched him through the tail of his eye while the dwarf did somersaults and pulled his face into a grotesque; the Roman Maximinus laughed and leaned toward his colleague to share his laughter, but the Kagan watched the dwarf almost with distaste.

Dietric had heard—they had all heard—that in spite of the Romans' presence in the palace and at this great feast, the Kagan had refused to talk over the matters that the Romans had come to Hungvar to discuss. Dietric was pleased at that: it would show the Romans that Attila could not be toyed with. Looking across the hall—he was standing behind his father, as Ardaric's cupbearer—he could see Attila full-face, and he began to see how such a man could be more noble than the Romans who believed their Emperor a god.

Every man of importance within two or three days' ride of Hungvar had come to this banquet. The wide hall was packed with tables and benches; the men sitting on them were crowded shoulder to shoulder even in so great a space. On the wooden plank walls hung rugs and tapestries from all over the world. The floor was covered with mats woven of rushes—Ardaric

had said that the Kagan preferred not to have his carpets
ruined by people walking on them.

The ceiling beams were black with soot from the torches,
and the roar of conversation sounded like a waterfall. All the
men sitting at the tables were of high birth, each dressed to
his own standard of elegance—the three kings of the Ostrogoths had come, wearing Greek and Egyptian cloth, and
Ardaric himself wore woven cloth trimmed with fur, but
Edeco and Scottas and the other Huns, who took precedence
over the Germans, wore fur and leather studded with jewels,
feathers and rocks in their hair, and symbols painted on their
faces. When Edeco had come in, Constantius, serving the
Kagan as herald, had announced him as Master of Horse.
Dietric was pleased with himself for knowing that was a jab
at the Romans.

The dwarf danced clumsily down the middle table toward
the Kagan, while the men seated near him tried to trip him
and catch his feet; a few slashed at his legs with their knives.
Artlessly the dwarf eluded them, his stubby arms raised above
his head and his ridiculous short robe flapping around his
thighs. One of the men lunged forward with a knife and the
dwarf dodged nimbly to one side and somehow a tall pitcher
of beer overturned and drenched the knife-bearer. A roar of
laughter went up. At the head of the hall, the Kagan frowned.
He wore the blue silk tunic he always wore on such occasions;
his huge round head was sunk down between his shoulders.
His arms lay on the arms of his chair, his hands fisted. Beside
him, the Romans in their embroidered gowns, with their fine-
boned faces and pale, soft skin, seemed womanish and frail.

"Dietric," Ardaric said quietly. "Fill my cup."

Dietric backed up two steps, turned, and jogged down the
hall toward the tables where the serving vessels stood. Along
the walls the Hun guard was stationed, Tacs among them, and
when Dietric passed Tacs he smiled and lifted his hand to
him.

"I told you it would be well," Tacs called after him.

Dietric signed to him to wait and stopped at the table. The ewer with the wine Ardaric was drinking had been taken away, and he leaned up against the table to wait for it. Tacs walked up to him. "Did he tell you what happened? I was—"

Edeco shouted at him from across the hall, and Tacs looked around. Dietric drew back out of range. Edeco with a torrent of Hunnish insults ordered Tacs back to his place and not to leave it again. Tacs gave a look around, surprised at such unexpected discipline, and returned to the wall. Laughter spread around the room, and now even the Kagan laughed. The blond boy who had taken the ewer away brought it back—a cupbearer to one of the Alan chiefs who sat at the far side of the room. Dietric picked up the ewer to carry it to his father's place.

The dwarf had reached the dais. He went down on his knees before the Kagan and touched his forehead to the table. On either side of him, the sons of Attila were sitting; among them Dengazich smiled and smiled and his eyes never stopped moving. Ellac sat like a lump, shoveling food into his mouth. The dwarf babbled something in gibberish, bowing and knocking his head against the table, and yet there was little humility in it, only insolence. Attila never smiled. After a little, he spoke to Constantius, sitting on a stool at his keee, and Constantius took a purse from his robes, opened it, and laid a gold coin on the table before the dwarf.

The dwarf snatched it up and whirling raced down the table toward the door, whooping and leaping into the air, kicking dishes and cups of wine into men's laps. The Roman Maximinus, shaking with laughter, reached out and laid his hand on the arm of the other Roman. The door slammed behind the dwarf and the Romans both leaned back, smiling, all at ease. A moment later a monk appeared before the dais.

Ardaric was turned away, explaining to his Burgundian neighbor that the Kagan would not laugh at the dwarf because the little man had once belonged to the Kagan's brother Bleda. Dietric poured wine into Ardaric's cup. Reaching for it, Ardaric saw the monk and spilled wine over his hand.

Dietric took a napkin from his shirt and gave it to his father. The monk was speaking Latin, facing the Kagan, his arms raised. "What is he saying?" Dietric asked.

Ardaric's lips were pressed hard together. He listened to the monk a little while longer and said, harsh-voiced, "He is reminding the Romans of a promise that he could preach here for the conversion of the Huns. He is a fool. You see that he has only angered the Kagan."

Dietric took the ewer back to the serving table, all but running in his haste, because the table was close to the dais. The monk talked on, but the Romans were fidgeting, and as Ardaric had said, the Kagan was angry. He spoke sharply to Constantius, who rose, but before Constantius could speak Edeco was on his feet and calling Hunnish names.

Three of the guards jumped forward from the wall and climbed across an intervening table to reach the monk. Yaya was among them. Dietric clenched his teeth. He set the ewer down and turned to watch. The three Huns picked the monk up and carried him roughly away. The monk gave one shout; afterward, the whole length of the hall, he fought silently, but he might as well never have moved at all. The Huns ignored it. Yaya was twisting the monk's arm. The man's black hood fell off his head and dragged along the floor. The Hun standing guard on the door opened it and let them out and shut the door again.

Maximinus was talking to the Kagan, smiling, but over his cheekbones the skin showed white with strain. He leaned forward, giving emphasis to what he said by tapping his forefinger on his knee. The Goth Vigilas, interpreting, came up between them, but before he could finish translating the Kagan said, "No. Just tell him that when he comes to my palace, I shall provide the entertainment." With his hand he cut them off, both Maximinus and the interpreter, and turned forward again. Maximinus lowered his eyes and sat back.

When Dietric got back to Ardaric's place, his father was laughing. "You see how he punishes them," he was saying to the Burgundian. "They are terrified that he will use the least excuse to turn on them and destroy them for their plot against him. He is a subtle man, the Kagan."

Dietric licked his lips. The memory of the monk struggling voicelessly in the grip of the three Huns stayed with him and made him uncomfortable. Looking around, he saw that no one else seemed to be bothered, yet most of the men in the hall were Christians. An instant later he realized that the monk was probably a Catholic and all the Germans Arian. He himself was Arian. But he knew that he should have gone to help the monk, somehow—they were both Christians, after all, and the Huns were pagan.

The roar of conversation thundered in his ears. Across the hall, Tacs was sitting down with his back to the wall, his lance tilted up beside him. The door opened and Tacs looked around. Dietric followed his gaze. Yaya was coming in, smiling, trailed by the other two guards.

Dietric jerked his eyes away. "Father," he said. "Let me go outside."

Ardaric had been cocked forward across the table, listening to one of the Ostrogoths. He looked up over his shoulder and frowned. "I warned you to go before we came here."

"Please," Dietric said. He shifted his weight suggestively from foot to foot, and Ardaric waved to him to go.

The Burgundian was staring at them, a wide smile on his face. He wore his hair in a long scalplock down the back, like a horsetail. When Dietric started toward the door, he shouted, "At home, we tell them to let it run down their legs, Ardaric."

Everyone heard; the laughter boomed out up and down the

tables. Dietric's cheeks and ears burned. He stretched his legs, trying to look calm. At the door, he turned and saw the Kagan watching him, and he bowed stiffly from the waist. The Kagan with a laugh nodded to him to go on.

The little antechamber beyond the door was as crowded as the hall he had just left. Servants and slaves waiting to be needed sat or stood in the middle of the room talking. Platters half full of table scraps lay here and there on the floor, and the dogs and people ate from them side by side. Soldiers of the guards of the kings and chiefs at the feast sprawled along the walls, under the torch standards, playing dice and sticks or sleeping. The monk was not there. Dietric went to the door. A Hun guard opened it for him, and he walked outside, onto the porch.

When he was three steps outside the door, the wind blew a handful of rain into his face. There was no one on the porch and he could not see beyond it into the dark. He walked up and down the porch, enjoying the solitude and the quiet. The rain hammered on the roof over his head; it was leaking in fat drops at several places and puddles of water stood on the porch. Occasionally a gust of wind blew the rain across the porch, soaking Dietric's sleeves.

He did not dare go back to Ardaric wet, tracking mud across the Kagan's hall, so he could not leave the porch to hunt for the monk in the darkness. He tried to convince himself that he would never find him anyway. When he went back inside, there was a sour taste in his mouth. He thought that if he had been quicker he might have saved the monk. That the man was probably lying in the pounding rain, beaten and half-dead and drenched, filled him with shame.

Later he heard that someone else had saved him and that he was wandering in the wilderness preaching, but although Dietric looked for him whenever he left Hungvar, he saw no sign of him again.

Constantius said, "My Kagan, the Romans are here again."

Attila grunted. He had thought that the Romans would already be gone. Without taking his eyes from the sticks on the table, he said, "Send them away. Send them home. They bore me." Ernach, his youngest high-born son, had laid a trap for him in the pattern of the sticks, and he sucked thoughtfully on his tongue, discovering it. Ernach smiled at him over his folded arms.

"My Kagan," Constantius said, "it is not all the Romans, simply the secretary, Priscus; I don't think he is here on official business."

The Kagan picked up two of the sticks to move them, taking both at once into his hand. Opposite him, Ernach frowned and shifted his arms so that his chin was resting on his right fist and his left forearm lay flat on the table. The sticks were made of ivory carved with the totems of the Kagan's clan, picked out in gold: they were a gift from the dead Emperor Theodosius. He measured them in his fingers, considering his move, remembered that Constantius was waiting, and nodded.

"Send him in."

"My Kagan is wise."

Attila put down the first of the sticks in its new place, watching Ernach's eyes; the boy stiffened, alert, ready to seize the advantage Attila was giving him. That Ernach should take the game so seriously always amused the Kagan. He dropped the other stick casually into place, as if he saw nowhere else to put it and hardly cared. Ernach's small hand shot out and he began moving sticks. The Roman came in, walking briskly, the heels of his sandals skidding on the smooth floor.

"My lord Attila—"

"If you are here for the sake of Maximinus, you will tire yourself to no purpose. I don't deal with men in the habit of offering bribes."

Priscus had prominent cheekbones and nose, sparse pale hair, smooth skin; he was in early middle-age. Attila watched him through the corner of his eye. Ernach was still moving, re-arranging the entire game. Priscus colored slightly, but his eyes never lowered. He said, "But you are in the habit of accepting them, my lord Attila, as we all know."

Twice the man had used the Latin word dominus, something of a concession. The Kagan gave a short laugh. "It is undiplomatic of you to mention that. Do you have a bribe for me?"

"No. My mission today concerns nothing of the matters we discussed—tried to discuss—with you last week and the week before. When we came here, Attila, we had in our party a certain monk. Now that we are to leave for New Rome he is nowhere to be found."

Ernach's hands were flying over the sticks, neatening them up; he was smiling, full of triumph. The Kagan said, "That monk disappeared over a month ago. You never complained before."

"No." Priscus cleared his throat. "We thought—we were afraid of jeopardizing our mission. But you never intended to treat with us, the mission was forfeit from the beginning."

"Not through fault of mine."

"Nor of mine, my lord, I assure you. Perhaps we were wrong not to inquire after the monk before, but is that any reason to—"

"You act as if I have him somewhere," Attila said. He sat back—of the Roman diplomats, Priscus alone interested him. "As if I might snap my fingers and produce him from a cupboard."

"Don't you have him?" Priscus asked, uncertain.

Attila stared at him a moment. He was suddenly sure that Priscus wanted nothing more than what he asked for. Looking down at the game of sticks he moved one of the ivory rods absently across the table toward Ernach.

"No, I don't have your monk. Certain of the Alans who were

here that night found him almost dead in the rain and made him well again. They are a pious people, and although they are Arians and the monk seems to be persuaded that Christ is eternal, they are caring for him."

For a long moment Priscus said nothing. It always startled them that he should understand the subtleties of their religion. At last Priscus moved his hands, as if that freed his voice. "I did not know that. Where is he now?"

"With the Alans, who I am pleased to discover by your questioning have not betrayed me as other Germans have. Go away, Priscus. I am tired of Romans."

Ernach was moving again. The Roman stood, thoughtful, his eyes following a game the Kagan knew he did not understand. At first Ernach moved with confidence and certainty but with each stick he grew more aware of how Attila had trapped him; his hands slowed, and at last he stopped moving entirely and sat back, his eyes rising to his father's. The Kagan smiled at him.

"You have beaten me," Ernach said bitterly.

The Kagan sat back, lacing his hands over his bulging stomach. It was another hot day, unusually hot for this season. The little stabbing pain that never quite left him now was poking insistently at his belly, and he reached for his ivywood cup. Priscus had gone.

"You move too elaborately," he said. "I keep telling you, my child, that the best moves are the simplest. We will play again."

FOURTEEN

⊂⊧

THE UNUSUAL HEAT OF THE spring led them into a blistering summer. Under the cloudless brassy sky and the sun, the plains around Hungvar baked to dust; the constant wind lifted it and blew the fine grit everywhere, through walls and into chests and cupboards, into food and drink and people's hair. Although he railed at his women to take special care with his clothes, everything Ardaric put on was gritty. The dust got between his teeth and into his eyes and made him short-tempered and sarcastic.

The Kagan's palace was no haven from the dust, although the Huns seemed to endure it better. Ardaric was spending much of the day with the Kagan, Edeco, Orestes and his brother Onegesius, and anyone else knowledgeable about the particular problems they were dealing with. Slowly Ardaric's plan for the attack on Rome was assuming shape, under the pressure of the different minds bearing on it, like a sword under hammers. He enjoyed the work—it was the kind of thing he did best—although he disliked the Huns he had to work with and hated Orestes and his brother.

Dietric was constantly in his thinking. Nothing he tried kept his son from running to the Hun village whenever he could get away. Ardaric piled extra responsibility on his back but the young man worked furiously and got it all done and went off to laze around and pick up lice and get drunk or worse with the Huns of the Kagan's guard. Twice Ardaric nearly mentioned it to the Kagan but he decided that Attila would only put him off, if he took no insult that Ardaric did not want his son friendly with Huns.

Gradually Ardaric came to see that there was nothing he could do. Yet it nagged at him like the dust in his clothes and his food, even though he could see, when he made himself look at Dietric calmly, that the boy was no worse for it all.

Ever since the Huns had defeated the Burgundians and forced their chiefs to pay tribute, a few years before, the Burgundians had been struggling to make an alliance between the Kagan and themselves that would at least raise them above the level of tribute-paying slaves. All through the first of the summer, Hungvar was packed with Burgundian envoys, each one offering the Kagan a little more than the one before. The followers of the various rival chiefs fought among themselves, bribed every Hun they talked to, and brought their offers to Ardaric every other day, hoping to get his support: whichever chief the Kagan chose to treat with would of course become king over all.

The Kagan paid little attention to the pleas and offers of the Burgundians, leaving these negotiations to Ardaric. The plan against Rome held his full attention. Finally, just after the full moon of midsummer when the heat always seemed at its worst, Attila called Ardaric before him, listened to his summary of the Burgundians' offers and activities, and chose the man he would accept. In token of their alliance he would marry the Burgundian's eldest unmarried daughter, a girl named Ildico.

On the first day of the ceremony, the Kagan appeared in front of his palace and announced the coming marriage. All the palace guards were there, many Hun subchiefs, and all the Gothic chiefs who happened to be near Hungvar—Ardaric, mounted on his white horse and surrounded by his own retinue, saw Widimir the Ostrogoth and several of his relatives, two or three Alan chiefs, Rugians and Heruls and even a Frank. With the summer coming to its climax all the tribes were moving around. They wore their richest clothes, sitting on their lanky German horses in the bright, windy heat, waiting for the Kagan to appear. In the windows of the Court of Women, Attila's other wives and their servants sat fanning themselves and eating oranges and watching. When at last the palace door opened and a dozen of the guard came out in double file, a sigh went up from the crowd.

Now the Kagan himself walked out onto the porch, and the sigh became a cheer. The crowd in front of the palace pressed forward. Ardaric's horse shifted and half-reared at the noise. Beside him, on foot, Dietric dodged out of the way. His face shone with sweat and excitement; a summer spent with Huns had tanned him dark as oak, and the scattered hairs of his new beard glistened like gold.

The Kagan raised both hands and came forward to the edge of the porch, into the sunlight. To the right of the crowd, the Huns began to chant, "Attila, Attila, Attila." Their arms waved in the air over their heads like the branches of trees. Ardaric looked over at Widimir the Ostrogoth and saw how he sat motionless in his saddle, neither cheering nor waving, although all the men around him waved and cheered.

He cares little for this, like me, Ardaric thought; he hardly knew Widimir but suddenly he felt a kinship with him.

The Kagan spoke in Hunnish, announcing that he would marry Ildico, the daughter of the Burgundian chief Gundar, and make an alliance between their peoples forever. Dietric translated it for Ardaric. With his right hand Attila gestured toward the palace door, and it opened, and attended by several old women the bride came out. In the Kagan's party her father beamed and looked at her proudly. She was tall like most Burgundians and her hair, pale as ice, hung in a thick braid down to her heel; they had woven pieces of red silk into it. She was younger than Dietric, hardly old enough to marry, but she looked boldly around her, as if she might actually become the Khatun of the Huns. Ardaric could see her pretty breast rise against the cloth of her gown. The women led her forward and Attila took her right hand. All the Huns and many of the Germans cheered her by name.

The girl was as tall as the Kagan, and seeing them together, the fair, pretty child and the Hun like a huge squat toad, Ardaric made an involuntary sound in his throat. He could not cheer. Dietric was hanging onto one of his stirrups and shouting merrily as any Hun. Ardaric looked again at Widimir and saw him silent and motionless, his face carefully wiped clean of expression, and the sense of a bond between them grew stronger in his mind.

OVERHEAD, THE SKY WAS white with stars. A soft wind blew, filled with the sweet scents of the grass, the trees by the river. Attila eased the heavy cloak on his shoulders; it was too hot to wear anything so heavy. Far down the plain, the torches blazed in a red ring, windblown and crackling in the blackness of the night.

With his attendants around him in a mass, the Kagan rode slowly down toward the ring of torches and could not help but smile. She was a beautiful girl, eager and willing—many of them were not willing, which spoiled it—but what she represented was more important. The Burgundians held the territory between the Rhone River and the Rhine and the Alps, and now that he controlled it he knew that he would have Italy in its turn.

When he held Italy, everything would be well. There would be food enough and the boundaries were defensible, and the subject peoples would be easy to handle; there the Hiung would surely recover their numbers and their strength. The soft wind that blew into his face smelled of the steppe, the hundred tiny flowers and grasses crushed underhoof to perfume his wedding night.

Now he could hear the wailing of flutes; he could smell the oil burning in the torches. Outside the ring of blazing light were gathered the people who must witness this marriage— the chiefs of all the other subject tribes, the men he had made into kings so that they would be happier servants. The torchlight reflected off the gold of their ornaments, the sheen of their eyes turned toward him.

He slowed his horse to a walk, to draw out the ceremony and make it more solemn. Beside him, Ernach, holding the Kagan's standard, spoke softly to his skittish horse. Another time Attila had ridden like this toward a ring of torches but then the witnesses had all been Hiung, and he had gone not to a bride but to a grave. Even while he had ridden toward his brother's body, he had wondered if he could justify his murder —how he would explain what he had done to the men who waited to judge him.

But when he came at last into the ring of torches and faced them, all men older than he, who was then still a young man, the uncertainty fled him, and like iron he stood and told them that he had murdered Bleda and would now be their only chief. Bleda had preferred Romans and Germans to his own people, he told them. Bleda had wanted to release the Emperors from their annual tribute.

Now Attila was close enough to the torches to see Ildico and her attendants waiting just beyond. She would step into the circle after he did, acknowledging her inferiority. If he had been only a chief or a king they would have entered the ring at the same time, because she was the daughter of a chief. But on the night he had faced the elders over his brother's body, he had hunted for a way to explain how he felt toward his people, and he had remembered certain stories the grandfathers told, and he had named himself the Kagan of all the Hiung. Although his clan was the largest of the Hiung, there were a dozen others; the elders stirred, more angry at his presumption

than at Bleda's murder. But they were afraid to defy him. When
no one called it blasphemy, it became the truth: he was the
Kagan.

He reined in his horse at the edge of the circle of light and
looked around. They all watched him. From his earliest years
he had felt eyes watching him, every waking hour. He looked
calmly from side to side, at the Lombards, the Thuringians, the
Rugians and Ostrogoths and Gepids, the Heruls, the Alans and
Scirians, Suevians and Quadi, all kings, obedient to his wishes.
Smiling, he dismounted and with his sons attending him
walked into the red-gold light of the torches.

ALONG BOTH BANKS OF THE
river, great fires blazed, twice as high as a man, to celebrate
the marriage of Attila. Tacs, on the gate watch at the stockade,
could remember when the Kagan had first ordered the lighting
of such fires; for a long while the Hiung had believed that
the fires were part of the German wedding ceremony and the
Kagan was deferring to the German taste. Later on they found
out that the Germans all thought the fires a Hiung rite.

Tacs leaned against the gate post, half-drunk, listening to the
sounds of the summer night. In the Court of Women, Kreka
Khatun and the other wives of Attila were celebrating in their
own way. The wild music of flutes and tambors spilled from
the windows, and Yaya, who had gone over earlier to spy on
them, said they were dancing. The palace was completely deserted, except for the sentries on the doors and one or two
slaves inside.

"Tacs," Dietric called, from outside the gate. "Are you
there?"

"Ayya. Come in." Tacs scrambled down the ladder to the
ground. "Did you bring it? Ah!"

Dietric rode in, leading a horse packed with two great kegs

of beer. "I think my father guessed, he locked up the brew-house. Have they started?"

Tacs shook his head. He took the leadrope from Dietric; they went off across the stockade. "I don't think so. If they have, we shall start it all over again. We can't be the only ones sober." They passed under the windows of Kreka Khatun's suite, on their way to the guards' bonfire at the back of the stockade; through the windows, the whirling figures of the women were visible, but Tacs turned his eyes away, because it was taboo to look on dancing women.

"Dietric," he said. "You have to keep watch on me and Monidiak—don't let us get too drunk."

"Is that possible?" Dietric asked, smiling. They rounded the corner of the Court of Women and started across the little field toward the first the others had made.

Tacs laughed. "I hope so. He and I have to stand watch on the Kagan's chamber, and it won't be good if we're drunk."

FIFTEEN

⊂╪

ONSTANTIUS STOOD UP
again, the white cloth of his gown bunched in his fists. "You
must waken him. They are all waiting."

"Let them wait," Monidiak said. He had rested his spear up
against the wall beside the door; he leaned himself up beside
it, his arms folded over his chest. Tacs, who was sitting on the
floor on the other side of the door, looked up at him and over at
Edeco, obviously struggling to make up his mind. Edeco's frown
had brought his eyebrows down over his nose, and his mouth
worked in and out; his eyes turned constantly toward the
Kagan's door.

Constantius gave Monidiak a black stare and sat down again.
In the narrow antechamber there was only one bench. Edeco
and Constantius were squeezed together on it like two lovers.

"What do you think?" Edeco said.

"I?" Tacs asked, startled. "Nothing. She is a pretty girl."

Monidiak smiled. "I like women with more fat on them to
roll around on."

"You, cousin," Edeco said, "have all the fat you need, between your ears."

Monidiak put his head back and laughed. One corner of
Edeco's mouth pulled down, as if he had thought of something
unpleasant, and he turned his eyes toward Constantius.

"I think you are right. We should go in. He never sleeps so
late, and he always calls out if someone knocks."

Constantius bounced up onto his feet and started toward the door. Tacs stood up. The Kagan would probably be angry and he wanted to get out of the way. Edeco knocked again on the door, pounding on it with the end of his fist. All of them stood with their eyes on the door, their breath caught in their lungs, listening. There was no answer. Edeco took hold of the iron latch and pulled it, but the door was bolted, and he stood back and kicked the door open.

With Constantius in his footsteps Edeco went inside, saying, "Attila, we all ask your pardon."

Tacs settled down again beside the door, holding the haft of his spear between his knees. Cheerfully Monidiak said, "I hope he doesn't hurt them."

"Tacs!" Edeco shouted, from inside the chamber. "Tacs, come here. Monidiak, shut the outer door and guard it."

Tacs jumped to his feet. The ragged edge in Edeco's voice raised the hair along his spine. He thought, The Kagan is dead. He darted through the door and into the chamber. Behind him the outer door slammed with a thud. He saw Edeco's face green-white behind his tan and Constantius kneeling on the floor with his hands clasped before him. An instant later Tacs saw the blood.

The girl was sitting huddled in one corner of the Kagan's draped couch. The curtains were drawn together enough to throw the Kagan himself into shadow. He lay on his back in the dimness, his mouth open, and his face was covered with blood. Under the couch blood lay in a pool, half-dried; the bedcovers were caked with it.

Edeco was talking to him, but Tacs could not hear. He could not look away from the Kagan. Finally Edeco took him by the shoulders and shook him until his head hurt. Tacs gave a little whimper, and when Edeco let him go he raised his eyes up to the taller man's.

"Edeco, what will happen to us now?"

"Be quiet," Edeco said. "We will think of that later. You

must stay here and stand guard over the Kagan's body. Can you do it? Monidiak will do it, if you—"

"I will," Tacs said. "I can do it, let me."

"Don't leave him," Edeco said. "Constantius, come with me."

Constantius sobbed. His trembling hands, ridged with rings, hung in the air before him, and he spoke pleadingly in Latin to the dead Attila. Tacs with his spear went to stand beside the Kagan's couch. The broken, foreign sound of Constantius' prayer made his skin crawl. He looked at the girl.

"Did she kill him?"

"No," Edeco said, his voice rasping. "No, she did nothing. See how it is with her." He went to the couch and lifted the girl up with one arm around her waist. Her body flopped against his side. Her eyes opened wide but no sense appeared in them. Edeco pulled her arm up over his shoulder. She laid her head down against his chest and her eyes slowly closed.

"Come with me, Constantius," Edeco said, and with his free hand pulled the fat little man toward the door. "Monidiak, open this door."

The door opened, and the three of them went out, Edeco's head in the middle between the girl's on one hand and Constantius' bald freckled scalp on the other. When they had gone, Monidiak looked in. He saw the Kagan and his face turned the color of milk. His eyes met Tacs'; neither of them could speak, and Monidiak went out and shut the door.

Tacs sat down on the floor beside the Kagan's head. The smell of drying blood filled his nose. At first he could not look at the dead man but bit by bit he turned his eyes toward him and saw how he lay, with his knees pulled up toward his chest and his body bent forward in agony. The blood had poured out of his mouth and nose. His hair was matted with it, his mustaches solid with it. Tacs' heart filled with pity, and he began to cry. Every word the Kagan had ever said to him flooded back into his mind. He could not bear that Attila should have died in such pain, with only a girl nearby, too frightened

to call for help. Putting his head down on the couch beside the
Kagan's, he wept and decided that he would never be happy
again.

After a little while he heard footsteps outside the door and
jumped to his feet, grabbing up his spear. Over a dozen of
them filed into the chamber and stood looking at the man on
the couch. Tacs passed his spear nervously from his right hand
to his left.

Ellac said, "The girl must have poisoned him." He said it
twice, in a voice without expression. Behind him little Ernach
burst into tears.

"No," Dengazich said. He came up beside Ellac and rested
one hand on his shoulder. "The Kagan was sick. Once when I
was with him he was seized with pain in his stomach." He came
up to the couch, heedless of Tacs, as if to touch the body, and
Tacs stepped between him and the Kagan.

"Let me by," Dengazich said impatiently. "He was my
father."

Tacs could not speak. But when after a moment Dengazich
moved to one side and tried to get past him, Tacs came between him and the couch again, and Dengazich shrugged and
went back with the others.

All the little boys were crying. The older ones took them
by the hand and led them out. Only Ellac and Dengazich remained behind. Ellac's eyes were shining. He said, "If you will
support me as the Kagan I shall make you second only to me."

Dengazich laughed.

The door opened again and Edeco came in, with Scottas,
Orestes, and two Hiung chiefs. They stood behind the two sons
of Attila and looked at the body and spoke in murmurs. Orestes
and Scottas went out, and a dozen other Hiung chiefs and
subchiefs came in, two and three at a time, looked at the dead
man, and went out without speaking.

Kreka Khatun, with Ernach beside her, appeared in the doorway, took one look at Attila, and went away with her hand

over her eyes. Ernach lingered, his reddened eyes sharp on Ellac's face. Tacs sat down on the floor, holding his spear upright. Edeco stayed in the chamber leaning against the wall opposite him, and whispering to each other, Ellac and Dengazich stood to one side. Tacs could hear them; by the expression on Ernach's face, he could, too. Ellac was trying to convince Dengazich to support him and Dengazich was putting him off. Now and again, Dengazich's eyes rested on Tacs, and at last he poked Ellac and told him to be quiet. Ellac looked over at Tacs and clamped his lips shut. Before they noticed him, Ernach slid back from the door and disappeared.

Now Ardaric came in, alone, first of all the Germans. When he saw the Kagan dead, he blanched. He opened his mouth but said nothing; after a moment he shook his head. Turning to Edeco, he said, "You know I suffer this as deeply as you do."

"Yes," Edeco said.

Ardaric shook his head again and left. Tacs said, "Why did he say that?"

Edeco looked away.

The Ostrogoths' three kings came single file through the door, their jaws locked and their faces full of strain. Ellac and Dengazich left while they were there. The three spoke to each other softly in their own dialect; Tacs could hardly understand it but all they talked about was the blood. Before they went out again, the shamans came.

There were five of them, The Fluteplayer among them but not their chief: that was Megiddo, old and stooped and mute. He wore a tunic made all of raven's feathers, because he was of the Shai clan that had the raven as one of its totems. While the other shamans watched, Megiddo leaned over and sniffed at the Kagan's face and put out his thin hands to touch the Kagan's body. The shamans moved around Tacs on the floor without speaking to him or looking at him. Each of them smelled different, although each one also smelled of the same crushed herbs. When they all had looked at the body, they stood in a little circle and made speech with their hands, the only language that Megiddo understood. Whatever they said was spoken quickly, and all but The Fluteplayer left.

The Fluteplayer said, "Edeco, the Kagan had a sickness that we had given him some charms against, and we believe that he died of the sickness. So there is no reason for revenge."

Edeco glanced at the Ostrogoths, who were watching from the back of the room. His eyes went to the Kagan's body. "What sickness was it that makes a man bleed so much?"

"Who knows?" The Fluteplayer put his head to one side, and his gaze slid toward the Ostrogoths. "There is a kind of truth in it, when he caused so much blood to flow." Taking a step backward, he looked down at Tacs and said softly, "Be easy, little frog. Every man dies." With his snakeskin coat draped over one shoulder, he walked out the door.

"He drank so much blood that it killed him," one of the Ostrogoths murmured, and the other two nodded and pressed closer together. "If he had known Jesus Christ—" They went swiftly out after The Fluteplayer.

Tacs looked back over his shoulder at the Kagan. He felt like a man whose father had died.

WHERE THE RING OF torches had stood for the Kagan's wedding, men were raising a platform of wood high as the head of a mounted man. Ardaric had mentioned something about that place being sacred to the Huns, but when Dietric pressed him, he did not know why.

"They go there to see their rites performed," Ardaric said. "When Bleda was—died, they brought his body there to be . . . whatever is done to dead Huns. The Kagan proclaimed his mission here."

Now the curly summer grass was trampled down and stained with soot from the wedding ceremony. Dietric took a step toward the ring, but before he had gone more than a few strides, Ardaric called him sharply back.

"I told you," Ardaric said, when Dietric had come back to his side. "Leave them alone. This time you must obey me. If you don't, I'll have you bound and kept in the sleeping loft."

"Why?" Dietric asked, but Ardaric had already turned back to his conversation with the Ostrogoth Widimir. They had come out to see how the work went on the Kagan's pyre, but now they were paying no attention to it. Dietric fretted. At first, when he heard of the death of Attila, he had been frightened, like a child afraid of something unnamed in the dark, but now he was filled with exhilaration. All his life Attila had ruled over them. Under the Kagan everything had been laid out precisely, with no room for surprise. Now there would be changes, new things, new men rising to importance. Ardaric and Widimir were discussing that—Ellac and Dengazich, the Kagan's only sons old enough to assume the Kaganate. Dietric thought, I will support Dengazich, he is part Goth. He wondered if the new Kagan would lead them against Rome; this time he would be old enough to fight. His horse lowered its head and cropped the crisp grass.

Brown in the late summer sun, the plain stretched off around them, gently rolling toward the horizon. Down at the pyre, a new wagonload of wood was being carried up. The pyre, half-finished, crawled with men working on it. Dietric's horse took another step toward that place, cropping the grass, and Dietric strained to kick it into a gallop and race down there. But he had heard a new tone in Ardaric's voice he was afraid to ignore.

He had not seen Tacs since the night before the Kagan's death, but he had met Monidiak down by the river, who said that Tacs was guarding the body of the Kagan. "He and Yaya," Monidiak said. "It is an honor, but I would not have it."

"Why not?" Dietric asked.

Monidiak's thin eyebrows rose. "So close to a dead man, for

two days in a row? And the Kagan's spirit is stronger than an ordinary man's."

Dietric imagined the Kagan's soul crawling out the mouth of the corpse and seizing Tacs by the throat. He hunched his shoulders, uncomfortable at his own vision. The Kagan's soul was in Hell, beyond doubt—he had defied Christ. Another wagon was rumbling down toward the pyre; Huns on horseback galloped around it. The Kagan's soul was surely safe in Hell.

"Dietric," Ardaric snapped.

"Yes, Father."

TACS COULD SMELL THE PERfumes and spices and herbs heaped up on the wagon behind him. He was exhausted; in the two days since the Kagan's death he had hardly slept. His coat weighed on his shoulders and his eyes felt gritty and burned in their sockets. The darkness around him was full of horsemen, crowded together, moving and bumping together in a river of bodies. In front of him, Ellac rode under the Kagan's horsetail standard. Ernach beside him carried the War God's Sword that the Kagan had found on this plain. Dengazich rode among the other sons of the Kagan, carrying nothing.

Edeco said, "See how the fire blows in the wind." His voice was hoarse and weak. He had spent the days since the Kagan's death talking and giving orders and he had lost his voice from it.

Before the sons of the Kagan went men with torches, and other men with torches rode in two long files down either side of the funeral train. On each corner of the wagon that bore the Kagan's body was a torch. The air stank of the burning. In the windblown light, faces looked hollow and wild. The horsetails swinging from the crossbar of the Kagan's standard caught the light in streaks. Tacs gathered the spittle in his mouth and spat it to one side. Ellac might carry the horsetails but Ellac would be no Kagan. No true Kagan would have left Edeco to do all the work. None of the Kagan's sons had shown reverence enough even to sit by the body. Now they pretended to mourn. Tacs thought, I will follow none of them.

Off in the dark the Germans rode in a mass, in a course parallel with the wagon's, but they had no place in this. It was for the Hiung to mourn a Hiung Kagan. Tacs wondered where Dietric was. Monidiak had said that they had met since the Kagan's death; Dietric was pleased with the honor done Tacs. Unaccountably, Tacs' eyes filled up with tears. That had happened often in the past two days.

Before them on the wide plain stood the hallowed ground where Rua was buried, where Beguz was buried, and Tinnuma, the great chiefs who had led the Hiung through the swamps after the white stag. There every Hiung chief for four generations had been brought to his body's last sleep, even though he died on the far side of the world. The Kagan would not be lonely there. His pyre was a dark spot on the plain, unlit as yet by any fire.

Before Tacs, in the mass of the Kagan's sons, Dengazich began to chant. Tacs bit his lip. After only a few words he remembered the song, although he had not heard it in many years. It was the old song of a son for a dead father.

On all sides, men picked up the chant. Tacs had almost forgotten it; the old words returned to him and filled him with wild dreams and memories. Beside him, Edeco said softly, "Dengazich spent a day with the shamans learning it. The Kagan would be pleased." Softly, nurturing his sick voice, he joined the chanting. Tacs licked his lips and the words came into his mouth and he sang them, although his voice broke and wavered, and tears ran down his cheeks. He felt both an unbearable sorrow and a strange uplifting joy.

Singing, the procession rode slowly down to the pyre. The

horsemen spread out and surrounded it, holding their horses shoulder to shoulder. Their voices welled up in the darkness like the beating of a drum. Ellac and Dengazich and the rest of the Kagan's older sons dismounted beside the wagon and lifted up their father's body. They carried it up onto the pyre and laid it on its back on top of the wooden platform. Bringing up the urns of perfumes, the sacks of spices and herbs, they massed them around the body, tipping the urns so that the rich stinking oils flooded down and soaked the wood. One by one the young men climbed down and mounted and drew back into the crowd. The last to go was Ellac. He came on foot to Edeco and without a word took the torch from him and lit all the torches around the pyre.

Where before it had been dark, now it blazed all over with light. Tacs could see the Kagan's face, yellow in the light, the eyes sealed and the mouth firmly shut, all the blood washed away. In his chest his heart trembled. The reek of burning stung his nose and hurt his throat. The black pony squealed and pressed its shoulder against Edeco's horse, and Edeco's big chestnut whirled and broke into a trot. The horses around them began to move. The black pony, thrusting its nose out, stretched its legs.

All chanting, the horsemen made a ring galloping around the pyre and their horses lengthened stride until many of them were moving at a flat blind run. Most of them chanted the song for a dead father but many sang another song, and as the others learned the words that song spread—the Kagan's death-song.

Tacs rode in the circle until he felt the black pony slowing down, bored. He nudged the pony out toward the edge of the galloping ring of horses, reined it to a walk, and started back toward the Hiung camp. They would be galloping all night and all the next day and the night beyond that, too; when a man got tired he would go and sleep and another would take his place. Tacs could hardly keep his eyes open. He let the pony take its own pace into the camp, and he dozed off and did not wake up until the pony stopped in front of Yaya's aul and Ummake came out and touched his arm.

A T DAWN THEY WERE STILL galloping around the pyre on the plain. Dietric could hear them all the way up to the village of the Gepids. When he got up just after the sun rose, he stood in the chill grey air putting on his clothes and listened, and the sounds put his teeth on edge. He went to the window and opened it. From here he could see nothing, even when he stuck his head out and tried to see over the roofs of the neighboring houses. But he knew what they were doing.

Everybody else was already up. He was the last one down from the sleeping loft. In the hall below, the house-slaves were busy with breakfast. Dietric pulled on his coat—so late in the summer, the evening chill lasted on into the morning—and pushed in among the men grouped around his father at the fire. A house-slave brought him a bowl of broth and some bread. Ardaric was still eating. He looked up and saw Dietric and poked his elbow in the direction of the Huns.

"What do you think of them now, eh? Yelling and howling like beasts. Is that a mourning fit for such a man as the Kagan? Pah."

Dietric sat down and chewed on his bread.

"They are all drunk," another man said. "Or mad."

"Dietric could tell you what they are," Ardaric said slyly. He ate fast and wiped his fingers on his thighs. Sitting back, he planted his hands on his widespread knees. "What are they drinking, Dietric?"

"The blood of German babies."

Ardaric laughed but the men around him twitched and gave Dietric stares full of horror. Putting his bowl down on the floor, Ardaric called the dogs over to lick it clean. With the dogs around his calves growling and rattling the bowl, he said,

"We are going. Yesterday I spoke to the elders and our priests. Today we must pack everything and tonight we will start leaving. It must be secret. Only God knows what they would do if they knew we were going."

All the sense flew out of Dietric's head. He stared witless at his father. The other men spoke in agreement, in relief. Dietric turned his eyes down to the half-finished bowl of broth on his knees. He knew he would never see Tacs again.

W HERE DID HE COME FROM?" Monidiak asked, and sat down on Tacs' left. Tacs shook his head. He had drunk so much that he could not focus his eyes, and he saw the monk in the center of the aul only as a moving shadow between him and the firelight. He could smell The White Brother with each breath. His stomach heaved, and for an instant he hovered on the verge of throwing up. Ummake sat beside him, singing in her low beautiful voice. Tacs felt a wave of love for her, even though she was Yaya's wife. The thick, hot air of the aul, stained orange by the firelight, was difficult to breathe.

Monidiak was watching the monk, whose arms rose and fell like the beating wings of a crane, in time with a song that came from somewhere nearby. Jabbing his elbow into Tacs' ribs, Monidiak said, "That is the one the Kagan threw out of the hall, that night when the Romans were here. He is a shaman of the Christians. What is he saying?"

"What?"

"What is he saying?"

Tacs thought that out, trying to make sense of it, and slowly lifted the jug in his hand and sipped from it. The wine was heavily laced with The White Brother. His stomach churned at its oily texture. Gradually he realized that the strange song to which the monk's arms moved was the voice of the monk singing Latin. He wished he could see the monk's face; a man could hardly judge another's words without looking at his eyes, but all Tacs could see were the splotches of red and brown and gold and dark brown that moved and swayed, in time to the swaying of the monk and his song.

"About spirits," Tacs said to Monidiak. "The Ancestor of the Christians. Something about Christ, too." He raised his jug again; his wrist could not hold its weight and he spilled wine all over himself. Monidiak was eying the monk intently.

"Perhaps it was this shaman who made the sorcery against the Kagan. For having him thrown out into the rain."

Tacs laid the jug down carefully and watched it roll on its lip around and around on the floor. Ummake took it and quietly got up and carried it away. Tacs said, "The shamans say there was no sorcery." He shut his eyes, but that was even worse; he could not tell if he were upright or falling, and his stomach rose; he opened his eyes again.

"So they say," Monidiak said, "but how else does a man die like that, except by sorcery?"

"What?"

Monidiak shook his head. "I'll talk to you in the morning." He sat back, his legs tucked under him, and began to clap in rhythm with the voice of the monk.

Ummake came back, smiling, and sat down; she had brought another jug. "All full again." In the heated ugly darkness her eyes were cool and beautiful. Tacs hung on them, speechless. Ummake looked down and away, telling him with the motion of her head not to look at her. Yaya's wife. Tacs picked up the jug, supported it with his free hand, and drank. The darkness thickened around him. Occasionally the monk's words reached him but they were not words for which he had meanings. The monk over and over said the Latin word that appeared to mean breaking taboo, but it was not the same, the taboos made no sense, they were derived neither from a man's ancestry nor his way of life. Several other men had joined Monidiak clapping in time and the sound crashed on his ears. The monk said the word that should have meant the cleansing of one who had broken taboo. Tacs began to shiver. He was ashamed of getting drunk when the Kagan lay dead outside. He got up and, crouched over, moved to the door.

Outside the aul, the air was warm and gusty. In the aul next to Yaya's, a woman was wailing the dead-chant, a tuneless, listless cry. Farther away there were others wailing, on throughout the camp. In the far distance were the shouts and singing of the mourners at the pyre.

Tacs walked between the two auls and was sick and vomited, and for a moment he rested, on all fours, his head hanging down. He felt ashamed and unhappy. Finally he straightened up.

His eyes had cleared. When he stood, he could see down through the auls to the plain and the pyre beyond. Bonfires lit up the plain in patches. Around the great flaming pyre the ring of horsemen galloped in the dark. The warm wind breathed on Tacs' skin. Filled with a zeal for mourning the Kagan, he went searching for the black pony. He thought of how the Kagan had led them and taught them and watched over them, and his chest clenched with grief and loss. He walked into the rope fence of the horse pen and hung on it, fighting to get his breath back.

"Tacs."

He pursed his lips and whistled for the pony.

"Tacs." Yaya staggered up to him and put his arm around his shoulders. "Where are you going? Come inside and get drunk with me."

In the midst of the horses something moved, and the backs and flanks before him shifted; the black pony appeared. Tacs reached for its mane. Yaya pulled him away.

"Come drink, little frog. Come inside with me. You have great magic for escaping your enemies, and my enemies and yours are the same, am I not Marag's brother?"

Tacs leaned against Yaya's arm. "Yaya. My friend. I love Ummake. You must always take care of Ummake."

"Yes, of course." Yaya chuckled. The pony came up to them —it had crawled under the fence—and shied back at the stink of wine. Tacs stumbled forward and wrapped his arms around the pony's neck. Yaya came after, reaching out one hand; the pony laid back its ears and braced its forelegs, snorting.

"I go to mourn the Kagan." Tacs pressed his face into the pony's mane.

Yaya came closer; the pony jerked violently back, dragging Tacs with it, and Tacs smelled that the pony shied not from the wine but from the smell of blood. Yaya's hands and chest and hair were covered with blood, still wet enough to glisten in the light from the next aul.

"There are other ways to mourn," Yaya said.

"What happened?"

Yaya threw his arms wide and nearly fell over. "They don't even fight, they are like fish in a weir, all you do is cut them a little."

Tacs climbed onto the pony's back. What Yaya had said made no sense to him. "I go to mourn the Kagan."

"Just a few Germans." Yaya stumbled away between the auls.

Tacs stared after him. Yaya reached the door to his own aul and ducked to open it, letting out a spill of light and noise. Tacs moved the black pony around by the pressure of his legs on its barrel and rode it forward among the auls until he found one with a waterskin hanging outside to cool. When he had drunk he spilled water on his hands and scrubbed them. Here he could not see the plain and the bonfires; all around him under the pewter moonlight the round auls stood like the hives of bees, and from them rose the keening of the women like the whine of bees. On his hands the water glistened. He remembered how the blood on Yaya had glinted, and a pang of fear cut through him. He looked quickly over his shoulder and squeezed the pony into a trot, headed down toward the funeral pyre and the ring of galloping horses.

SIXTEEN

⊂⋕

IN THE MORNING YAYA WAS
dead. Monidiak found him out by the horse pen with wounds
in his back and chest. They took him to the dead-aul, where
Ummake could make him ready for burial. None of the horses
had been stolen and nothing of Yaya's was gone from his body.
Monidiak said, "He had many enemies. But it is unkind of a
man to take such advantage of the Kagan's burning."

Tacs looked at Ummake bending over Yaya's body; she was
weeping in silence, and her hands moved softly over his arms
and legs, caressing him. Tacs looked away and said nothing.
Although the sun was bright and the wind warm, he was cold
inside his shirt.

After Ummake had said she had no need of him, he took his
pony and rode around behind the Kagan's stockade toward the
Gepids' camp. On the way he passed the pyre. The Kagan had
been burned entirely and the fires allowed to go out. The bones
had been collected and put into a gold box. Only a heap of
blowing ash lay on the plain, with a torch pole like a standard
thrusting up at each corner. Around the pyre the plain was
beaten and trampled in a ring as wide as a dozen horses.

Passing the stockade, he heard and saw some of the furious
activity that filled it. They were packing everything onto mules
and into wagons, to be carted away. Where? Ellac and Dengazich and the others would attend to that. He rode down the
little slope to the river and along its bank, through the dried-up

marsh, toward the camp of the Gepids. The ground rose into a little hill, and he stopped the pony on its height and looked across the river into the camp.

It was smaller than before. At first he would not believe it, but he forced himself to accept what his eyes told him. There were fewer houses, especially at the far end. He wondered if it were here that Yaya had found his Germans like fish in a trap, needing only cutting. But the Gepids were certainly going. Sometime during the night they must have packed up some of their houses and rolled away. There were fewer people in the lanes of their camp, and Tacs could see no women or children.

He lingered a while, watching the Gepids; he had taken for granted they would not follow Ellac, but that they should go away so quickly unsettled him. Twice he decided to go and find Dietric and twice changed his mind. At last he turned his pony and rode back toward the Hiung camp.

The Fluteplayer was sitting outside his aul, drinking from a bowl figured inside and out with serpents. His wives bustled around him and in and out of the aul. Tacs left the pony a way away to keep from raising dust around the shaman. When the wives saw him coming, they hid inside the aul, but The Flute-player only sat sipping from his bowl. Tacs sat down beside him and waited for him to speak.

The Fluteplayer said nothing, and at last Tacs cleared his throat and said, "It's a fine day."

The Fluteplayer set the bowl down. Tacs saw that it had held only broth. The shaman folded his arms over his chest and eyed Tacs. "You are the third who has come here today and each of you has started out by saying what a fine day it is. How can it be a fine day that sees the bones of Attila go into the earth? Why can't you start out by saying something I could not determine for myself?"

"Who else was here?"

"I shouldn't tell you, but I will, because it disturbs me. First was Edeco, your master, the Chief of the Guard, coming to ask whose magic was stronger, Ellac's or Dengazich's. Second was Dengazich, asking if he should follow Ellac or do what he himself believes proper. And now you. I hope you have a better question."

"Why should they ask such things of you?" Tacs said, surprised.

"Precisely why it disturbs me. What do you want?"

Tacs wet his lips. "Do you know that Yaya is dead?"

"No. Yaya of the Shai Hiung or Yaya of the Mishnigi?"

"My friend Yaya who was with me in the Kagan's guard, Yaya of the Mishnigi."

"Ayya. I didn't know."

"He was murdered. We found him this morning near the horses, but nothing had been stolen from him and no horses were gone. There were many wounds in him. Some of them never bled."

The Fluteplayer whistled between his teeth. His eyes focused beyond Tacs. "Ah."

"And the Gepids are leaving in the night, a few at a time, houses and all. I think the women and children are gone already."

"Yes. Tell me about the other thing—about Yaya."

Tacs hunched his shoulders. "I saw him last night and he said something. . . ." He told The Fluteplayer everything that Yaya had said and what he, Tacs, had seen—the blood covering him.

The Fluteplayer's head settled down between his shoulders. He went on whistling through his teeth, and his eyes looked vacantly into the air. The women had come out of the hut and were tending the fire and the pot of meat hanging over it. The Fluteplayer's eyes moved to the side and forward to look into Tacs'.

"This is clearly shaman's work, not like what Edeco and Dengazich asked. You were clever to tell me. Now listen to me. Today we shall put the Kagan into the ground. Tonight after darkness comes you must meet me here with a horse for me and all your gear packed up, and we shall go south together. Don't worry about them." He gestured toward his wives. "They can go back to their families who are better able than I to care for them. I think this is the last shaman's work that I shall do."

"What is happening?" Tacs asked.

"Nothing more than we should have guessed at. The Kagan once. . . ." The Fluteplayer pulled at his lower lip. "There is a reckoning for everything, and an economy in the world so that often all reckonings come at once. Be here tonight." He got up and went inside his aul and shut the door.

Tacs stayed a little while longer, pretending to fix the laces on his boots, but The Fluteplayer did not come out again. At last he went back to the black pony and mounted. Ummake would need help with Yaya—Monidiak was up at the stockade, with Edeco—but Tacs did not go immediately back to the dead-aul; he rode out of the camp toward the river on the chance he might catch a glimpse of Dietric.

Hiung children played in the dry marsh along the river. Their screams and laughter rang across the plain. Tacs rode up to the highest point on this side of the river and strained his eyes toward the Gepid camp. The late summer wind lifted the dust of the marsh and blew it like a veil between him and the Gepids. Everything was brown and sere, even the fringe of willow trees along the edge of the river. He stayed on the hilltop a long while, no longer hoping to see Dietric, only watching the Gepids, puzzled. At last he rode back to his own people.

When he reached Yaya's aul, Monidiak was there, eating. Tacs came in and sat down beside the fire. The aul was stuffy and the air odorous and still. Yaya was in the dead-aul, but Ummake had come back and was putting his belongings into sacks. She wept constantly, snorting every few moments to stop her nose from running. Tacs dished up a bowl of the gruel on the fire and ate, scooping the thick grain soup into his mouth with his first two fingers.

"Well," Monidiak said, "don't you want to hear what Edeco is doing?"

Tacs grunted. He put down the empty bowl and wiped his hands on his sleeves. "What is Edeco doing?"

"He is talking to Scottas and Orestes and his brother, Onegesius, Constantius and Ferga and Millisis, everybody important. Ellac is trying to make them proclaim him Kagan but they will not." Monidiak's voice was edged with triumph. "Ellac will not be the Kagan, nor Dengazich. Everything is changed, it's all new, all fresh."

Tacs thought of the Gepids leaving Hungvar. In the hot, stuffy aul, his skin was covered with a thin unpleasant rime of sweat. "What about the Germans?"

"What? Oh. They aren't important now. When we have gotten our own affairs straight, we shall bring the Germans back."

German chiefs from every tribe subject to the Kagan's will had been in Hungvar for the wedding and the funeral. Now they were gone, scattered across the world. Tacs said, "We will never bring them back. There will be no new Kagan."

"No—we don't need a Kagan. A council of Hiung chiefs—"

Tacs shook his head. "Nothing will be as it was. What is he doing here?" He pointed across the aul toward the monk, who lay curled up asleep against the wall.

"He has been kind to me," Ummake said. "Let him alone." She snuffled and rubbed her nose.

"Does he speak Hiung?"

Ummake turned away, her hands full of grain, and poured it into a stone jar.

Tacs got up and went across the aul to the monk's side, shook him until the man's eyes opened, and sat back. Like a child waking up the monk lifted his head and looked around, full of trust. His eyes fixed on Tacs' face and he smiled.

"Go," Tacs said, in Latin. "Go away. You will only get into trouble here."

The monk pulled himself up onto his haunches, shaking out the sleeves of his rough black gown. He smoothed both palms across his head. In the light from the smokehole and the fire, his thin face looked all hollows and ridges. His eyes were pale as water, shining.

"Did you hear me?" Tacs said, impatiently.

"You are hasty. I was told Huns had no sense of time," the monk said. He sat down cross-legged. "You speak excellent Latin, where did you learn it?"

Tacs banged his hands on his knees, angry. "You must go. Wickedness will come to you if you stay here."

"No. Wickedness will come to me only if I let it. Christ Jesus is my armor against sin."

"Tacs," Ummake called sharply. "I told you, he has been very kind to me. Leave him alone."

"Yaya wouldn't want him here." Tacs glared at the monk as if he could lift him up on the end of his stare and hoist him out of the aul.

Ummake threw a cup at him. "Yaya is dead." Her face was slimy with tears and mucus; she scrubbed it roughly with her sleeve. Her eyes moved to the monk and her face altered into gentleness. "Come here, friend." She held out one hand.

The monk smiled. "Friend," he said, in Hiung; so he knew some of the language after all. He went toward her, bent over, across the aul.

"Ummake," Tacs said. "Why do you. . . ." He watched her, helpless; she broke off a chunk of bread and handed it to the monk, patted his hand and smiled at him, as if he were a favorite dog.

With the bread in his hand, the monk turned to look back at Tacs. "Please. Come translate for me." When Tacs hesitated: "Please."

Tacs went over to them. "Ummake. What are you doing?"

"You all went off to your own doings," Ummake said. "You left me alone with Yaya. Everybody else is either drunk or asleep or working at something. This one helped me carry Yaya around the dead-aul. He helped me wash him and dress him. He comforted me."

"He is a Roman," Tacs said.

The monk was pulling at his sleeve. Finally Tacs looked around at him. "What do you want?"

"I want to thank her. And to tell her of the comfort and love of the Lord Jesus Christ."

For a moment Tacs was wordless. Finally he burst out: "Her husband is dead, and you want to tell her about Roman things —German things—"

"It is now that she needs it," the monk said.

Ummake was sealing jars of food with mud. She had rolled up the wide sleeves of her shirt nearly to the armpits. Tacs watched her a moment, her strong arms and her hands, her eyes lowered to her work. Her hair hung down over her shoulders, matted and tangled. Tears splashed on her hands.

"He wants to tell you of the demon Christ," Tacs said. "He says it will comfort you."

Ummake shook her head. "I shall have all my comfort very soon. Tell him so." Her hands went on packing mud into the necks of the jars. Her eyes watched her work. "Ask him to stay with me."

Tacs turned back to the monk. "She says she will not listen. Stay if you want." He backed off. If the monk made her feel easier, maybe there was good in it. He remembered what The Fluteplayer had said and went across the aul to find his bows and extra clothes.

Monidiak came after him. "We shall have to take Yaya out to the plain today. I am leaving. Without me there will not be enough."

"Good. Find Bryak." Tacs threw back the torn cloak he had been sleeping under and looked over his equipment. He needed arrows. Suddenly he heard what Monidiak had said and glanced behind him. "Where are you going?"

"With Ellac. He wants to go up by the Lakes and gather the people there. The shamans are calling for all the Hiung to meet on the Nedao River at the auroch crossing to elect a new chief. We will gather at the beginning of the Stag-Fighting Moon."

"Why didn't you talk to me first?"

"Oh." Monidiak struck him lightly on the arm. "We will all come together at the Nedao, anyway. We shall see what happens there. I knew you would not follow Ellac. Are you going with Dengazich? He is too young."

"Are they fighting?"

"Not yet. But Dengazich is talking about Bleda, and the elder son set aside in favor of the younger."

Tacs thought, Everybody is leaving. Within a few days, Hungvar would be deserted. "The Gepids are going away."

"Of no importance. Whoever we make Kagan will ride them down."

"We will make no new Kagan."

"It doesn't matter. The Germans would never dare stand against us, anyway."

Tacs picked up one of his arrow cases. "Last night I saw Yaya and he told me that he had been killing Germans. That was who killed him, the Germans. For killing them. Be careful. Do you have any extra arrows?"

"Take Yaya's."

Tacs' heart jumped. The thought of taking a dead man's arrows revolted him. But when he looked into his arrow cases, he saw how few were left.

"Ummake," he called.

She was folding up a sleeping mat; the monk sat beside her, looking off into nothing. When Tacs called, she raised her head.

"I need arrows," Tacs said, ashamed of asking.

"Take them."

Tacs went across to the wooden chest against the wall and got down Yaya's bows and his cases of arrows. Ummake had often made arrows for him, although most people said it weakened arrows if a woman made them. There were three full cases. Tacs took two of them and left the third for Ummake to leave with Yaya.

In the midafternoon, when they had all packed up everything in the aul, Bryak came, and they took Yaya's body from the dead-aul and rode out onto the plain. Tacs and Monidiak carried the body between them on a horse and Bryak rode in front carrying Yaya's bows and his spear. Ummake with the monk beside her followed the body. Tacs led his three extra horses; Ummake had Yaya's mare on a leadline.

They went away from Hungvar to the north. The long summer drought had parched the steppe grey-brown. The sky burned so blue that it hurt to look at it. Not long before sundown they came to a spring where a tall tree promised plenty of wood. Ummake sat down in the shade, with the monk beside her, while Tacs and Monidiak gathered wood and Bryak drove four sticks into the ground at each corner of the mat Yaya lay on. The three of them lashed sticks together for a platform, raised it up on the sticks, and laid Yaya on it with his bows and spear. After they had piled the goods and food under the platform, Ummake took the bridles and saddles from her horses and drove them away. The mare was already grazing near the spring and the three saddle horses jogged away to join her.

Ummake sat down again under the tree. From her pack, she took the crown of wood and ribbons that she had worn to her wedding and put it carefully on her head. She got out pots of paint and painted her face for mourning. Putting everything away again, she sat still with her hands open in her lap.

Monidiak walked around the platform, pretending to see that it was secure. Bryak stood looking fixedly at the northern horizon. At last they went to their horses. Monidiak looked back toward Ummake; Bryak mounted and rode over to Tacs, who was standing beside the platform.

"You will come to the Nedao, won't you?" Bryak said.

"I don't know," Tacs said. There was a lump in his throat. He reached out blindly and clasped Bryak's hand. Monidiak led his horse over and each of them hugged Tacs by turn.

"You will come," Monidiak said.

"Maybe . . . I could go to New Rome."

Monidiak laughed. "Or you could turn into a sparrow and fly away. We will look for you." He threw his reins over the head of his dun mare and vaulted up onto her back. "Keep safe." He and Bryak kicked their horses away, waving to him.

Tacs turned slowly from them, back to Ummake. The monk was sitting there looking into the air; he did that often, his hands clasped and his lips moving slightly. Tacs went to Ummake and squatted down beside her.

"Good-by." He leaned forward and pressed himself into her arms. She embraced him; her cheek brushed against his, warm and soft.

When he stood up, she said, "Wait."

Tacs set himself. He looked furiously at the monk, knowing she would speak of him. Ummake said, "You must take him with you."

"Ummake. You are mad. He can walk. He has legs."

"He is a city man, a Roman. He would die."

Tacs glared at the monk. "You. Come with me."

The monk lifted his head. "Oh. Now?" He got to his feet and started toward Tacs' horses. Tacs followed him, and when the monk stopped and looked back, took him by the arm and pushed him ahead. "But what about her?" the monk asked, and immediately frowned. Tacs pushed him to the sorrel mare.

"Get on."

At first he thought that the monk would refuse, but the Roman hesitated only a moment. He took hold of the sorrel's mane and hauled himself awkwardly up her side and onto her back. Tacs shook his head so that the monk would know he disapproved and leapt up onto the back of the black pony.

They started off toward Hungvar. The monk kept twisting his head to look behind them. Tacs only turned once. He saw Ummake sitting under the tree, staring off into the distance the same way the priest had, and on the platform Yaya's clothes fluttering in the wind.

The monk said, "I wish I could have told her about Jesus." He avoided Tacs' eyes and looked straight ahead, toward Hungvar.

SEVENTEEN

TACS GALLOPED BACK TO
the Hiung camp, dragging his led horses behind him as fast as
he could, half hoping that when he came to the edge of the camp
and looked back, the monk would be gone. But he was not,
although his hair flopped in his eyes and his coarse black gown
was twisted around his body. Tacs rode up the embankment
that ran along the southeastern edge of the camp and reined in.

"Now you must give me back my horse. There is the camp."

The monk glanced into the packed bustling camp and said,
"Please don't leave me alone here. I speak no Hunnish—only
a few words."

Tacs waved to the north. "The Gepids have a camp here, on
the hill beyond the river. You can walk over there."

"Please," the monk said. He took a breath to steady his
voice. "I am afraid. Please don't leave me alone."

Tacs studied his face, intrigued; something in the monk's
voice made him believe that the man was struggling less with
fear than with his pride. Tacs said, "Why do you want to go
with me?"

"All my life I have wanted to bring the Word of God to the
Hun people. Now I am among Huns, and I find myself afraid,
but if I shrink now I shall never succeed."

Tacs could make no sense of that. He looked around at the
Hiung camp before them, sprawled along the slope below the
stockade. People were taking down their auls all along this
side of the camp. Skeletons of the auls stood here and there,

peeled branches curved like ribs up to meet the lodgepole in the center. Children and dogs and goats were gathered in clumps near the skeletons, waiting to be loaded up.

"You mean," Tacs said, "you want to live with Hiung people."

"Yes."

"Why?"

"The Germans already know Christ."

Tacs laughed. "Yes. Well, you can come, I suppose. But I don't know where we are going—I am going with The Fluteplayer, who is a very wise and great shaman."

He started off along the edge of the camp. The monk followed after, keeping his horse clear of the two led horses. Behind him the sorrel mare's suckling colt and the black mare's filly played while they ran.

Already the air from the Hiung camp smelled stale, as if the camp were long deserted. Tacs rode into it near The Fluteplayer's aul and wound his way through people rushing around packing up their gear. A train of six wagons rolled slowly away from them; on two of the wagons, auls had been built, and an old man sat inside one of them, looking out the door.

The Fluteplayer's wives were taking the hides down from the frame of his aul and rolling them up. All their furniture and all The Fluteplayer's glass jars and sacks and other equipment were gone. In the middle of the half-naked aul, The Fluteplayer sat on his heels and played his flute.

Tacs dismounted and hitched the led horses to the aul frame. The black pony he left to wander at will. The monk stood uncertainly with his reins in his hand, and Tacs pointed to the aul frame.

"Tie her. She's very quiet, see her baby?" He patted the sorrel colt, which came trotting up and poked his nose up under the mare's flank. When the monk had tied the mare fast, Tacs pushed him down and forward through the gap between two ribs of the aul.

The Fluteplayer looked up. "Who is that? Sit down. You came before I said you should. Just as well."

He was sitting on the last of his fine carpets, and he moved backward to give them room on it. Tacs pulled the monk down beside him. The monk sat with his legs crossed, like a beggar in a city.

"He wants to know who you are," Tacs said to the monk, indicating The Fluteplayer.

The monk nodded. His head and face were shaped like a wooden mask, all flat spare planes. "Please tell him that I am Aurelius, a servant of the Lord Jesus Christ, a citizen of the City of Rome and lately an inhabitant of New Rome, where my father was a civil servant and my mother the daughter of a Senator."

When Tacs had translated this, The Fluteplayer smiled and said, "He has a straightforward way to him. Tell him that I have been waiting for some sign of what course I should follow and I believe that he is a message to me. I will go to New Rome."

Tacs jerked his head up. "But—"

"You will take me and you can do whatever you choose, when I am there. Tell him."

"But he wants to be with the Hiung."

The Fluteplayer shrugged. "What he wishes makes no difference to me."

Tacs translated to the monk everything that The Fluteplayer had said. The monk lifted up his eyes to him, smiling. "My dear friend, you know my desire to live among your people. I don't want to go back to my own. Tell him I may be a message to him but now that he has received his sign I must find some way to stay with your people. He does not need me with him now."

When The Fluteplayer had heard that, he said, "Tell him he may come back to the Hiung later, but now is impossible. The clans are scattering until the hunting season. Most of the people will be in groups of two or three families. They won't come together until late in the autumn, to elect new chiefs and hold a great hunt. Who would take him with them—a man who can't help them hunt or herd or keep a camp but who would eat as much as any of them? Tell him, he will understand, his face is intelligent."

The Fluteplayer picked up his flute where it hung against his breastbone and warbled notes from it. Tacs grimaced. In Hiung what he had said was all easy to say but in Latin it took many more words and lots of explanation. At the end of it the monk looked over at The Fluteplayer, his face heavy with resignation.

"I see. God's will be done."

"He understands," Tacs said.

"I expected that he would," said The Fluteplayer.

WHEN AURELIUS HAD FIRST mentioned his desire to preach the Gospel to the Huns, his superiors had denounced him for the sin of pride. The penance he received only fixed deeper in his soul the sense of his mission. For years he struggled to reach Hungvar. Finally a diplomatic envoy agreed to take him. When at last he came to Hungvar, he was pitched out unceremoniously into the wet, in a humiliating and degrading spectacle witnessed by dozens of the barbarians, and it took him the better part of the summer to detach himself from the pious Alans who rescued him: having no priest of their own, they were determined to keep him, even though they were Arians and he believed the orthodox doctrine. At last he found his way back to Hungvar, arriving in the midst of the funeral. The screaming, the fires, the people rushing frantically in all directions should have terrified him, but instead they filled him with a passionate and fearless exhilaration. He plunged into the first occupied hut he came to and began to preach.

Of course the Huns hardly knew what was happening before them, but understanding would come when they had accepted him, and the Word of God poured from him. He preached less to his audience than to himself. Part of his vocation in becoming a monk was that thinking about Christ always made him happy.

The next morning when the last of the Huns had fallen asleep or left the hut, he went out into the open to breathe and orient himself. He enjoyed the look of the camp; it reminded him of a nursery full of untidy children. While he stood at the hut door admiring what he saw, some of the Huns came back, carrying a dead man. They ignored him, he might have been invisible. Among them was one who sobbed and struck aside the hands of those who tried to give comfort. Aurelius realized that this was a woman and the wife of the dead man.

He followed them a little way into the camp, fascinated by the woman's choked, inconsolable grief. The men left the corpse in a large empty hut, and the woman began to straighten the body, still crying. Aurelius went to help her.

At first she acted as if he were not there, but gradually her restraint dissolved, until at last she was talking in a stream to him, even though she knew he spoke no Hunnish. Together they washed her man's wounds and put fresh clothes on his body, and all the while, she talked.

The man had been hacked to death with knives. Aurelius at first was unable to look at what he was doing. The woman— her name, she made clear, was Ammarka—handled the body as if it were only meat. But suddenly, washing the caked blood from the body, she laid her cheek against its chest and moaned, and Aurelius saw that she handled it so deftly because she knew it so well. The sliced and filthy body took on another aspect for him.

But now he was riding south again; he was not meant to be the Apostle to the Huns. The horse he rode traveled at a bone-cracking jog. He could not get a grip with his knees and each stride nearly jarred him loose. They were riding through a moonlit night full of the voices of owls, with the river to their left and the wide plain stretching pale and cool to the southern horizon. Ahead of him, the two Huns rode chattering away like women. Before them they drove the two loose horses and the colts.

The sorrel mare stopped to nurse her colt; she had done so once before. Aurelius was afraid to urge her on because the colt might starve. He knew Huns valued their horses above anything else. When the Huns noticed him, they reined in and sat on their horses waiting. The older man, who was tall and lean, picked up his flute and began to play. Their horses lowered their heads and grazed.

Aurelius eased his weight gently from side to side to stretch his cramped muscles. The mare started forward again, pulling her teat out of the colt's mouth. The other foal had lain down; its mother prodded it with her nose, but the foal refused to rise.

"Wait," Aurelius called to the Huns, who seemed ready to ride on. He pointed to the foal on the ground. "We must stop to rest."

"We have hardly left Hungvar," the younger man said; he was in one of his more patient humors.

Aurelius nodded. "I know that. But if you want me to go with you, you will have to realize I am no Hiung."

The older man laughed at Aurelius' use of their name for themselves. He and the younger man spoke for a while. When they had done talking, the older man played his flute and looked around. Dropping the flute, he nodded and pointed toward the river and said something.

"We can camp there, by the river," the younger man said to Aurelius. He was angry again; he snatched the sorrel mare's leadrope from Aurelius' hands and rode off at a gallop. Aurelius took a handful of mane and tried to hold fast to the horse with his legs, as he had been told. But his knees and thighs were sore from so much riding, and halfway to the river he fell off.

The younger man pretended not to see and raced on toward the river. Aurelius stood up. The other Hun jogged over to him, laughing, and said something in Hunnish that included the word Hiung. Bending down, he slapped Aurelius good-naturedly on the chest and rode off. Aurelius was left to walk. His legs hurt from hip to ankle and his back was sore. Before he reached the Huns beside the river bank, they had built a fire. He lay down in the circle of its warmth, rested his head on his folded arms, and fell asleep.

THE MIDMORNING SUN WAS already baking hot, even in the half-shade of the trees along the river. Tacs sipped water from the gourd The Fluteplayer had given him and leaned out to pick another handful of the berries. His fingers, tingling with thorn-scratches, were stained deep red with the blood of the berries; the sour taste of the occasional unripe fruit lingered on the back of his tongue. Up ahead of him, The Fluteplayer was playing on his flute, and the monk was probably with him. Tacs drank more water. Reining the pony back out of the berry bushes, he rode at a fast jog around behind the grazing horses and herded them on along the river bank.

Sunblasted, the plain stretched off into a haze of dust. For once the wind had fallen calm. The two colts played at fighting one another; dust and pollen clung to their long lashes and to the bristles of their young manes. Ahead, still out of sight, the sorrel mare whinnied, and her colt answered her and loped toward the sound. Tacs whistled. A moment later The Flute-player whistled back.

They had decided to follow the river as far as they could,

because there was always something to eat there, and they could fish if they needed meat. The Fluteplayer had brought dried meat and fish and a sack of grain, but that he wished to save for the journey south. Tacs at first tried to talk him into leaving the monk behind, so that they could go faster, but The Fluteplayer refused. He said that he liked the monk, and anyway, with the two foals they had to move slowly. Tacs herded the loose horses down a little glen and around a copse of trees.

The Fluteplayer dropped his flute and waved. Beside him, the monk looked over his shoulder at Tacs; his thin white face was smeared like a child's with berry juice. Tacs trotted up to them. He reined in beside them, and the sorrel mare called to her colt and let him nurse.

"Find out what he is trying to tell me," The Fluteplayer said. He stabbed his chin toward the monk. "All this morning he has been trying out different languages, as if he has something of importance he wants to ask."

Tacs drank another mouthful of water and handed the gourd to the monk. "Do you want to say something?"

The monk's head bobbed. Instead of drinking from the gourd, he splashed the water over his hands and scrubbed them together. The berry juice would not wash off, even when he rubbed his fingers on his sleeves. At last he gave up.

"I meant to ask him who he thought had created all this." His arm moved in a circle, taking in the river, the trees, the berry bushes, everything.

Tacs stared at him, wondering if he had understood. At last he drew his eyes from the monk and looked around him, to see why the monk thought all this had been made. It astonished him that the Romans should have such craft at their disposal, that they could conceive of an entire river and its banks actually being constructed, and to such perfection of detail.

"Well?" The Fluteplayer asked.

"He is mad." Tacs shrugged.

"Tell me what he said. I will decide what he means."

"He wants to know who made all this. The river, and the trees."

The Fluteplayer gave the monk a startled look. Gratified, Tacs watched him look all around, just as he had. Finally the shaman's eyes returned to the thin white face of the monk.

"Ask him what he means."

The monk was looking from one to the other, and between his eyes a small frowning crease had appeared. He cleared his throat. "I mean, does he believe that God made the world, and everything in it? Or that the Devil made it?"

Tacs snorted. "Ah. I understand." To The Fluteplayer, he said, "Now he is trying to teach us of his Ancestor and the demon Christ. He is asking if we believe that his Ancestor made everything in the world."

The Fluteplayer nodded, his face clearing. "I see. Excellent. Now we may exchange many thoughts and I shall learn answers that have puzzled me always. But we must get moving again—the colt is finished. Come along."

They started off again, the three of them abreast. Tacs while he translated kept his eyes searching the thick brush and trees along the river for more berry bushes and for fruit trees and small game. The horses grazed while they moved, and the colts played with each other and lay down now and then to rest their legs.

"Of course we do not believe that your Ancestor made everything in the world," The Fluteplayer said. "We have our own Ancestors, some of them very powerful, to whom we owe honor and prayer, but it would be arrogance to say that even the greatest of our Ancestors might have actually—" He milled the air with his hand, searching for words, and gave up. "They protect us, as long as we honor them, and they teach us magic and how to cope with demons, but certainly they never made a tree, or. . . ." He looked at the monk, leaning forward to see around Tacs' body. "Does he understand?"

The monk said, "I understand, I suppose. But this is exactly why I have come among you. What you have described is an imperfect awareness of reality, the result of ignorance and darkness into which all men were cast when God drove our first parents from the Garden of Eden."

The Fluteplayer listened to that in silence. For a little while, riding through a stand of tall trees, he said nothing in reply. Tacs, coming on a little problem in translation, had used the Hiung word demon-king for God. Dismounting, he poked among some mushrooms sprouting around the base of an enormous oak tree.

"Don't pick those," The Fluteplayer called. "They are poison. Come back here."

Tacs trotted after the black pony, which was walking along between the sorrel mare and the bay gelding that The Flute-player rode. "There's a ford up ahead," Tacs said, "and a road south."

The Fluteplayer brushed that impatiently aside. "Tell him that I can see we shall have to make simple things clear to each other before we can get to such large questions as he wants to ask."

Tacs could see no value even in the simple things. The monk was full of Roman idleness, making games out of ideas that were perfectly clear at a glance. He translated what The Flute-player had said to the monk.

For once the monk did not rush forward into speech. The little crease remained between his eyebrows; his clear pale eyes stared unwinking at The Fluteplayer, intent.

Ahead, the deep shade of the trees was broken by the bright sunlight glistening on green bushes. Tacs could see by the way the shrubs grew there that a trail passed through to the river. He squeezed the black pony forward, sniffing the air for a scent of fruit.

"Tell me," the monk said. "Do you Hiung believe that—"

Tacs yanked his pony to a stop. "Fluteplayer—see—what is

that? See there?" He pointed ahead, toward the lone tree at the edge of the trail, and kicked the pony forward. At first he had thought it was some kind of moss on the tree, but now he knew that it was not. He galloped up to the tree and reached out to touch the hair hanging from the trunk; he could not make himself touch it, and he drew his hand back to his chest. The others rode up beside him.

"What is this?" the monk cried. "Jesus save us!"

Tacs nudged his horse forward, craning his neck to look at the other trees near the ford. His mouth had gone dry and his heart beat painfully in his side. On three of the other trees, he could see clumps of hair, like this one, hanging from the boles; the wind came along and lifted up the hair and streamed it out.

When he looked around The Fluteplayer had pulled the hair from the tree next to them. Tacs gasped. He shrank to one side, repulsed. The monk sat stiff and silent on his mare while The Fluteplayer turned the hair over and over in his hands. It was clotted and matted with blood; the withered patch of scalp had shrunk to the size of a man's palm.

"Ostrogoths," The Fluteplayer said. "They take scalps. How many are there?"

Tacs pulled himself out of his daze. Riding forward into the middle of the trail, he counted the scalps hanging from the trees. Now he could see more than before—on one tree there were three, two very short, that he thought came from children. He trotted back to the other men; the colts dashed past him toward the river, kicking and biting at each other.

"There are seven others," he said. "They are all from Hiung."

The Fluteplayer sighed. He laid the scalp in the palm of his hand and stroked it softly with his fingers. "Go get them. We will bury them." He looked over at the monk, who crossed himself and began to murmur under his breath.

They took down the scalps and laid them together in a deep hole under the oak trees. When they found a raven feather still tied into the hair of one scalp, they decided that the dead were

Shai Hiung, and The Fluteplayer remembered all that he could of the funeral arrangements of the Shaigi. They did what they could, lining the hole with stones and bits of bark. It filled Tacs with grief and terror to handle the scalps, but The Flute-player stroked each one and laid it lovingly into the ground, all in the same direction so that they would travel together. The monk helped where he could and when he could do nothing sat and stared away and spoke to himself.

It was midafternoon before they were finished. They rode on, turning south away from the river along the trail they had found. The monk and The Fluteplayer talked, but they spoke only of immediate things, and they rode at a faster pace, the colts keeping nearby their mothers. Tacs' eyes swept constantly over the plain. He felt as he had when he found Yaya dead.

"Why would anyone have done that?" the monk asked, out of nothing. "Torn the hair from the heads of corpses—tiny children, too."

From habit, Tacs did not answer but translated, and The Fluteplayer said, "Many reasons. The Ostrogoths believe that when a man's body is dead his spirit goes off to some other land and lives there in a form like the one he had when he died, and a man without hair would be ridiculous and without honor."

"What happens to a Hiung when he dies?"

They left the river far behind. The Fluteplayer twisted to look back toward it. Tacs could see by the way he moved that he too was anxious.

"When we die and our bodies are properly tended, that is the end of it," The Fluteplayer said. "As it should be. If a man lived on after his death it would be unseemly. Of course the spirits of the people dwell in the totems and the holy places. But if a part of a man's body is hung up on a tree, without the proper rituals, his spirit will go wandering off like some stupid Ostrogoth's causing everybody trouble." He spat.

"If a man knows Jesus Christ," the monk said, "when he

dies, his soul finds its peace and joy in Heaven, with God."

Ahead of them, beyond the close horizon of the next hill, a feather of smoke was rising into the air. Tacs bit his lip. The other two did not see it and went on arguing.

"Why should a man die at all," The Fluteplayer was saying, "if after he is dead his spirit goes on just as before?"

The monk waited until Tacs had gotten through half of it and said, "Jesus Christ has rescued us from death."

The Fluteplayer scowled at him. "I don't want to be rescued. If there were no death life itself would have no value. No! Listen to me—I—what is that?"

"Smoke," Tacs said.

The Fluteplayer reined in. His eyes swept the blank plain around them. Under his breath he said something Tacs could not hear. With the ends of his reins he flogged his gelding into a gallop. They followed him at a dead run toward the smoke. At first the colts kept pace with them but on the steep slope, they faltered, dropping back. The black mare stopped with her baby. The sorrel mare's colt neighed in fright and the mare neighed and turned back toward it, and the monk could not rein her around. Tacs left him and galloped after The Fluteplayer, pulling his bow out of its case while he rode.

Someone was screaming. He reached the crest of the hill, and saw below him a burning wagon. There was only one, and that poor and old. The ox lay dead in its traces. The screaming came from the wagon. The Fluteplayer was already halfway down the slope to it. Tacs kicked the black pony after him. He could see the bodies sprawled on the ground beside the flaming wagon, with their gear scattered around them. Tacs' hair stood on end. The screams rose in pitch, sharp with pain; they made Tacs feel like screaming back.

The Fluteplayer leapt from his horse and rushed toward the wagon, and the screaming abruptly ceased. When Tacs galloped up, he saw that there was a man tied to the wagon wheel. His hair was all burned away, and his eyes were gone; the flesh of his head was crisp and oozed blood and fat. The Fluteplayer had killed him with his knife.

"Germans again," The Fluteplayer said. He thrust his knife into its scabbard and knelt beside another body.

Tacs drew a deep breath. His nose and throat were clogged with the reek of the half-cooked man. Riding in a circle around the burned wagon, he crossed the trail the Germans had made riding away. The hoofprints of a dozen or more horses led straight south across the dry grass. If he rode after them, he would bring them within sight. His legs tightened around the black pony's barrel and he pulled the top off a case of arrows, but The Fluteplayer called sharply to him and brought him back to his side.

"You must help me. These must be . . ." His voice trailed away; he was looking somewhere else. Tacs followed his eyes. A girl lay sprawled in the dirt on the far side of the wagon, near the dead ox. Her pale German hair was spread out in the dust. Blood covered her, and nearby there was another puddle of blood. The Fluteplayer walked toward her and Tacs followed him. He stopped following when he saw that she had been pregnant, and her belly slit open and her baby pulled out and trampled.

"She was his wife," The Fluteplayer said, coming back toward Tacs.

The monk was running down the hillside toward them, on foot. Out of breath, he staggered the last few yards and stopped, his chest heaving and his breath rasping in his throat. To steady himself he took hold of Tacs' pony by the mane. His eyes moved slowly over the dead people—the two old people crumpled on the ground on this side of the wagon, the burned man, and the Gothic wife and her baby. He put one hand on Tacs' knee and patted it. Tears streamed from his eyes.

"Tell me again," he said, and paused to get his breath. "Tell me again that it is a grace to die."

EIGHTEEN

⊏⊨

AT SUNDOWN THEY WERE
still burying the bodies; besides the five dead people Aurelius
had seen at first, they found two more bodies inside the charred
wagon. The monk had tried at first to help them in their hor-
rible work. Slowly he realized how useless he was to them.
When it became evident that they would be there after dark,
he gathered wood for a fire, and while the sun vanished into
low clouds along the horizon, he laid out the fire and lit it.

The two Huns paid almost no heed to him. All afternoon,
while they got the bodies ready and built platforms of sticks
for them, they argued with each other. The monk suspected,
from their gestures and the few Hunnish words he knew, that
the younger man—his name was Tox—wanted to hunt down
the Germans who had slain these people. The older man, the
shaman, seemed more consumed with grief than minded of
vengeance. Often during the afternoon he wept.

The monk could not fathom why they had buried the scalps
but were hoisting these bodies on platforms—why, for that
matter, they had buried their master Attila in the ground and
laid out Ammarka's dead husband under the sky. Throughout
the afternoon, whenever he tried to pray, his mind turned instead to the things that the shaman had told to him through
Tox. It frightened him to find no point at which his viewpoint
touched the viewpoint of the Huns. It was as if, expecting to see
a little river, he had come out instead on a cliff overlooking the
limitless ocean. There was no room in their lives for Christ.
Their ignorance seemed without boundary.

In the dark, Tox called him over, and he stood with them while they raised the corpses up and heaped what was left of the family's possessions around the platform. Clearly they needed some minimum number of people to bury their dead, and it did not matter if the witnesses were Hun or not. Afterward, the three walked back to the monk's little fire and sat down around it. The shaman put his forehead down on his raised knee and was silent.

Tox put more wood on the fire and hurried around, pulling open his packs and arranging equipment for cooking beside the fire. The monk looked around them. After a lifetime in cities he could not adjust himself to sitting about outside. He missed the snug close feeling of a roof and walls. Most of all, the darkness and emptiness behind him made the back of his neck creep and kept his ears stretched for the sounds of the night. It occurred to him that their fire surely could be seen from far off on the plain. The Germans who had bound a living man so that a fire would consume him bit by bit could be watching them even now.

He tried to pray and again could not. The vision of the dead woman, of the bloody trampled mess beside her, hung lurid before his eyes. He stared into the fire and tried to empty his mind. The weight of the dead he had seen pressed against his imagination.

Opposite him, the shaman raised his head and spoke to Tox, who answered him with a word. The shaman turned his eyes on Aurelius. At that moment Aurelius was so burdened with a leaden despair that he could not summon the energy to look politely away. He and the shaman stared straight into each other's eyes.

Almost at once, Aurelius began to feel better, and the shaman smiled. He spoke to Tox, who was pouring water into an iron pot. By the look Tox gave him, the monk knew that the younger man did not approve of the question. Tox said, "He asks why you are—why you became a monk."

"Ah."

Aurelius hitched himself closer to the fire. His stomach was cramped with hunger. Holding his hands out to the warmth of the flames, he considered how he had first recognized his vocation.

"I feel very close to Christ. I want other people to feel what I feel when I think of Christ, and I want other people to find salvation."

Translating, Tox with two long sticks rolled hot stones out of the fire and dumped them with a splash into the iron pot. Clouds of steam rose into the firelight. The shaman hunched his thin shoulders. Tox got up and went into the darkness, and the shaman spoke directly to Aurelius. Ghostlike, the translation came out of the dark behind him, and Tox appeared with a coat that shimmered in the light from the fire. The shaman put it on; Aurelius saw that it was made of snakeskin.

"But you monks—I am told—are not healers?"

"Christ was a healer," Aurelius said. "We heal souls."

Tox gave each of them a bowl of steaming hot grain soup. The shaman dipped one bony finger in, tasted it, and put it aside to cool.

"Let me say a blessing," Aurelius said. "For us all."

"Do what you want," Tox said. He got himself a bowl. Aurelius saw that he was not going to translate: an assertion of power. Aurelius looked at the shaman.

The shaman spoke to Tox in a mild voice; Tox answered sullenly, and the shaman's voice became chiding and paternal. Surly as a child, Tox turned to the monk and said, "He says you may say it and I am to tell him what you say."

"Thank you." The monk kept his voice polite. He cleared his throat and said the Pater Noster, pausing every phrase for Tox's translation. He wondered if this were the first time the prayer had been voiced in Hunnish; it sounded like a pagan incantation. When he had finished, his gruel was cool enough to eat.

The shaman said nothing. He ate his soup slowly, wiping his lips now and then. Occasionally he would stare at Aurelius, full of curiosity. At first the shaman's bold, condescending arrogance had unsettled the monk and made him resentful, but now he was used to it; he even respected it. Putting aside his bowl, he said, "And how did you become a shaman?"

Of course he had used the German word, and the man opposite him obviously recognized it; before Tox had finished translating, he was answering. His voice was suddenly light and almost joking. "I used to be convinced that all the shamans were frauds. I thought they only pretended to be wise and powerful so that people would be afraid of them and in awe of them. I saw how rich they all were and how other people treated them. So I took to keeping company with the shamans, so that I could find out how they committed their frauds. Finally they approached me to become their student. So I am now a shaman."

Tox, translating, kept his eyes on the shaman's face; finished, he asked some question, and the other man laughed and nodded and told him to be quiet.

"Well, then," Aurelius said. "Are you frauds?"

The shaman turned his hands palms up. "I cannot say. There lies the joke of it. I am a fraud, perhaps, but I am not sure."

"Come, now, you must know if you are a fraud."

"I think I am. I have made up a trick that I do with a bit of thread. I pretend to suck out the demon that makes a man sick; I hide the thread in my mouth and cover it with spit and blood and that I appear to suck out of the sick person."

Enthralled, the monk studied him a moment. The shaman smiled. "Do you see the joke?"

"No. I am fascinated, though, by the—"

"The joke is that when I play my trick on them, usually the people get well."

That Aurelius could not believe, but before he had a chance to doubt, Tox spoke to the shaman. While he and the shaman talked, Aurelius got himself more soup. The feeling of being mercilessly exposed on the vast plain returned to him. He ate quickly; the gruel was almost tasteless, and although it filled his stomach he could not satisfy his tongue.

Tox broke off angrily in the middle of a sentence and pouted at the fire. The shaman spoke to him and Tox refused to answer. Again the shaman spoke, his voice this time edged with contempt, and he gave Tox a push on the shoulder.

Like a dog snapping, Tox whirled himself away from the other man's touch. Aurelius jumped. The two Huns faced each other, their eyes black in the firelight. Tox's body was rigid with anger. When the shaman spoke to him Tox burst out with a cascade of words.

When he had ranted for a little while, the shaman cut him off and gave him some command, gesturing to him. Tox glared at him. The shaman repeated it and made the same gesture, with more force, and muttering Tox turned around and began to clean up the cooking gear.

Aurelius' body slumped. It was alarming to see the power that the shaman held over Tox. Yet the little Hun hardly seemed to resent it or to chafe under it. Already he was happy at his work again, scraping the iron pot with his fingers and licking them clean.

The shaman said, "My friend, I am sorry to tell you this. We shall have to ride on tonight. I know you are tired but we cannot be here tonight. Also we must get away from the Germans. We will ride slowly so that you can rest, perhaps."

"I understand," Aurelius said. "I will try to keep up."

AT MIDNIGHT THE BLACK mare's filly lay down and would not go farther. Tacs dismounted and tried to push the foal up onto her feet, but the black mare thrust herself between them and nearly bit him. The filly was already as tall as Tacs; she climbed up onto her long legs and stuck her nose under her dam's flank to nurse.

The Fluteplayer rode over and watched a moment. After a while, he looked up and swept the horizon with his eyes. Behind him, the monk sat slumped on his horse. The Fluteplayer said, "We can't stop here. We are still too near the river."

Tacs said, "You go on. I will come after you in the morning." He thought, If I can get away I will hunt down the Germans.

"No," The Fluteplayer said, as if he had heard what Tacs was thinking. "We can leave the horses. The mare can do for herself, and the filly is almost big enough to wean."

"She is my best mare," Tacs said. "Let me stay here with her, I can catch you when the filly is rested."

"I do not wish it so," The Fluteplayer said.

Tacs looked down at his hands, furious. Everybody seemed to be winding shackles around him. He thought of abandoning The Fluteplayer and the monk to themselves. Without him they would be almost helpless, unable even to talk to each other. An instant later he pictured himself alone on the wide plain.

"She is an old mare, anyway. And this filly isn't so good." Turning to the black pony, he vaulted up onto its back. "Let's go."

They rode off toward the south. The sorrel mare's colt was a little older and kept up without difficulty. In the moonlight the horses seemed to lose their color: they all looked to be black. The Fluteplayer picked up his flute and made tentative notes on it, hunting for a song.

Overhead, the moon rode steadily across the sky. There were no clouds and the wind had died. In all directions the plain ran off to the horizon, without feature, confusing to the eye. Twice the monk and The Fluteplayer talked, asking and answering their incomprehensible questions; Tacs translated almost without listening. His muscles were cramped and aching and his leg joints hurt. Once, when the other men had been long silent, he dozed off.

The moon set; the darkness lifted. A flock of birds flew overhead, calling out in shrill voices. On the horizon streaks of
white appeared. The air was growing warmer against his cheek.
He reined in, almost without thinking, and stared into the
eastern sky.

The other two also stopped. Slumped on the sorrel mare's
back, the monk had fallen asleep. His gown was crumpled
loose around him like a half-shed skin. The Fluteplayer dismounted and walked around, stretching his legs out like a
crane; his knees crackled with each step. Tacs watched him a
moment, unable to find any of his usual love for him. When
he looked back at the horizon, the sun was rising.

Against the white of the sky there was a sudden flash of
green. Beneath it the light turned too bright to watch. Tacs
put up his hand to shade his eyes. A west wind sprang up,
rustling the grass, and raced off busily toward the sun. Brilliant,
implacable, the sun lifted into the sky. All around them, the
plain burst awake, teeming with small animals and birds.

"We can stop, if you wish," The Fluteplayer said. He stood
at Tacs' knee. "Find us a place to camp."

Tacs licked his lips. The sunrise had left him exhilarated.
He searched the plain around them for a ravine or dimple that
might mark a spring. His eyes came to the monk, fast asleep
on the mare; the colt had come up for something to eat, and
the mare was also dozing, her lower lip sagging.

"Why don't we wait here?" Tacs said. "Until he wakes up,
at least."

"Good." The Fluteplayer sank down where he stood and
began to play on his flute. Dismounting, Tacs searched for
something to make a fire, so that he could toast some grain
to eat.

At NOON THE BLACK MARE
caught up with them, walking along their track, with her
filly behind her. Tacs was so glad to see her that he gave

her a handful of parched wheat. The Fluteplayer had decided that they should stay where they were until dark. Wrapped in his clothes, the monk slept on the ground; Tacs had noticed that he preferred to have something solid behind him, and he heaped his saddle and the packs up against the monk's back. It amazed him that the monk could sleep so soundly, with the shaman playing his flute and the horses moving around and the wind running in the grass.

In the afternoon, Tacs slept, waking every once in a while to turn over and look around him. At sundown he got up and checked the waterskins. Although the water was brackish and tasted like dirt, there was enough for two days more—by then, he was sure, they would have found a spring or a stream. He packed the bay gelding, saddled up his black pony, and went to wake the monk.

The Fluteplayer was sitting on the ground shredding blades of grass with his teeth. While Tacs put the bridles on the horses, the shaman and the monk sat together and tried to talk with their hands. But of course they could say nothing to each other. At last The Fluteplayer called to Tacs.

"Ask him why he believes that all men have the same Ancestor when there are so many different kinds of men."

Tacs led over the horses. When he had translated it, he said, "We have to go now. I think tomorrow maybe we will see the mountains."

The two men rose and came to their horses. Tacs cupped his hand to boost the monk up onto the mare's back. The monk picked up his reins.

"I don't mean that God the Father is actually my ancestor and yours—not as your father is your ancestor. I mean that God is our spiritual father, having created us all from nothing, as He created the world."

The Fluteplayer mounted the bay gelding, sitting on the packs. To Tacs, who was circling them to go to the black pony, he said, "You have translated it wrong."

"No," Tacs said. It had occurred to him before that the monk believed his Ancestor and the Demon-King to be the same, but that was only a sign of Roman ignorance.

"Tell him that I have studied of demons and spirits for my whole life, under men who studied all their lives, and so on, back to the beginning of all magic, and never has anyone spoken to me of a single master demon who made everything that is."

They rode on; the monk was thinking, his head down. At last, he said, "I begin to understand. Maybe you can tell me what God means." He looked over at Tacs. "You."

"Me?" Tacs started. Frowning, he fixed his eyes ahead of them, trying to find words. "Oh, well—some great magical . . . thing that can do as it wishes with me."

"A good being—a loving being?"

Tacs shook his head. "I don't understand you."

The monk said nothing, only held him in his eyes. It was still light enough to see his eyes. Tacs, confused, looked at The Fluteplayer; he could not conceive of a good or loving demon. The Fluteplayer said impatiently, "Tell me what he has said to you."

When Tacs explained, the shaman made a good-natured face. "So it is not a demon he has been talking about. I begin to see now. Tell him that he has suggested an interesting idea and he must let me think."

Tacs could not imagine what idea he meant. They rode on in silence—the monk hardly ever spoke to Tacs. The waning moon rose, one side flattened. When it had stepped into the sky to a height of two fists, Tacs dismounted and gave all the horses some water. He felt the black mare's bag and found it almost empty, shriveled to the touch.

When he went back to the pony, the wind brought him the smell of smoke. The hair on the back of his neck stood on end. Looking up at The Fluteplayer, he saw the shaman staring south, his back rigid, and his nostrils flared. A moment later the monk asked, "Isn't that smoke I smell?"

The Fluteplayer grunted. "It could be coming from miles away."

Tacs mounted the pony; they started off at a quick trot toward the smoke.

Gradually, the smell grew more intense, although every few moments the shifting wind carried it entirely away. When the moon stood near the peak of the sky, they came to the edge of a deep ravine. Tacs led them east along its rim. The ravine was only a dozen feet wide, but the banks were sheer.

"Look!"

Ahead of them, a red glow colored the upper edges of the ravine's banks. Tacs nudged the pony forward. The others followed him single file, the mares calling to their foals. In one place, the ravine wall had collapsed into a soft slope; Tacs headed the pony toward it, and the little animal pricked up its ears, snorted, and slid down on its hocks.

He reached the floor of the ravine in a shower of pebbles and dirt. Above him on the rim The Fluteplayer and the monk were trying to force their horses down the slope. Tacs galloped down the ravine toward the fire. The hot smoke stung his eyes; it amazed him that he could hear no screams, when the crackling of the flames filled his ears. A deadfall loomed in his way, and he swung the pony around it and rode out into a wide meadow.

He reined in. In the middle of the widened ravine, a fire burned, as big as a house. Flames sprouted and flickered still at one end of it but most of it was only glowing ash. Tacs rode excitedly forward. He could see parts of wagons half buried in the flames. On the far side of the fire he found the bodies.

There were many of them, perhaps as many as twenty, all Ostrogoths, lying in rows with their throats cut. His heart bounded. So Hiung had done it. Now the fire seemed like a beacon set to call him across the plain to witness this revenge. He counted the dead Germans, delighted. There were eighteen of them, including the children; the Hiung had even cut the throats of the dogs.

The Fluteplayer and the monk were coming, calling to him. Tacs shouted to The Fluteplayer to come and see. He could not keep the pleasure from his voice, although he wanted the shaman to be surprised.

Rounding the fire, The Fluteplayer snatched his horse to a stop. Shadows hid his face, but by the set of his body, Tacs could see he was not pleased.

"What's wrong?" Tacs cried.

The Fluteplayer said nothing. He reined his horse around to walk down the line of bodies; he looked at each one as if they had been long friends. Tacs stared at him, bewildered. The monk rode around the fire. When he saw the dead Germans, he whimpered like a dog. Tacs knew that it was the monk who had caused The Fluteplayer to look so gently on the Goths. But before he could even raise his temper, the rustle of branches behind him brought him around, poised.

The sound died at once, but the pony was staring, prick-eared, into the dark beyond the firelight. Tacs tightened his legs, and the pony minced forward on its toes, its nostrils wide. The monk called out. Tacs ignored him. The pony hated Germans; therefore it was a German that hid in the scraggling bushes along the ravine wall.

Beyond the firelight, he held the pony back while his eyes adjusted, and in that stillness heard the German in the brush move again. The pony snorted. Tacs eased up on the rein, and the pony bounded forward into the bushes; from the thick undergrowth the Goth ran, bent over, racing for the darkness down the ravine.

Tacs let out a yell. The pony on its own lunged after the Goth, and Tacs held back a little to make a race of it. The Goth screamed—it was a woman. She ran for the shelter of the brush against the ravine bank, but the black pony crashed after her through it, and she turned and tried to climb the sheer wall, clawing at the earth and bringing down stones and dirt in a rain around her. Tacs rode up behind her and seized her by the hair. He laid his rein against the pony's neck and it whirled, and at a gallop he dragged her back toward the fire. With each stride she screamed. He remembered the Hiung tied to the burning wagon and her screams delighted him. Within the light of the fire, he flung the woman to the ground and jumped down to kill her.

Like an animal, the monk leapt on her. She started up to run again, and with one hand he thrust her down and stood astride her body, facing Tacs. "No," he said. "In the name of Jesus Christ."

Between his feet, the Gothic girl lay weeping. Her legs worked from side to side. Tacs looked for The Fluteplayer, and the shaman appeared and walked calmly to the monk and put one hand on the man's arm. He said nothing. The monk met his eyes and after a moment stepped aside. The Fluteplayer knelt beside the girl and turned her onto her back.

Tacs sat down on his heels near the last of the fire. "I don't understand you anymore," he said. "What has this idiot monk done to you?"

The girl at first only wept, but when she opened her eyes and saw the shaman above her, she surged up violently from the ground, attacking him and trying to run at the same time. The Fluteplayer grabbed both her wrists in his left hand and held her still almost without effort. With her arms locked in his grasp she hung in the air and stared at him; her body shuddered with each breath. The firelight lay against her face, shining on her round pale eyes.

"Tell her that we won't hurt her," The Fluteplayer said, over his shoulder.

"Why should she live?" Tacs asked. The monk stood looking from one to the other, his face lined.

The Fluteplayer said, "Do as I tell you, frog."

Tacs dropped his chin to his chest. He felt the pressure of everything that had happened since the Kagan's death. After so much Latin, he had trouble finding his German again. He told the girl what The Fluteplayer had said, and without waiting to see if she answered, he went around the fire to the lee side, took the packs off his horses, and lay down in the warmth and went to sleep.

NINETEEN

⊂╪

IN THE MORNING, AURELIUS and the Gothic girl said their prayers together. The monk kept his voice loud and steady, to show the Hun shaman how pleased he was to have another Christian to pray with, although he knew that the girl—her name was Greita—prayed only because he forced her to.

Of course she spoke no Latin. He had to communicate with her through Tox. He was beginning to see a classical irony in having to strain every idea through the Hun.

When they had prayed, he told her with gestures to stay where she was. Tox had cooked them a broth of dried meat and herbs and water, and she fell immediately to eating. The monk crossed the ravine to the shaman, who was sitting in the shade of the wall playing on his flute. Sitting down beside him, Aurelius tried patiently to express himself with his hands and his few Hunnish words.

He did this as often as he could, to break Tox's power over them, but naturally it never worked. The ideas he wanted to express were too general and abstract. He found it easy enough to tell the shaman Greita's name and that he, Aurelius, felt responsible for her, but he could not get the shaman to understand that he wished her taken at once to her own people.

All the while, Tox moved around the ravine, restless as a beast, gathering wood, widening the space of their camp, and clearing the brush away from the small spring at the far end of the meadow. His black pony followed at his heels. The monk thought that Tox had noticed them trying to talk but was waiting to be called. The shaman watched politely while Aurelius gestured in the air, drew pictures in the dirt with a stick, and pointed at various objects within seeing range. Once or twice, his eyebrows cocked, the shaman asked something in his own tongue and tried in his turn to explain with signs, but at last he shrugged and smiled and waved to Aurelius to stop. Lifting his voice, he called Tox over.

Tox said something in a voice sulky with injury. Abruptly Aurelius saw that he was offended by their attempts to do without him. The shaman laughed at him and said something, and Tox looked over at the monk.

"He asks what do you want now?"

"I was trying to say that the girl should be returned to her own people as soon as possible."

Tox's face darkened; he was in a bad temper. "But all her people are—" He broke off in the middle of a gesture toward the charred debris of the wagons and in a flat voice translated to the shaman.

"All of her people are dead now," the shaman said; Tox translated with a sleek unctious satisfaction in his voice.

"I meant her tribe, her clan—the larger body of her people. Other Goths or Germans, people who speak her language, who. . . ." Tox was translating; Aurelius let his voice trail off. He kept his eye on the Gothic girl, for fear that she would try to escape and Tox would take the chance to kill her.

"The best thing we can do is leave her here," the shaman said. And when Aurelius started to protest: "This spring must be well known—every caravan coming south will water here, and she can go with the first Goths who pass this way."

Aurelius said, "Surely you don't mean to expose her again to death at the hands of your own people."

"How are we to take her back to her people, then?"

The monk had not considered it a problem. Now he saw that it could be difficult. He frowned, surprised. "Well—if we can find a Gothic camp and let her go within walking distance—"

"Without them finding us," the shaman answered. "They would surely kill us if they caught us."

"Perhaps not all the people in the world hate each other."

The two Huns looked away. Tox said, "The Germans and the Hiung have always hated each other. But before, the Kagan was alive." He looked beyond the monk toward the girl. "You might take her to the Germans." He spoke over his shoulder to the shaman, who made a noncommittal gesture with his hand. Tox looked back at Aurelius. He fought to keep the pleasure from his expression. "Of course you would have to stay with them when you did. With the Germans."

Aurelius laughed at him, and Tox clenched his teeth and dropped his gaze. Clapping his hands together, he turned his shoulder to the monk and spoke to the shaman. The shaman began to nod and his eyes went to the girl and to Aurelius. Finally he said something, pointing to the monk with his chin. Tox turned back to him.

"I know where some of the Gepids will probably be camping now. The son of the King of the Gepids is—was a—my friend. It will be two or three days' ride but we can take her there and they will get her back to her own kind."

"Excellent," Aurelius said. "Thank you."

THAT NIGHT THEY RODE ON. The day spent in the ravine had eased the stiffness in the monk's bones and toughened his muscles. He began to feel comfortable on the sorrel mare's wide back. The plain under the failing moon was now familiar and he could recognize some of the things he saw and heard—the cry of an owl, the indent on the surface of the plain that marked a spring.

The girl rode the horse that the shaman had been using; the shaman took the black mare. Through Tox, he and Aurelius talked, the monk relating the history of the Creation.

He had noticed that the primitive understanding of barbarians admired the stories of the Old Testament more than the subtler teaching of the Life of Christ, and the Huns were no different. The shaman listened patiently to him and asked his usual odd questions. He was entertained by the idea of the Father creating the serpent together with the Tree of Knowledge, before He made Adam. Although Aurelius guessed at the reason for his amusement, it rattled him to think about it and he pushed it out of his mind.

The next day they spent on the open plain; the monk slept soundly until the early afternoon and spent the time until they started off again praying with the girl. She spoke her prayers in her own language but he had learned enough German to follow what she said. When their prayers were done, he sat meditating in silence, thinking of Christ's Passion. It troubled him to see that the girl did not meditate; although she sat still beside him, her eyes followed the two Huns.

They rode on. The plain became low rolling hills covered with trees and underbrush. Scudding clouds crossed the horned moon. By the configuration of the stars the monk guessed that they were traveling southwest. The wind moaned and chuckled in the trees around them, and the air smelled oddly sweet.

Throughout the night the clouds thickened, and just before dawn the rain began. At first the drops were small and few. Tox drew rein and looked quickly around; at a fast lope he led them across the meadow before them and into the trees. Aurelius hung onto the mare with both hands, bent over; the branches of the trees struck him on the back and across the face and shoulders. He felt himself slipping.

Abruptly they stopped; the horses crowded together. Tox had brought them to a place where a hillside gave them some shelter from the wind. In this shelter they made their camp. The rain increased to a steady drenching downpour. The wind was cold and uncertain, sometimes blowing away from them, and again lashing the stinging icy rain straight into their faces.

Yet Tox had a fire lit almost before the others had taken the harness and packs from the horses.

They had camped in a copse of trees; Tox made a kind of tent around the fire, using the trunks of two trees to support it. Aurelius crawled into the space around the fire, where the shaman already sat, and stretched his arms and body to the warmth of the flames. When the girl appeared—she had gone off on a womanly errand—Aurelius called to her and drew her against his side into the heat of the fire. Her soaked hair clung to her cheeks and her coat was sodden. She pressed herself against him like a puppy seeking shelter.

Warily, she lifted her face toward the shaman, sitting across the fire. The Hun stared down at her. His thin nostrils flared. Pointedly, he looked away, and the girl snorted. In her own language, she rattled off a flash of words that Aurelius decided uncomfortably were curses. The shaman contrived to look down at her as if from a great height.

For a moment, Aurelius read something like self-mockery in the shaman's disdain for the girl. But an instant later the shaman was looking into the fire, his face slack with boredom. The girl had her hands buried in her coat. Aurelius put his hands out to the fire. They would probably have meat broth again tonight, and his stomach was clenched tight for want of more substantial food, but in spite of that and the rain, he found himself in good spirits. When Tox came up with his pack slung over his shoulder, the monk got up to help him.

As soon as he was out of her way, the girl hurtled forward. Her hands flashed out of her coat; in one of them she had a knife, the blade gold in the firelight. With the gold tip leading, she launched herself forward into the shaman. He grunted. Stunned, Aurelius watched his black eyes widen over the girl's head. He slumped forward, and the girl plunged on past him. Before she could scramble clear of the tent, Tox had her by the hair.

He knocked her down on her back and pinned her with his

foot, her hair wrapped around his wrist. His eyes fell to the shaman. The monk looked down. The shaman was curled around his middle in the firelight. Blood ran down the dirt under him toward the fire and hissed in the hot ash.

Aurelius crawled over to him. Awkwardly, he tried to straighten out the shaman's crooked angular body. Something in the feel of the man's limbs and the texture of his skin convinced him that the shaman was dead. His fingertips felt the death in him. He leaned forward on his outstretched arms and waited for the shaman to come alive again.

He returned to himself when he thought of the girl. Straightening up, he looked hastily for her. But Tox had not harmed her; still holding her by the hair, he was down on his knees beside the shaman's body.

"I'm sorry," Aurelius said. Tears filled his eyes. "I'm sorry."

Tox shook his head. Raising his clawed fingers, he raked his nails across his cheeks, scratching his skin across the deep ritual scars. He made no sound; his eyes were vacant. Lines of tiny beads of blood popped out on his cheeks. Dropping his hands to his lap, he shut his eyes and moaned.

After a moment, Aurelius went around the fire and brought the girl back to sit beside him. If she ran he knew that Tox would kill her. If she stayed with him, perhaps he could keep her alive. He himself was void of everything, even fatigue. With the girl's arms clasped firmly in his own, he sat listening to the rain and did not try to pray.

TWENTY

A RDARIC CAME OUT INTO
the common hall of his new palace, with Tentius behind him,
and was startled to see that it was almost dark. The women of
the house were carrying trays and platters of food to the table,
and most of the men had gathered there, waiting to be fed.
The air smelled deliciously of gravy. Ardaric paused to let
Tentius catch up with him.

From the corner beside the hearth, a monk came forward,
blocking Ardaric's way. "My lord King," he said. "Today
some of your men took prisoner a companion of mine. Please,
order him released."

Ardaric stopped still. He looked the monk over curiously.
Under the man's deep tan he saw a trace of sunburn, as if he
had come only recently into the full sunlight. The monk's
intent unswerving eyes irritated him; waving the Roman on
toward the tables, he scowled down at the monk, who stood
with his arms folded and his eyes lifted to meet Ardaric's.

"This man you want released is a Hun," Ardaric said. "The
Huns are not men, they are animals. They are not Christian,
and I cannot see why a man of Christ would consider one of
them his *companion.*"

The door banged open and Dietric came in. He looked
quickly around the room, marked the Roman, and seeing
Ardaric strode toward him. Taking his father by the arm, he
drew him off two steps.

"Father. It is Tacs they have taken."

"Tacs," Ardaric said, startled. Dietric's eyes were a hand's breadth from him. Over his son's shoulder, he saw the monk, also staring at him, steadily, like a Hun. "What would you have me do?"

"They have hamstrung him," Dietric said.

Exasperated, Ardaric stepped forward, thrusting him aside. The monk came up to him again, his mouth open to talk, and complaints spilled from him. Ardaric's blood beat loudly in his ears. Tacs had never been his friend, his only friend in all that tribe had been the Kagan, and now the Romans were saying— He thought of having the monk taken prisoner also, but as soon as the idea came to him he knew he did not dare, not a monk and a Roman. He felt stuffed up, all his thwarted will pressing up into his throat.

"Go," he said, and gestured the monk away. "There you see my son. He will see that you are properly cared for. Dietric, take him, treat him as he deserves, a Roman and a monk. Just take him away." He went swiftly down the hall toward the tables, where the Roman envoy sat among his servants eating and the rest of the men were waiting for Ardaric to join them.

The monk came after him, actually reaching for his arm. "You must release that man."

Ardaric gave him a wild look and shook him off. Dietric came to the monk to take him by the sleeve and pull him away toward the other end of the hall. Ardaric went around the tables to his place; Thrygyrth was sitting beside him, and after he had sat down, Ardaric whispered, "You said they were alone. Was this monk with them?"

"No, no," Thyrgyrth said. "I swear it, there was only the Hun and the girl. There was no one else."

Ardaric muttered an oath. With quick abrupt strokes of his knife he sawed off bits of meat and thrust them into his mouth. From the other end of the table the Roman smiled at him and nodded. Ardaric kept his eyes away from Tentius and his servants. The Roman's messages, so welcome to him before, now stirred him to mistrust. He remembered how they had offered Edeco money to kill Attila. It seemed far in the past now, and yet it had been less than a year ago. He would be a fool to take the Romans at their word.

Dietric had led the monk off to sit beside him, opposite the Romans; he was conspicuously serving the monk with his own hands, so that everyone would see that he honored him. Ever since they left Hungvar, Dietric had been acting mysteriously. Ardaric put down his knife and stood. Seeing him on his feet, half the table rose, and he waved to them to sit again and walked toward the front door. Passing Dietric and the monk, he kept his eyes averted.

After two days of rain, the yard outside his palace door was deep with mud. The rain had stopped and torches were lit on either side of the door and beside the gate. The light fluttered on the puddles of standing water. Overhead, there was no moon, no star, only impenetrable black. Ardaric walked along the edge of the yard, where the ground was firm. With each stride his feet slipped sideways in the mud. He took the torch from beside the stable door and threw back the bolt and went in.

Of course, if they had caught the Hun's horse, he would have known immediately who it was. The cleverer of the two escaped, he thought, and laughed. The dark stable smelled of wet manure and wet horses. He started to light the torch he had brought, but the window in the back of the stable was open, and he used its light to find his way down past the tethered horses to the hayrick.

The Hun lay there on a pile of straw, his hands bound and tied to an iron ring set into the wall. It was Tacs. Ardaric let his breath out in a sigh. He reminded himself that Tacs had been only Dietric's friend. Blood caked thick as mud covered Tacs' lower legs, and fresh blood leaked down and sullied the hay.

The draft from the window was freezing and raw. Ardaric

leaned awkwardly across the Hun to shut it, and the hay rustled. Looking down, he saw Tacs' open eyes on him. He lurched back, and the glitter of the man's eyes followed him.

Ardaric slammed the window shut and strode to the door. With one hand on the latch he stood listening. The horses moved, champing their hay, covering whatever sound Tacs might be making. Yet he felt as if he could still see the Hun's eyes on him. He pulled open the door and went out.

There were Gepids in the yard, spreading straw over the mud. Under their eyes, he forced himself to walk slower, more casually. I am a king, he thought. I am their King. But his legs carried him faster, faster toward the light and warmth of his hall.

Tentius was waiting for him beside the door. Coming inside, Ardaric realized he still carried the dead torch and leaned it up against the doorframe. The Roman took him by the arm. "Let me understand what troubles you, my lord." With a crooked finger, the Roman summoned beer for them; he led Ardaric to the hearth and when the girl brought the ewer, took it from her and poured Ardaric's cup full.

"It is of no interest," Ardaric said. He took a long steadying draught of the beer and wiped the foam from his mustache. "Tell me more about how I may serve my lord the Emperor."

Aᴌᴌ ᴇᴠᴇɴɪɴɢ ᴡʜɪʟᴇ ʜᴇ waited for an opportunity to talk to the Roman envoy alone, Aurelius imagined fiery conversations with him: the envoy infinitely cynical, the monk inspired by Christ to a furious contempt for worldly diplomatics. In his mind he developed for Tentius an elaborate character, like someone in a play.

At last, late in the evening, he found Tentius alone in a corner near the hearth, sipping German beer. Dragging up a chair, the monk sat down beside him.

"Well, fellow citizen," Tentius said, and sat forward, almost eager. In the face of his friendliness Aurelius lost his bearings. The Germans were either already in bed or going there, ignoring the two Romans. Aurelius looked off into the room. The wooden walls around them bled pitch and smelled of the forests; the warmth of the fire mingled with a draft leaking through the floorboards.

"How have you made out among our friends the barbarians?" Tentius asked.

"Well. Excellently."

Tentius scratched his nose. "Yes. They seem to be Christians, granting an obstinate insistence on the Arian heresy."

"I have not been among Christians," the monk said. "I have spent the last few months among the Huns."

"Have you." Tentius' eyes widened. "A field innocent of the plow. Did you convert any?"

"No."

Tentius made a gesture of sympathy. They fell into silence, each looking elsewhere. Presently, Aurelius raised his head, determined to force the envoy into opposition.

"Are you a Christian?"

"Of course."

"Then how can you do what you do here?"

"What am I doing here?"

"Do you deny that you are influencing the Gepid King to attack the Huns?"

Tentius smiled. "Of course I don't deny it. The Huns are not Christian; they threaten the Christian Empire; they must be done away with somehow. Do you find my actions reprehensible?"

"To murder is against the law of God."

Even in his own ears, he sounded pompous and even shrill. The Roman closed his eyes. "Yes," he said. "But there are philosophical problems even in eating, these days. My goal is to serve the Emperor. It is for the good of Rome that the Huns be broken. I leave the philosophy to men trained in it."

Aurelius took air into his lungs and let it slowly out. Where he had expected opposition, he found only lack of interest. Tentius sipping his beer made a face with each swallow, and Aurelius said, "You don't care for the beer? They must have wine."

Tentius set down his cup. "I was told to admire their ways."

His eyes closed again. It was in the monk's mind to ask him why the Emperor ought to be served at all, but the possible answers depressed him. He thought of The Fluteplayer and a sense of loss quickened in him, for a moment he could not speak. Of course there was nothing to be said. He wrapped the skirt of his gown around his calves, to ward off the draft, and like Tentius, huddled down in his chair and waited to be led off to a place to sleep.

IN THE MORNING, TACS WAS gone. The rope that had tethered him lay cut in half on the fouled straw, and when Ardaric sent for the monk, his men told him that the monk was gone as well. No one had seen them go. Dietric stood on Ardaric's left hand, his eyes full on his father's face, throughout the questioning. Even when Ardaric spoke to the three men who had stood watch at the gate all night, Dietric showed no interest.

None of the gate guards had seen the monk or the Hun or anyone else; none of them would admit to having left his post. Ardaric sent them angrily away and sank back into his chair, which was fashioned like the Kagan's chair at Hungvar. Around him, the usual morning business cluttered the hall, servants going and coming, and the women at work with their looms and their chatter. Dietric was still watching him.

"You are disrespectful," Ardaric said. "Who taught you to stare like a common lout of a Hun?"

"Excuse me." Dietric looked away.

"One of them must have left the gate for a while. Or how

else could the monk have gotten out? And how could he have carried Tacs at all? A little man, and not so strong—would you have thought him strong enough to carry a hamstrung man away?"

"No," Dietric said. "But, then, he did not. I did."

Ardaric swore. Lunging forward, he seized Dietric by the arm and pulled him up to face him. "What do you mean? You did, ah? You took him off?" It was a relief to be able to lose his temper justly. He slapped Dietric on the cheek.

"I carried Tacs as far as the river," Dietric said. He acted as if Ardaric had not touched him. "The monk could not. Their horses were there, after that they needed me no longer."

Ardaric slapped him again. The heat of his rage burned in his face. His palm struck Dietric's cheek as solidly as an axe chopping into wood. Dietric turned his head to let the blow slide off; even so, it must have hurt, there was the bright mark of Ardaric's hand, but Dietric seemed not to feel it. His eyes met Ardaric's without flinching. Ardaric slapped him a third time. "You are a fool, you are mad." He threw his son's arm at him. "Go. Think on your sins awhile and come ask for my forgiveness."

Dietric said nothing. He stood there a moment, to the left of Ardaric's line of sight. Ignoring him, Ardaric fixed his eyes on a point across the room. After a little while, Dietric went away down the hall toward the door.

Above Tacs' head the white branches of birch trees rose into the burning sky. His legs hurt with a measured throbbing. Whenever he thought of how they had captured him, his eyes watered with rage. He had recognized two of them—friends of Dietric's. He rolled his face into the dirt and ground his teeth together.

The monk was coming back. He could feel his footsteps through the dirt under his cheek. He lifted his head. It was funny to see the monk dressed like a Hiung, in Tacs' second coat and shirt and a pair of baggy Hiung trousers. The brown cloth the monk held streaming in his hands was obviously part of his cassock. The monk knelt and carefully took off the bandage on Tacs' legs and pressed the fresh one down in place along his calves, where it hurt.

"You should have stayed with them," Tacs said.

"Don't be stupid. Who would have tended you?"

Tacs had not considered that. He moved so that he could see what the monk was doing—folding up the used bandages, also part of the brown cassock. Tacs made a sound in his throat. "The Fluteplayer would make me well better than you."

"I know," the monk said. He passed one hand across his narrow face. "I wish he were with us. I'm sure he would know far better than I what to do."

"The Fluteplayer knew everything."

"He certainly knew a great deal."

They had laid the shaman out under the sky the morning Tacs and the girl were captured. At least the girl was gone. "Is there water to drink?"

The monk stood up and went out of Tacs' range of vision. He shifted himself to look, and saw that they were camped in a little cleft of shade, with a short steep bank on either side lined with birch and ash trees. Obviously they were close to the river. He was lying on branches covered with what remained of the monk's cassock. Against the far bank, ten feet away, the monk had piled the packs and a bundle Tacs had never seen before. He brought a gourd of water to Tacs and sat down beside him; in his free hand he held a loaf of German bread.

"Your friend gave us food, too."

"My friend." Tacs propped himself on one elbow.

"The King's son. Who brought us here."

Tacs shook his head. The water ran cool down his throat. He remembered nothing except being sick and fevered in the

filthy Gepid stable like a slave. "Dietric? Did he bring us out
of there? Where is he?"

"I suppose he went back home."

"Is he coming back?"

"I don't think so. He said we should go as soon as you could
travel, that they will find us here easily enough if they decide
to look."

"Did he tell you who he was? He was young, wasn't he—
younger than I? With light hair and eyes—a good-looking
man, wasn't he? In a German way."

"All he said was that he was your friend. He is your friend."
The monk tore the loaf in half and gave Tacs one piece. "It
must have been Dietric, of course."

Tacs put the bread down and pushed himself upright. The
monk started toward him but did not try to stop him. With his
fingers Tacs probed through the bandages on his heels. His
feet ached all over; he could not move them and when he tried
the pain shot up through the backs of his legs.

"I can still ride. You have to go back to Ardaric—Dietric
will take care of you." Maybe the monk could talk Dietric
into leaving, and Tacs could meet him somewhere else. But
the monk was shaking his head.

"Now, listen to me, my friend," the monk said. "I would go
to Hell rather than to that place again. Don't try to argue with
me. If you want to leave—I can see you do—you must leave
me here. I can make my own way, I did so before."

Tacs grabbed hold of his arm. "That was in summer. Look
at the trees. It will snow soon. You don't know the winters
here. If you won't go with the Gepids, come with me."

"Thank you. But I cannot."

Tacs muttered in his throat, watching the monk through the
corner of his eye. He ate a bite of bread. He wished he could
see Dietric—it was maddening to be told that he had been
here, had brought him here, without Tacs' seeing him. He
finished the bread and dusted the crumbs from his knees.

"Do as you wish. It will be dark soon, I will leave then. I think you should come with me. In any case I will give you a horse. Take anything else you want. I can hunt on the plain, so you take the food. Have you seen anything of my black pony?"

"Yes—he has been grazing with the mares, but he won't let me near him."

Tacs nodded. "I thought he would come back." There was no sense in going directly to the Nedao River; no one would be there yet. Lying back, he looked up into the sky past the birch trees and thought of where he would travel to, the hunting he would have, between now and the Stag-Fighting Moon.

TWENTY-ONE

⊂≣

T ACS! TACS!"

Tacs reined in, looking around behind him. In the vast mobbed sprawl of the camp he could see no one he knew. The dogs were snapping and growling at the pony's hoofs, and it kicked at them, snorting. Tacs bent down and whipped at the dogs with his bow. When he straightened he saw Monidiak plunging toward him through the tangle of auls, meat-drying frames, laundry, and campfires.

Dropping his bow, Tacs spread his arms and whooped. Monidiak leapt his horse across a pile of garbage and dove from his saddle into Tacs' arms. They fell backward together and landed on a baby, which screeched; the mother rushed out of her aul with a whip and flogged them, screaming curses.

"Monidiak," Tacs cried, and crushed his friend in his arms. The woman's ox-hide whip slashed across his shoulders; the tip caught his cheek like a hot coal. "Oow. Let's get out of here. Monidiak, Monidiak!"

Shielding his head with his arms, Monidiak sprang up and ran out of the woman's camp. Tacs scrambled after him on hands and knees. That made him less visible, and while the woman with her whip cracking over her head pursued Monidiak, Tacs reached the black pony, wrapped his hands in its long mane, and let it drag him away to safety. Monidiak was laughing and begging for mercy. Behind the woman, the baby had found a pretty stone and was trying to eat it.

"Monidiak," Tacs called. He hauled himself onto the pony's

back. Monidiak dodged away from the whip's last crack, made a fig at the woman, and jogged through the camp after his horse. Tacs followed him. When he had picked up his trailing reins, Monidiak turned to smile at him.

"I knew you would come. What did you do with The Fluteplayer? Is he with you? Where are you camped?"

"I just got here. The Fluteplayer is dead."

Monidiak's eyes widened round as a German's. His smile drooped forgotten on his face. "The Fluteplayer is dead? What happened?"

"It's complicated. A Goth killed him. Where are you camping?"

"Come with me." Monidiak vaulted up onto his horse and led off. "Another for the Goths."

"Yes. They are killing every Hiung they can find. I have seen as many people dead, since I left Hungvar, as I ever saw in a war." Since he left the monk behind, he had come on signs of other massacres. He had to drop back to follow Monidiak —the Hiung camp was so crowded that the trails between the auls were only wide enough for one horse at a time.

"So I have heard. In the north we saw very little of it. Bryak is here, too. We have both heard enough stories of butchery to guess how complicated yours is."

He led the way down almost to the bank of the river. Tacs had left his other horses a day's ride away on the plain, thinking that he would bring them here when he had found a good campsite, but now he decided to leave them where they were. There was no room for extra horses here. Every inch of the river bank was covered with Hiung campsites.

Monidiak and Bryak had no aul, and they had made a lean-to of brush and hides against three living trees. Bryak was there already, feeding sticks and horse dung to a fire. When he heard them approach, he raised his head.

Monidiak began, "See whom I have—" and Bryak bounded to his feet.

"Tacs!" He rushed forward, and Tacs slid down from the pony to embrace him.

"Ah," Monidiak said. "Now at least there are enough of us to bury someone. Come in out of the wind."

Tacs gave Bryak another hug. For over a month, since he left the monk, he had been alone; now his throat thickened and tears started in his eyes at the touch of friends. He was leaning on Bryak, and he said, "Help me—I can't walk anymore."

Kneeling by the fire, Monidiak gave him a sharp look. Tacs laid his weight on Bryak's shoulders and let him drag him to the fire.

"Germans," Monidiak said. He reached behind for a jug.

"Gepids."

Bryak and Monidiak looked at each other. Tacs pulled the stopper out of the jug and sniffed. "Pah. Wine? I want some of The White Brother."

"We don't have any. Tacs, there is no way to get anything anymore." Bryak slapped his thighs. "Nobody has anything more than he needs for himself. We have nothing to trade for it, anyway."

"Get me my pack," Tacs said. He stretched his legs out awkwardly in front of him and with his hands pulled them around to cross at the ankles. Monidiak swore.

"It isn't bad," Tacs said. "I can do anything anyone else can, so long as I can hang onto my pony. You should see—I can ride him without a bridle now." He leaned toward the warmth of the fire. "It was Ardaric."

"Did he kill The Fluteplayer? Where was Dietric?"

Tacs shook his head. "You remember that monk."

Bryak dropped Tacs' pack on the ground beside him, and Tacs took one of the gourds from inside his blankets. "Here. I found him growing wild and made tea."

Monidiak howled. They both fell on him, hugging him and pounding his shoulders with their fists. Sitting back, they passed the gourd among them. Tacs told them how The Flute-player was killed and he himself crippled.

"At first, I didn't mind so much. Now I think of King Ardaric and I want to kill him."

"Ah." Bryak smacked his lips. "This is as good as any of The White Brother I have ever had."

"Maybe we can kill him," Monidiak said.

Tacs nodded. "We should kill them all. I saw such things, coming here—" He broke off to drink; Bryak was riffling through his packs.

"Three more gourds full and a big bag of dry leaves," Bryak said.

"Be quiet," Monidiak said. "All you can think of is getting drunk. We have a revenge to take."

"Against King Ardaric? Don't be foolish. How could three ragged Hiung take vengeance against a King?"

"Against every German in the world."

Bryak sat back. "That's more possible. Give me the gourd."

"Who is here?" Tacs asked. He looked from one to the other, feeding on the sight of their faces.

Monidiak rubbed his hands together. "Ellac—I came with him, that's how we got such a good campsite. And Dengazich and Ernach are camped over there. They are allies now. You shall see Ernach soon. You won't believe he is still a boy, without his cicatrice. He is much like the Kagan. Orestes is here —that Roman who served the Kagan. But they say he may go, the Kagan's sons are slighting him, and many people say a Roman has no place in a Hiung kurultai. Edeco, Scottas, Millisis. Megiddo is not here."

Tacs made a noise in his throat. With The Fluteplayer dead without successor, Megiddo, the raven-sorcerer, was sole master of most of the tribe's magic. "Who killed him? Which of the shamans are here?"

"Ferga," Bryak said. "I think Sallac."

"Megiddo is alive," Monidiak said. "He is up by the Lakes, with most of the other elders. None of them is here. Only the men who were great because of the Kagan have come here—them, and the warriors."

Bryak cleared his throat and got up. "I will get something for us to eat." He went away. Tacs looked over at Monidiak.

"What's happened? Why have the elders and the shamans stayed away? They should be here. When we elect a new Kagan—"

"They say there will be no Kagan," Monidiak said. "Let's have something to eat. I'm hungry." He got up and walked away.

Tacs looked at him, alarmed. Monidiak was Edeco's cousin —perhaps Edeco had been talking to him. Edeco was a devious man sometimes and afraid of things that did not exist.

All that day, they sat by their fire and ate and got drunk and exchanged lies about their deeds and adventures. Tacs had meant to go looking for his brother Ras, but from what Monidiak had said, he suspected that Ras had not come here. He remembered that Ras had been unenthusiastic about the Kagan even before Attila died.

By sundown, they were all too drunk to stand. The roar and traffic of the camp seethed around them. After the sun set, a freezing gusty wind blew up, but the people built huge fires that lit up the whole camp; reflected like copper in the river, the fires blazed in a narrow band up and down the river bank. The uproar and the comings and goings of people never faltered. The women and children went into the auls, but the men in groups wandered from fire to fire, talking and drinking. Most of them wore the paint of a blood feud, and Tacs went to another campsite, begged two pots of color, and with his friends painted his face as well.

All night, other Hiung walked or rode up to them, talked a moment, and traveled on. Most of them were around Tacs'

age or a little older or younger. Each had his own story of a
German massacre, or of Germans massacred. After a while, all
the stories sounded the same, and Tacs and Monidiak and
Bryak offered the same expressions of anger and revenge and
mourning. Tacs was so drunk that the camp looked like one
long fire, with shadows moving back and forth across the
flames. The words of the men talking to him became only a
trickle of clear noise against the dull general roar. Dimly, he
saw Ellac, surrounded by torchbearers, parade with his followers through the camp. He thought that Edeco himself came
by and spoke to him. When he could not see anymore, he
dragged himself into the shelter of the lean-to and curled up
out of the wind and fell asleep, to dream of all-consuming fires.

THEY ARE CAMPED UP
ahead," Ardaric said. "All up and down the river on the north
bank." With his right hand, he gestured crisply toward the
water at the edge of their camp. Dietric, sitting on the tailgate
of his father's wagon, folded his arms over his chest. The
thought of the Huns so close tightened his back muscles. He
wondered where Tacs was, if he was not dead.

Ardaric was walking in slow circles around the wagon, looking out over his warriors. He had camped them in a horseshoe
bend of the river and stationed his wagon on a little hill near
the center that commanded it all. Even Dietric was impressed
with his father. Perhaps because of the Romans, or perhaps
just for Ardaric's sake, every German nation east of the mountains had sent fighting men, and somehow Ardaric had managed to call them together at a defensible place within two
days' ride of the gathering Huns. Dietric was glad at least that
the Roman ambassador had left. Ardaric was walking towards
him, and he drew his face impassive.

"Shall I trust you?" Ardaric said truculently. He slacked

his weight against the side of the wagon, bracing himself on his hip.

"For what?"

"If you meet your pig-nosed little Hun friend, will you go off with him?"

Dietric could not help but smile. "Maybe."

"Unh." Ardaric struck him in the side, hard. But they had stopped even trying to talk to each other about some things, and after a moment Ardaric went on.

"Take as many warriors as you can find to follow you and go look over their camp. I will send others, there is no use in lying."

Meeting his father's eyes, Dietric tried to think of a nasty reply, but when Ardaric's eyes widened, he realized that he was staring and turned his back and walked away. He felt oddly out of breath, as if he had been running. The strain between him and Ardaric wore on his nerves. He walked up to the nearest group of Gepid fighting men. They turned to face him, and he picked three at random, hardly knowing their names. "Get horses, we will go out to scout the Huns' camp. Meet me by my father's wagon."

They went off quickly to get ready. Dietric walked around to the lines of horses tethered beside the river. Before they had left his father's new stockade, he had taken a young cousin on his mother's side to carry his arms for him. This boy was sitting on the river bank daydreaming, and Dietric sent him to ready his horse. Sitting down where the boy had been, he changed his boots.

He had never fought in a war, and it was only good sense for Ardaric to use him as lightly as he could. He doubted that Ardaric really thought he would betray his own people to the Huns. Sometimes he suspected that Ardaric was as tired of the trouble between them as he was.

The more he saw of Ardaric's ordering of the growing

mass of German warriors, the more he appreciated why the Romans had chosen Ardaric to flatter and cajole and bribe into turning on the Huns. But it made him angry that Ardaric would let himself be the Romans' tool. He had said that once to his father and Ardaric had knocked him off his horse into a river.

His horse-boy brought over the chestnut gelding and held him while Dietric mounted. "Get me my coat," Dietric said. "The one with the fur hood, I'll be gone all night."

"And your sword," the boy said.

"No, just the coat. Bring it to my father's wagon." Dietric booted his horse up the slope, away from the river.

The horseshoe bend was half full of German camps; Ardaric had said when they needed more room they would have enough men to make a more open campsite secure. Riding up to Ardaric's wagon, Dietric could see along the river to the south, in the direction of the Huns, but of course they were far out of sight downstream, beyond the leafless trees. He reined in his horse at the wagon's tailgate, next to Ardaric, who was making charcoal marks on one of his charts. Two men held the chart before him, one at each end.

"Three men only would follow you?" Ardaric asked, without lifting his head. "You have no sword."

Dietric dismounted and hooked his reins over the tailgate. Going around to the other side of the wagon, he saw the three men waiting, and beckoned to them to come forward. They were all burdened down with weapons; one even carried a hammer.

"Get rid of all that," Dietric said. "Leave it here. It will only slow us down. If we meet Huns, we will have to run."

"He loves Huns," Ardaric said. He snapped his fingers, and the men holding the chart ran around in front of Dietric. Startled, Dietric's three men gave him wide-eyed looks and backed hastily out of the way. Ardaric pointed to a scribble on the chart.

THE DEATH OF ATTILA 251

"Here is the river. Here is our camp. Do you make it all out?"

Dietric could not decipher any of the lines and marks on the chart. He knew if he said so Ardaric would shout at him, so he nodded.

"A day's ride south of here on the far bank is a shattered tree, lightning-struck, the first scoutings say three turnings of the river from here. Just beyond that is the Hun camp. Remember everything you see, especially the lay of the land beyond them and across the river from them. They say the river is much wider there than here. Tell me how much wider and where the nearest ford is. I never have enough information."

Ardaric slapped the man with the chart on the shoulder, and he and his fellow carried the map hurriedly off. Ardaric glared at Dietric and his men. "You know what the Huns will do to you if you are caught. These things—" he striped the head of the hammer with his bit of charcoal— "will do you no good. He is right. Leave them. If you are not back in three days, I will claim your horses." He made a charcoal cross on the front of Dietric's shirt and went away, shouting.

Dietric's horse-boy ran up, carrying his coat. The three men looked around them uncertainly, whispering to one another, and at length put their weapons under Ardaric's wagon. Dietric strapped his coat behind his saddle. Abruptly he realized that it was the Hun coat that Tacs had given him. He stood running the tip of one forefinger over the faded embroidery on the sleeve; finally he undid the straps that held it to the cantle of his saddle.

"This coat will not do. Get me one from my father's wagon."

The boy sprang off to do his bidding. Dietric pulled himself up into his saddle. It was midday. If they made good speed, they would come upon the Huns just after moonset. The boy returned with a sheepskin coat; when he had lashed it in place, Dietric reined his horse around and threw the Hun coat in the nearest fire.

Tacs LEANED FORWARD AND
quietly took the jug from Monidiak. Even so, Edeco saw him
and looked in his direction. Smiling, Tacs nodded to him.
Edeco jerked his eyes away, back to Dengazich, who was rant-
ing on, milling his arms around his head. Tacs drank from
the jug, stoppered it, and set it down in his lap.

Dengazich said, "The Germans are gathering half a day's
ride up the river to the north. I went there myself with my little
brother Ernach to see what was happening. We came within
bowshot of the German camp."

He raised his arms over his head, and all the men watching
him grunted. Tacs leaned forward and whispered to Monidiak,
"Probably from across the river. That isn't so brave."

Monidiak laughed, and Edeco gave them both a hard look.
Dengazich went on talking about how vile the Germans were
and how he and his little brother had defied them. Ernach was
sitting beside Edeco, behind Dengazich; he sat on a bearskin
and wore a bearskin cloak. The Kagan had worn a bearskin
cloak. Ernach was paring his fingernails. He looked even
younger than he was.

Dengazich said, "Ellac hasn't even gone to see the Germans.
How does he know where they are?"

"You just told him," Bryak said, and everyone around him
laughed. It was big, noisy laughter, too; no one was much afraid
of Dengazich. Dengazich made himself laugh.

Edeco stood up. "Bryak. Take yourself elsewhere."

Bryak started to get up, but Tacs and Monidiak put their
hands on his shoulders and forced him down again. Around
them, the men called, "No—no—he stays." Someone shouted,
"He is a better Hiung than this half-Goth!" and there was a
howl of agreement.

Monidiak leaned back on one elbow to speak into Tacs' ear.
"You see how much support Dengazich has. It's too bad that
Ernach is so young. See how angry Edeco is."

At that moment, Ernach lifted his head to look at his half-brother, railing on before him. Tacs said, "He reminds me of the Kagan—see, about his head and his shoulders?"

Edeco started to his feet again, and Monidiak quickly straightened up. Dengazich was describing the German camp. They had of course buried themselves in a horseshoe bend of the river.

"It will surprise no one to hear who leads this slave army," Dengazich said. "Perhaps it will surprise Ellac, who gives no thought to such things. But it will startle only fools to be told that King Ardaric leads this army against us."

Tacs started. Monidiak leaned back toward him again. "Ardaric!" Tacs stretched out his arms, and hauling him up to his feet, Monidiak and Bryak half-carried him out of the pack of listeners, toward the back of Dengazich's campsite. When he glanced over his shoulder, Tacs saw Edeco looking after them, and Dengazich had stopped talking and was pacing up and down before the audience.

"We shall have our revenge," Monidiak said. "For everything, even Marag."

Tacs had to struggle to remember why Ardaric might be guilty of the death of Marag, more than a year before. They reached their horses, standing in the shade of a tree, and mounted up. Bryak swung his tall bay horse in a tight circle. "What are we going to do?"

Monidiak laughed. "We will show Ardaric that he isn't safe from us. Remember the last time we raided him?"

Tacs said, "Let's go somewhere and plan this. We aren't going just the other side of our camp." He tightened his legs around the pony's barrel. "Stop yelling, do you want to get something thrown at us?"

They rode down a short slope toward the river. Bryak and Monidiak were giggling and suggesting painful tortures for Ardaric should they chance on him. Tacs could not make himself happy. He could see no way to take revenge on Ardaric

without getting himself killed. He was unsure what he wanted
to do, but he did not want to die. It made him morose to think
how little control he had over that.

E VEN IN THE DARK, THE HUN
camp was easy to find: they were making no effort to hide it,
and Dietric suspected they didn't even have sentries out. The
whole upper bank of the river was brilliant with fires for half
a mile of its length. With his men behind him, he rode along
in the darkness on the opposite bank, in the quiet, trying to see
what was happening around the fires. Behind him the three
men swore and guessed at what they saw. Finally Dietric
snapped at them to be quiet.

"We will split up here," he said. "You two—Edric, Rotar—
go back to that ford we passed. Stay there until tomorrow
night. Hide—keep the trail in sight so that no one will sneak
up on you. Count the number of Huns that cross that ford. I
—we will join you tomorrow after sundown. If we aren't
there by midnight, go back without us. Edric, you are chief.
Don't get caught." He turned to the third man. "Otho, come
with me."

Otho had no chance to protest; Dietric kicked his horse into
a canter, going south to circle around the Hun camp. He could
hear the other man's horse lumbering after him in the dark.
Dietric swung east to reach the river below the camp.

Like a puddle of light, the camp shone on his left hand until
the dawn came and the rising of the sun blotted out the color
of the fires. In the blue early morning light, Dietric reined in
under a tree and dismounted. He had been riding almost one
full day, and his legs were so stiff he could barely walk. Behind
him he heard the soft explosion of Otho's breath as the big
man sat down.

The rolling plain, scattered with trees, ran off to the river in the distance. Dietric could not hear the Hun camp, but only because the wind was dead wrong. He could see almost to its far side; he could see the people coming from their auls and stretching their arms and yawning. He even recognized one man, who had ridden to Sirmium with him and Tacs.

It still bewildered him that they had put out no sentries. He supposed they were so sure that the Germans would never dare attack them that they did not bother. Of course they could also be too disorganized. Watching the camp, he saw how haphazardly it was set up, how little space there was, how many of the auls held only men.

There were far fewer of them, too, than in the village at Hungvar. He had expected twice as many, after they summoned the entire nation. Perhaps they were early and the bulk of the Huns would arrive in the next few days. He lay down on his stomach on the ground and began to memorize the terrain around the camp.

"My lord," Otho whispered.

Dietric looked up over his shoulder. Otho held out a waterskin. "Are you thirsty?"

"Ah. Yes." Dietric rolled over onto his back, sat up, and reached for the waterskin. The ground tilted down here, as if swooping back into the wood, and he hoped that and the underbrush would hide them. He drank from the waterskin, lifting his head between each small sip to look around.

"Good. Take the horses back into the wood and tie them. Stay there."

"Are we going to stay here awhile, my lord?"

"Until dark. But keep a watch. They don't have any guard out but they are coming and leaving in all directions." A group of Huns had just ridden from the camp, going up-river. He strained his eyes to count them.

"Tell me what to do," Otho said.

Dietric handed him back the waterskin. He wished he knew

what was happening in the Hun camp. The more he considered it the less he believed that they would make another man the Kagan. It would insult the dead Attila.

"Excuse me, my lord," Otho said.

"I've already told you what to do," Dietric said. Another band of Huns was riding up to the camp, herding half a dozen sheep before them.

"Do you think that we can beat them?"

"What?" Dietric said, startled. "Beat whom? The Huns? I don't know. I can't count very well, but I don't think there are very many of them here. If we can catch them like this, maybe we can beat them. My father—" He stood up to watch the camp. "My father will decide what we should do, he is a capable general, even the Kagan drew on his advice."

"But he doesn't know them as well as you do," Otho said.

"Yes," Dietric said hastily. "Now we have to get out of here." He could see the black pony jogging out of the camp to the open meadow; if the wind changed and the pony caught the scent of Germans, it would bring the Huns down on them. He dragged Otho by the arm back toward their horses.

TWENTY-TWO

⊂⊱

DENGAZICH AND ERNACH
had refused even to stay for Ellac's kurultai and left the camp,
taking with them a hundred warriors. When he heard it,
Monidiak snorted and clapped his hands together. "Now we see
their cast of thought." He sat down beside their fire and dug
into the glowing coals angrily with a stick.

Edeco had brought that news; he dismounted from his horse
and followed Monidiak over to the fire. Tacs looked up at him,
surprised. Edeco stood punching one hand against his thigh.
As usual he was frowning, but now he actually seemed upset.
"What's wrong now?" Tacs said.

Squatting, Edeco tugged off his gloves to warm his hands.
Around his neck he wore a chain of gold studded with blue
jewels. Tacs wondered if he had gotten it from the Emperor.

"We may as well all leave now," Edeco said, but he spoke
to his cousin Monidiak rather than to Tacs. "Nothing will
happen here. There are no important men here."

"You are important," Monidiak said.

Edeco looked at Tacs. "Where is your brother Ras?"

"Ras is not important," Tacs said. He hunched closer to the
fire. Dark was coming; the hot red glow of the innumerable
campfires lit up the sky.

"No. Not by himself. But he and all the other men like him
are important at a time like this, especially if they don't come."

Monidiak handed him a gourd of The White Brother. "Here.
Make yourself sober."

"They are all off leading their dull little lives," Edeco said.

257

He gulped down the tea without stopping to taste it, and made a face, surprised. "I thought it was wine."

"We are too poor to drink wine," Monidiak said.

"Too wise," Bryak said.

Edeco took another drink of the gourd. "Maybe both."

Tacs said, "You mean there will be no Kagan." He had thought so before but he had not been relieved until now.

"None of them can get enough support. You heard them before. They clapped at Dengazich." Reluctantly, Edeco passed the gourd on to Bryak, who drank and smacked his lips.

"None of them is any worth, either," Monidiak said. "What are we to do now, cousin?"

Edeco leaned back on one elbow. "That is why I am here, cousin."

"Ah?"

"None of you is married, none of you has a family. Come with me, fight for me, and I will make you all rich."

Tacs could think of nothing to answer. He licked his lips. Bryak said, "Where will you go?"

"Italy, maybe. Or Spain. Thrace. Somewhere good to fight in."

"What are we fighting for?" Tacs asked.

Edeco shrugged. "Whatever is there." He got his feet under him. "Tell me what you decide. I mean to gather many men— perhaps five hundred." He pushed himself erect and went away, leading his horse.

The night had fallen while he spoke. Beyond the light of their fire, in the crowded camp, other fires blazed, showering embers. Monidiak took the hares they had shot in the morning, got his knife, and began to joint them. Bryak was staring into the fire, his chin on his raised knee.

"Well?" Tacs asked.

Monidiak hitched up one shoulder. With his hand he scooped out the guts and organs of the hare. "Can you think of anything else to do? You know we really cannot take revenge on Ardaric."

Tacs said nothing.

"Edeco will see that we don't starve, we will see that Edeco has what he wants."

Bryak said, "He promised we would be rich."

"Almost as rich as he will be," Monidiak said. "I heard him. I will go with him."

Tacs took the gourd and drank from it. It depressed him to think that he had nothing else to do except follow Edeco. It seemed as if when the Kagan died, everything valuable disappeared. He thought of the Roman monk, wandering alone on the plain. For the first time he saw why the monk might prefer the wild country to a camp full of other men. He watched Monidiak joint the hare and throw the pieces into a pot. Turning the skin fur-side down, Monidiak scraped the fat off and dropped it in after the meat.

In the darkness at the edge of the firelight, a dog snuffled, and when Tacs glanced that way he saw a pack of four or five dogs, their tongues running out, and their eyes on the rabbit offal. Monidiak was spitting the heart. With a stab of his arm, Tacs snatched up the rest of the garbage and tossed it to the dogs.

"There was good meat there," Monidiak cried.

From the dark came the growling and snapping of the dogs. Tacs said, "You know what will happen to you if you eat rabbit hearts and livers."

"That's just a story. Wolves and wildcats eat them every day and are not cowards." Monidiak took the roasted heart from the fire and waved it in the air to cool.

"Italy, he said," Bryak muttered. "Maybe we could take Rome, after all."

"THE OSTROGOTHS ARE HERE," Dietric said. He shaded his eyes against the sun and looked around Ardaric's camp. Since he had left, the army gathered there had swelled so large the bend in the river could not hold them, and they were making camps on the far side, which was dangerous. Everywhere he looked he saw men talking or cooking over fires; they had flattened the bushes and stripped the trees of their branches to build huts and make fires.

Ardaric nodded. "They came yesterday. We shall have to find a new place to camp. How close can we move to the Huns?"

"Don't bother to move," Dietric said. "They must know you are here, and as soon as they can they will attack you."

"Let me make such decisions."

Dietric sat down on his heels. He glanced down the slope at the men camping on the far side of the river. "You should pull them in. Do you have sentries over there?"

"You must think I'm a fool."

"No. Not at all." Dietric thought of fighting, and his muscles stiffened. He felt vulnerable, soft all over his body to the sword. Hastily he pulled his mind back to the Hun camp.

"They don't seem organized. They have no sentries out. I don't think they had scouts, either. I watched the camp from several different points, all day long. Once I was so close I overheard them talking—I could hear two men arguing, I understood the words. Once. . . ." He searched Ardaric's face. "Once I saw many men all in a mass, listening to Dengazich talk. When he said something—that I did not hear—they all clapped. All of them."

"They liked him?"

"No," Dietric said. "They clap their hands together to show contempt."

Ardaric's eyebrows arched up. "Really. Of Dengazich?"

"Or of what he said. The same thing. And there are only about a thousand auls in the whole camp. Shouldn't there be more?"

"Auls? Huts. Yes. You have miscounted."

"No. There are less than a thousand. That means only a few thousand fighting men, at the most. And while I was there, I saw wagons leaving. If we wait long enough, there will be no Huns there at all."

Ardaric dusted off his hands, scrubbing his palms together. "But you think they will attack us when they know where we are." Reaching into the back of the wagon, he got out another of his charts. Setting one foot on a spoke of the nearest wagon wheel, he rested the chart against his knee.

"If they do not, we will outnumber them too much."

"If your estimate is right there are already two Germans to each Hun."

Dietric said nothing. Ardaric was staring down at his chart. Turning his head, Dietric looked out over the camp. The German warriors moved over it in swarms, full of industry, ordering their campground into ranks and files. Their yellow hair and yellow beards looked red in the bright sunlight. Here and there, a wagon stood, being unloaded. In the midst of it the river curled in a sinuous loop.

"Do you think they have elected a new Kagan?" Ardaric asked.

Dietric shook his head. "I don't know."

He turned back toward his father. Ardaric was watching him shrewdly. In deference to him, Dietric lowered his eyes. Ardaric said, "Do you actually miss them? Your Hun friends?"

Dietric got up and without answering walked away.

Aᴛ ᴅᴀᴡɴ ᴛʜᴇ Hɪᴜɴɢ learned that the Germans were marching toward them. From fire to fire the rumor spread among the few men left awake, and they woke up the men they could rouse. Nobody could agree who was to command them, but they all wanted to attack the Germans. Some of them took their horses and rode out of camp on first hearing the news. Others waited long enough to collect twenty or thirty men together. Most of them got out of their blankets, put on clothes, ate, pissed, and went around getting their war-gear ready and waking up their friends, with a view toward leaving camp around noon. The Germans, after all, would not disappear.

Tacs had been awake when the news first came. He called Monidiak out of sleep and sent him for their horses. Moving around their little campsite on his hands and knees, he put meat, water, and grain together and set it to cook in the coals of last night's fire.

Around him, men galloped constantly off in all directions. The hoofs of their horses lifted the dust into the air, thick as smoke. Three riders, shouting Ellac's name, trotted along the river bank through the haze, and here and there a warrior followed them, to gather under Ellac's standard. But most of them did not even lift their heads at the sound of his name. Bryak woke up; grinding his fists into his eyes, he staggered to the fire and slumped down beside it. "Ayya. What a night's sleep."

"The Germans are coming," Tacs said. He lowered his head down almost to the ashes and blew on the coals under the pot.

"How brave of them."

Bryak lay on his side to reach for a gourd of The White Brother. It was empty, and he let it fall, groaned, and straightened up. His eyes moved slowly over the camp around them. "Where is Monidiak?"

"Over there." Tacs was cutting bread; he gestured with his knife. Through the accumulated litter of the camp, Monidiak was walking toward them, leading their horses; on the black pony's back was a bundle of hay as tall as the pony itself. Bryak jumped up to help him.

They fed the horses and themselves, and afterward, while Bryak washed the pot, Tacs and Monidiak sat watching the other Hiung flood out of the camp. Many of those leaving waved and sang and shouted jokes back and forth. Tacs unhooked his bow and arrow cases from one of the lean-to's support poles. They had made some paint, and when Bryak came back, they sat in a little circle and painted each other's faces with their totems and the war-sign.

"I have a bad feeling about this battle," Monidiak said. "Everybody is too happy about fighting today."

Tacs whistled to the black pony. It walked around from behind the lean-to, wisps of hay trailing from the corners of its mouth. Tacs cajoled it into lowering its head for the bridle; with his left hand wound in the long black mane, he hauled himself onto his feet and saddled the pony up. "Don't be foolish," he said to Monidiak. "You will bring bad luck on us. Remember when we went to Italy. Everybody was in very high spirits then."

"We did not conquer in Italy."

Tacs shrugged. "We did not lose, either. Have we ever been beaten?"

"We were beaten in Gaul."

Tacs made a rude sound with his lips.

"The Kagan always said it was a victory, but we were beaten and he knew it, Edeco once told me so."

"What does Edeco know of it?"

Bryak came back, swinging the pot by the handle. "What shall I do with this?"

"Leave it," Monidiak said. It was his pot. He stood up and started around the lean-to for his horse.

"Are we coming back here?" Bryak called after him, and turned toward Tacs for an answer.

Tacs pulled his saddle-girths tight. He had tied his bow and arrow cases to the saddle and bound his cloak on behind the cantle. "We can get whatever we need from the Germans." He dragged himself up onto the pony's back and sat straight.

"Wait for us," Monidiak said, coming back leading his horse. Bryak dropped the pot and ran off the way Monidiak had come.

Tacs laid his reins on the pony's neck and sat watching his friends saddle their horses. The wound in his right heel was festering again; it had refused to heal, closing over only to break open again if he banged it or strained it. Now it itched and burned halfway up his leg. That frightened him, and he wished again that he could ask The Fluteplayer to heal him. Although he had seen people die by the hundreds, he could not get it into his mind that The Fluteplayer was actually dead, he felt as if the shaman were hiding somewhere, just out of his reach. For the first time in his life, he was afraid of the battle coming.

At that moment, he heard someone shout, and a horseman galloped along the river bank, weaving in and out of the fires, crying, "Everybody come—there is fighting in the river, they are driving us back—everybody come."

Tacs snatched up his reins. The black pony threw up its head and took two nervous steps sideways. Monidiak leapt into his saddle. "Wait for me," Bryak cried. He jerked his girths snug and ran back into the lean-to for his bow.

"Get me my lance," Tacs shouted. If they were fighting in the river, a bow would do no good. He reined the pony over to take his lance from Bryak.

Monidiak shouted, "Edeco!" and his horse bounded away. Following, Tacs saw Edeco, off in the middle of the camp, riding at the head of a hundred horsemen. Dozens more were joining him with every stride of his horse. Streaming west along the river bank, other men called to each other and banged their ox-hide shields, laughing. Tacs took his shield from his saddle and hung it on his left shoulder. Bryak, riding beside him, was flushed and laughing.

Now they rode in the middle of a tide of horsemen, all talking and shouting. Here and there, men sang, their voices hoarse with excitement. Bryak's wooden stirrup struck Tacs' left leg with every other stride. On his right rode a man cursing in a steady monotone.

Tacs turned his eyes forward. Always before he had loved the prospect of fighting, the action, the suddenness, the strain.

He made a face at himself for being afraid but the fear gnawed him still. All around him, his friends' voices sounded, but he could not make himself speak.

In a long parade of warriors, they rode down the bank of the river, keeping their horses to a quick jog. The sun rose blazing into the clear autumn sky; men who had ridden out wearing their cloaks took them off and stowed them behind their saddles. A waterskin came back through the crowd, and Tacs took a long drink and handed it on to Bryak. He strained his eyes to see. The dust of their passing hung in the air like a veil.

Bryak was muttering to himself. Tacs said, "What's wrong with you?"

"Why didn't we think to bring The White Brother?"

Tacs reached behind him, into his cloak, and got out his last full gourd. Bryak seized it with a cry of disbelief and joy. Pulling out the stopper, he put the mouth to his lips and up-ended the gourd. Tacs laughed at him, but when the gourd came back to him, he drank as much as Bryak.

The tea heated him and made him light-headed in an instant. His mouth dried up. The dust stung his eyes. His fear shrank to nothing and before the gourd had come back to him he was singing a gamesong with Monidiak. They passed the gourd back and forth among the three of them and two or three other men, until there was none left. Tacs hung the empty gourd on his saddle. A moment later they picked up speed, and the pony broke into a lope.

Somewhere just ahead, there was shouting. The noise rolled back into the ranks around them: "The river—the river—" Tacs took a firm hold on his spear. He could see no use for his bow. The pony stretched out into a dead gallop. Shoulder to shoulder, the big horses all around charged up a little slope, trampling down brush and knocking into trees. The dust covered everything. Tacs could see only the heaving bodies of the men and horses immediately around him. Monidiak's dark head with its red feather bobbed before him. Suddenly the ground swooped away; he braced himself, and the pony slid down a long steep bank into two feet of cold water.

To his right, there was a roar like drums. Metal clanged. The sudden crash of sound hurt his ears. To his left, someone shouted in German. Arrows sliced the water around the pony's legs. Tacs reined in and looked around him. The tight pack of men loosened—Bryak was two horses' lengths away, looking around as bewildered as Tacs. Now the sound of fighting came from three sides, and behind him more Hiung slithered down the bank into the river.

"Bryak!" Tacs waved to him and pushed forward. The pony laid its stubby ears back and at first refused to move, and Tacs beat it with the butt end of his spear until it jumped forward. Losing its footing, it fell sideways into the river. Tacs clung with his free hand to its mane. The current caught the pony, sweeping it downstream, and the pony righted itself and swam and scrambled up onto a gravel bank that projected out from the far side of the river. Tacs was soaked through; when the cold air struck him he gasped and started to shiver uncontrollably. Prodding the pony with his lance, he forced it toward the far bank.

The pony skidded and staggered along the gravel bank. Trees and thick-growing brambles covered the bank ahead of them. Beyond the bare, thorny branches Tacs could see people moving—Germans, their yellow hair plaited and their crosses around their necks. Tacs screamed for Bryak and charged up the bank. The pony put out its nose and crashed into the brambles without breaking stride. A thousand tiny thorns stabbed into Tacs. The Germans beyond wheeled to face him. He ran his lance through one man's chest and kicked another in the face.

The rest ran away from him, yelling. The White Brother

pounded in his blood. He had no time to be afraid; all he could think of was how to fight, chasing after the half dozen Germans fleeing him. He speared two of them and ran the pony over another. The others turned; more of them raced toward him, carrying swords and hammers. Their red mouths, fringed with yellow beards and mustaches, opened like the sucking mouths of fish. He could hear nothing save the tremendous featureless roar of the fighting. He gave it a scream of his own and galloped along the bank toward the ford.

They had caught the Germans crossing the river here, but somehow the Germans had managed to trap the Hiung instead. Tacs had never understood tactics. Ahead of him, between him and the river swarming with bodies, stood a wall of German backs. They weren't even fighting; there were no Hiung before them, and they leaned on their swords and watched. Tacs waved his spear at shoulder height and crashed in among them. The spear bounced off the heads and shoulders of the Germans. They swung to face him, and Tacs stabbed the one before him in the eyes. He was so close that he heard the man's gasp of pain. The falling body left a gap to the river, churned to a blood-spattered foam, and Tacs lowered his head and squeezed the pony toward it.

A dull throb filled his right leg, and he pulled out his knife and slashed down across the German holding him. The German shied out of the way, letting him go, and the pony jumped out into the river. It landed on men fighting; Tacs swayed over the rushing brown water, bodies leaping and screaming under the pony's thrashing hoofs. He jerked himself back into the saddle. Something hit him hard in the right hand. Water splashed in his face—it tasted of blood. Beneath him the pony bucked and kicked out, lunging forward on its hind legs, bucked again, and broke into a gallop. Sheets of water surrounded him. He heard Hiung screaming. The pony spun around and stopped dead, and they were in the midst of the Hiung again, safe and snug.

The Hiung cheered. They were struggling to force themselves all at once into the narrow ford. On the far bank the
Germans in orderly rows were chopping at the Hiung front
rank. They were too many to use their bows, and half the
Hiung apparently had not brought lances. Their horses stamped
and lunged and crushed the riders' legs between them. They
could not move forward past the Germans and they could not
drop back away from them. Tacs could not believe that he had
come through so easily from the other direction: the Germans
looked like a solid wall. Pressing his right rein against the
pony's neck, he worked his way to the edge of the battle.

The fighting was shoving him forward. Over the black hair
and straining shoulders of the Hiung in front of him he began
to see German faces. Each one of them reminded him of
Dietric. He wondered what he would do if he saw Dietric, up
ahead of him—reach him, somehow, take him away. Dietric
was his friend. Dietric had saved him from Ardaric. The pony
stumbled and went to its knees, throwing Tacs up onto its
neck, and for a moment he stared blankly into the muddy foam
of the river. The pony hurtled itself up again, snorting. Tacs
gripped his spear, took a deep breath, and forced his way past
two more men to the edge of the mob.

He saw no sign of Bryak or Monidiak until he was on the
very edge. They were ahead of him, being forced like him toward the Germans but holding back and looking wildly
around. Tacs imagined the Germans ahead as a maw they were
being fed to. A shout tore from his throat; to his surprise,
Bryak heard him and leaned out to pull on Monidiak's sleeve.
Tacs waved to them, and they fought their way back toward
him.

Tacs aimed the pony at the river and beat it into the water.
Again, the pony stepped into the deep water and had to swim,
and the current whirled it off, struggling to keep upright.
Tacs hung on with both hands. He could see where the gravel
bank reached out into the current, and he aimed the pony for

it. The pony swam strongly, blowing the water out of its nostrils. Tacs looked over his shoulder—Monidiak was following, with Bryak right behind him. Tacs turned forward. The pony stood spraddle-legged on the gravel bank, to its hocks and knees in the river, and shook itself violently all over. Tacs almost slipped off. With a snort that sprayed water from its nostrils, the pony started at a crisp trot along the gravel bank, toward the German side of the river.

They were mobbed on the river bank where Tacs had come out before, and he swerved to the left and drove the pony up six feet of sheer frozen mud into the thorns and briars along the bank. Reining in, he let the pony catch its breath. Monidiak raced up beside him. The bank came down under Bryak, and he went downstream a few yards and scurried up to join them.

The Germans were ranged before them, headed up-stream toward the ford, but already they were looking back over their shoulders toward them. Tacs set his lance and charged. Just before he reached the Germans, he saw that several other Hiung were following him across the river. He lifted his voice in a scream, half cheer and half war-call. Before him the German faces dissolved into a blur of pale flesh to be torn with his spear, and he hurled the pony into it.

Like the river, the Germans lapped around him, their heads even with his shoulders—even on foot, they were giants. He stabbed with his spear and used it as a long limber club. His breath caught in his throat. Their hands were clawing for him. Swords sliced around him. He knew that something had hit him from behind. Suddenly there were Hiung around him, pressing toward him, working through the Germans with their arms swinging. The Germans faltered. Their light eyes turned away from Tacs. He let his arm slacken to his side, and no one struck him. When he looked around, he saw no face lighter than his own.

Twenty or twenty-five Hiung had followed him across the river. In a pack they struggled forward, trying to break through

the mass of Germans and rejoin the other Hiung in the center
of the battle. Tacs hung back in their midst until he was rested.
Forcing his way forward, he wedged his pony into the front
rank against the Germans. One German lunged for him, his
hammer raised into the bright sunlight, and Tacs sliced his
arm with his spear and drew it back and plunged it into the
man's chest. The line of Hiung around him surged forward a
few yards. Two Germans braced themselves against Tacs, and
one he killed and one he wounded so badly that the man
crawled away into the German lines. Yet there were more in
front of him still. He had to lean forward over the pony's head
to reach them. With their long shields they struck aside his
spear. Their clumsy swords whirled in the air over him. He
striped their arms with the blade of his lance and their swords
dropped.

Gradually he realized that he was no longer moving forward. He could not see the Hiung in the middle of the river;
he could hardly even see the river itself. There were too many
Germans between him and it. Suddenly their number swelled,
and he had to back the pony up a step.

Turning the pony, he dropped back into the middle of the
Hiung pack. They were fighting on three sides now—the
Germans were encircling them. Tacs caught Monidiak's eye and
waved, and Monidiak came over. "Let's get out of here." Tacs
took a fresh grip on his lance and started toward the river,
hitching his shield up on his shoulder to protect his left side.

Monidiak and Bryak rode up beside him. They trotted toward
the river bank, jogging over foliage beaten to the ground by
the hoofs of horses. Seeing them go, the other Hiung broke
and followed them. The pressure of their horses behind them
forced Tacs and his friends into a lope. They raced down toward the river.

Abruptly, Germans appeared in front of them, dashing in
from either side to fill the gap. Tacs caught his breath. He
tucked his lance under his arm. The Germans faced them like

a wall of golden trees. The pony smashed into them, and the wall buckled, but beyond there was no open river bank, only more Germans. With a scream, Monidiak fell toward him in an explosion of blood. Tacs' mouth was full of blood; it dribbled down into his eyes and blinded him. He dragged in another breath through his raw throat and laid about him with his lance. The river was before him, somewhere. He saw blood leap from a bright slash on the pony's neck. Its body quivered between his knees. Ahead of him, in the haze of German faces, Dietric's face appeared. For a moment he thought of going to him and helping him, but he was too far away, and saving Dietric didn't seem important anymore. The river was before him at last. He kicked the pony in the ribs; the little horse skidded down the bank, and they stood in the cold water, safe.

The river was clogged with bodies. Above Tacs the trees along the bank shaded the water, and corpses floated in and out of the dappled shadows. They were Hiung bodies. More Hiung, still alive, dropped into the river around Tacs—the men who had come after him. Bryak was there, his eyes like holes burned into his face, and his mouth gaping.

In a mass they rode up toward the battle again. But before they reached it, they saw that the banks of the river were packed with Germans, on both sides, looking down at them. They came to the place where the current ran so strong, and like one man they decided to give up, to run away. Turning their horses, they charged the near bank, on the German side of the river.

In their midst, Tacs saw Bryak before him lunge up into a solid pack of Germans, and Bryak fell back into Tacs' path and half the bank collapsed on him. The pony wrenched its body to one side to keep from stepping on him. Tacs' neck ached from looking up into the faces of the Germans. He could not see them very well anymore; his eyes were full of dirt. Each time he breathed his throat burned. He gathered himself for one more strike. The pony clawed its way up the bank and pitched in among the Germans. Their hands and arms hacked at him. He saw no weapons, only faces, alien white flesh, and blue eyes. The pony slipped; dropping his lance, he leaned forward and clasped his arms around its neck. They fell for a long time, together, into the river, this time not cold at all, but hot with the blood of his people.

D IETRIC ENDED HIS PRAYER, crossed himself, and stood up. He could not believe that God had let him live. All around him, the dead and the wounded were heaped, and here and there lay parts of men, pieces of clothing, broken weapons. Save for the sturdiest, the trees and brush for half a mile along the river were hacked and flattened into the dust. He walked toward the river; his throat was caked with dirt.

When he saw the ford, he stopped, stunned, and Ardaric rode up beside him on his white stallion. Ardaric had not fought. From the ridge behind them, guided by his lookouts in the trees, he had directed the fighting, sending them here and there as the shape of their enemy changed. Now Ardaric looked down at his son and over toward the ford.

"You were right. There were only a thousand of them, all together. Maybe less."

Dietric put his hand on Ardaric's saddle to hold himself up. The bodies in the ford had dammed up the river, but while he watched, the water piling up behind the corpses mounted to the top and flowed over. The far bank was buried under the bodies of Hiung and their horses. On this bank there were almost as many dead, half of them German.

"If they had all come at us at once," Dietric said, "they would have beaten us."

Ardaric gave an indifferent shrug. He started along the river bank, looking over the dead. "It doesn't matter, does it?"

"No."

"You did very well. You are very brave, Dietric."

Dietric nodded. He followed his father along the edge of the river. Even here the water was loaded with corpses. Against his will he searched for Tacs.

"How they fought," Ardaric whispered; Dietric knew that he was talking to himself. He understood the tone in his father's voice. He who had never seen a battle had expected nothing like the sight of a hundred Hiung riders flinging themselves at him, like men in a holy fit, ignoring wounds and their own dead. He had seen them plunge through the German line, fighting a dozen men at once, as if they could not die. He had seen Tacs do that. He was sure it had been Tacs.

"Dietric," Ardaric snapped.

Dietric looked around. They had come to a place where the bank was sheer but the water ran slowly and more shallow. At the foot of the bank, in the shallowest part of the river, lay a heap of dead men and horses. One of them was Tacs. The black pony lay across his body, its head buried in the river. Beyond him Bryak lay dead.

Dietric started forward. His father rode up between him and the river, and Dietric saw that Tacs was still alive.

Tacs had seen him. His body stirred; all the bones of his chest moved broken under his skin. "Help me," he said.

Dietric could barely hear him. He took another step forward. Ardaric took him by the arm. "No."

Tacs wet his lips with his tongue. He was shuddering; his eyelids drooped like a madman's. "Help me."

Dietric twitched. "No," Ardaric said. "He would kill you." He turned his horse away from the river. Dietric for a moment could not take his eyes from Tacs'. But he knew Ardaric was right, that Tacs would try to kill him if he went too close. He went stiff-legged after his father, back toward the height of land. The night was sweeping in; he walked into the comfort and the safety of darkness.

A NOTE ON THE TYPE

The text of this book was set on the Linotype in Garamond
No. 3, a modern rendering of the type first cut by Claude
Garamond (1510-1561). Garamond was a pupil of Geoffrey
Troy and is believed to have based his letters on the Venetian
models, although he introduced a number of important
differences, and it is to him we owe the letter which we know
as old-style. He gave to his letters a certain elegance and a
feeling of movement that won for their creator an immediate
reputation and the patronage of Francis I of France.

Composed, printed, and bound by
The Kingsport Press, Inc., Kingsport, Tenn.

Typography and binding design by
VIRGINIA TAN